DYLAN'S
MONSTER

A Novel

Tom Faustman

CONNECTICUT

Blue Sky Ventures

175 Tryon Street
Glastonbury, CT 06033

Cover Design by CreateSpace

Manufactured in the United States of America

ISBN – 978-0-9887862-0-2
ISBN(ebook) – 988-0-9887862-1-9

If you have a loving family, you are a lucky man. A lucky man has the strength to do the impossible. This book is a testament to my blessings.

DYLAN'S MONSTER

CRINA

Crina Barbu had lived a full life. Now at age 84, she thought back to her childhood in Romania. When tata told the family they'd be moving to Philadelphia in America, she remembered thinking, "the city of brotherly love," as she had been taught in the village school.

At age 10, Crina was the star student of 5th grade, with grand hopes for the future. It didn't work out so grand. Life was hard in the Romanian section of Fishtown, a small neighborhood near downtown Philadelphia. The Catholic school she attended was mostly Polish, Czech and Romanian immigrants. The nuns were kindly, but insisted the immigrant children speak English correctly. Crina's first adjustment was being renamed "Lily." Sister John advised sagely,

"Crina labels you eastern European. Lily is a proper American name."

Crina's musings were suddenly disturbed as Sylvan banged the front door shut. Always courteous and gentle, Sylvan had been her kindly helper for nearly a year. But Crina had noticed a change; lately he had turned brooding and abrupt; something seemed to be bothering her Sylvan. Crina heard another thud.

To make sure it was him, "Is that you, Sylvan? I'm in bed, can't move too well today. Can you help me up? I need to use the toilet." Crina spoke with a slight accent, but her grammar and inflection were perfect. Sister John would be proud; Lily had become a proper American citizen.

From the other room, Sylvan bellowed something in an angry tone. Crina got worried, rubbed her fingers in anguish.

For the past year, Sylvan had been the most important person in her life. She met him when she pawned a porcelain doll, trying to get enough cash to buy more of her beloved Hummels. She returned to his shop frequently, they became friends. When he learned she had no living family, he soon did her shopping, got her mail, and drove her to the clinic. Everything she needed, like the son she never had. She called out again, but still no reply. She could hear him moving in his distinctive gait. A huge man, Sylvan would frighten most people. But for Crina, he had always been a gentle giant.

Till recently. Everything was different since she traded her savings for those beautiful rubies and diamonds. Sylvan had arranged it all.

"This way you can hold and feel your life's work, Crina. What pleasure is money?" Sylvan had assured her the jewels were a good investment and a nice complement for her Hummel collection.

"Those Jew bastards at the bank will milk you blind with interest and special charges." She had mused: Thank God for Sylvan. What would I do without him? But during his last visit, he got surly, knocking her roughly to the floor while helping her dress.

"Sorry, it was an accident," he had mumbled. But his face said otherwise.

Finally, Crina could wait no longer, hollered for Sylvan to help her to the toilet. She heard her "big boy" moving in the living room.

Suddenly he stormed into her bedroom, rushed up to her and put his hypnotic eyes inches from her face. Crina recoiled, but was unable to take her gaze from the feral stare. And then Sylvan did something even more disturbing, he started to sniff her, like a wolf over fresh kill, making sure there was no life. Sylvan made no other noise, just the unnerving sound of inhaling air. Crina caught her breathe, murmured robotically,

"What are you doing, Sylvan?" The question seemed to surprise Sylvan; he backed slightly away and said,

"Seeing if I can smell death." Crina wet her pants.

Sylvan instantly smelled her urine and got furious. "You silly bitch." Without another word, he threw back the covers and pulled Crina violently to her feet.

"Go clean yourself up you disgusting cow!" Crina started to collapse but Sylvan caught her. And then he dragged her into the bathroom and plopped her on the toilet, pulling her nightgown almost to her neck.

"Finish up. If you make a mess, I'll stuff your face down that toilet. You're disgusting." Crina was too terrified to tinkle; she sat still trying to understand Sylvan's rage. He inched closer, loomed over her.

Crina passed out.

੭

When she awoke, Crina was back in bed, all tucked in. She felt warm but soon sensed her wet sheets and nightgown. And then she remembered Sylvan's rampage. She listened to see if he was still there.
Nothing.

She looked at her clock radio. Ten o'clock. I think he's gone. She sat thinking; should I get up to call the police? But she realized how shaken she was. She didn't have the strength; better wait till tomorrow. Sylvan never comes over during the daytime.

Crina reached over to grab her favorite magazine, "Good Housekeeping." And then she noticed that the windows were now shut. That's odd, it's warm outside. Did Sylvan shut them?

But she soon got interested in a Shag carpet article, her thoughts quieted. Maybe it was just her imagination? Crina turned back to her article, read about the new carpeting fad sweeping America and sank into her pillows.

She loved reading about how the rich and famous decorated their houses. She never lost her belief that America was the land of opportunity. People's dreams really did come true. With that pleasant thought she dozed off. She dreamed about birds and their beautiful whistles. One summer a whippoorwill had settled in the neighborhood and regaled her morning and evening with its haunting refrain.

But then Crina realized that the sound she now heard was the teapot boiling, Sylvan was still in the house.

She shook her head, trying to get alert. The upstairs telephone was just outside her bedroom. She installed another phone there when her rheumatism worsened and she began spending most of her time upstairs. Crina listened again, the teapot was silent.

Had she dreamed it?

Sylvan words came back to her, "Seeing if I can smell death." That made up her mind. She pulled back the covers and sat on the edge of the bed to test her balance. She breathed deeply, slid to the ground. After a few steps, her strength returned, she moved softly to the door. Twisting the knob slowly, she pulled the door ajar. When it was about a foot open, a sharp creak sent goose bumps down her arms. She stood motionless.

Had Sylvan heard that?

After a few moments, Crina listened but no one stirred. Not risking another creak, she squeezed through the opening, looked down the hallway. The phone was about 20 feet away. Moving carefully, almost sliding her feet to avoid noise, she proceeded but had to rest every few steps.

Only 10 more feet to go. Sliding along, Crina finally reached the phone and lifted the receiver. She hesitated, not knowing how to get to the police. The persistent dial tone blared in her ear. Could Sylvan hear it? She covered the receiver to muffle the noise. Just when she decided to dial the operator, she heard the unmistakable sound of Sylvan moving from the kitchen.

Panicking, Crina put the phone down and began moving back to her room. Not wanting to alert him, she left the door slightly open and got into bed, pretending to sleep. Crina thought she heard her door open. Peering through shut lids, she saw Sylvan engulfing the entrance. He had a cup of tea and some cookies in his hand. He moved toward her. Blinking quickly, Crina pretended to come awake.

Sylvan was now beside her. He held out the tea, "I brought you a goodnight treat. It will make you sleep better."

She paused as if debating a decision, murmured, "Thank you." Sylvan nodded, backed away and went into the bath room. After a while, she heard the water running in the tub. Not knowing why, that terrified Crina.

Sylvan emerged from the bathroom and glared at her.

"Drink your tea then I'll give you a warm bath, clean that piss off you." His harsh tone brought back her fear. Trying to compose herself, Crina reached for the tea, but her hand shook and she spilled some on the floor. Sylvan's expression immediately became animated, fierce; he rushed at her, grabbed the cup before it fell to the ground.

Placing the cup on the saucer, he turned and walked to the door, "I have to clean that up before it stains. He left the room without shutting the door. Crina made up her mind, this was her last chance. She slid to the floor and walked as fast as she could to the phone.

Just as she rounded the entrance, she saw Sylvan standing by the telephone that she had forgotten to place back on the hook. His head jerked up, he turned slowly. His eyes were almost glowing with rage. He closed on her instantly and lifted her off the floor. They moved toward the bathtub and he roughly sat her down beside the tub, pulling the nightgown over her head, striping her naked. Without saying a word, he lifted her into the warm bath.

Crina looked at him wordlessly. As if reading her thoughts, he muttered, "You shouldn't have done that, Crina. Shouldn't have done that." Crina's eyes started to flutter, her heart pounded like a drum.

Slowly, Sylvan began to rub soap over her arms and legs. His ice cold hand jolted her, sending chills down her spine. Crina went rigid. Sylvan continued to stroke her, and oddly, had a conversation with himself.

"She had a nice cup of tea and cookies before bed. Then peed herself, like old people always do. She decided to clean herself up rather than lay in piss all night. She took a warm bath, got too tired and fell asleep. She probably dreamed she was choking, but it was too late."

Crina wondered what he was talking about. And then Sylvan wordlessly grabbed her head and shoved it under the water, as she finally understood.

In her last moments, Crina looked through murky water, saw his fearsome eyes brighten as he hummed, "Ding Dong, Ding Dong."

DYLAN

I still looked over my shoulder once in awhile. Since returning from Nam, my survival instincts remained on red alert. Had Percy gotten out of jail? Would he come after me?

My final days as an MP in Da Nang had been tempestuous. Sgt. Percy Pratt had tried to kill me. Thinking about the psychopathic Percy still gave me chills. Ah well, no use looking back. Time to move on. My girlfriend Laura said I'd changed some. "Still funny but more serious. We'll work on getting the old Dylan back. All you need is some lovin'." She laughed as I nodded vigorously.

Laura was younger than me, was finishing her last college semester in Paris. After I returned from Nam, our long romance was instantly rekindled; I knew she would be Mrs. Dylan Frazier one day.

"When you really grow up," was her smiling analysis.

My "sure you want to wait that long?" made her smile broader. She didn't want to leave so soon after I came home but I pushed her to complete the French study plan.

What was I thinking? When had I ever been noble?

I needed to find a job. While in Nam, I was surprised to learn of my talent for detective work. So with my M.P. background, I got accepted into the FBI training program and soon discovered the "bureau" part of the name wasn't whimsical, was shorthand for "bureaucracy."

I soon discovered my other gift--an inability to tolerate assholes.

One FBI instructor asked, "You got a problem following orders, son?"

I grinned back. "Not orders in general, just dumb ones."

Before he could react, I added, "For instance, in Nam when they told me to, 'Take the hill, I'd say, No thanks, I already got one.'"

The instructor didn't appreciate my rapier wit, encouraged me to find a new profession.

"The Bureau doesn't like wiseasses."

That's how I ended up in the investigation unit of Voyager Insurance. With my Military Police background, I was viewed as a natural for insurance claim investigation. My insurance training consisted of being locked in a conference room, reading large green books called, "Fundamentals of Health Insurance."

I emerged for air after a week and told my boss, Dave Hoban-- I was ready.

Dave looked at me funny. "You read those manuals already?"

I nodded, "Test me on the best ways to fake Hammer Toe."

Before he replied, I said, "Look for a suspicious guy limping around with the top cut outta one penny loafer and a throbbing pinkie poppin' out, right?"

Dan Hoban had a warped sense of humor, we became friends. I actually did read all the manuals, absorbed most of it, since I'd inherited my father's great memory.

But alas, I got nothing of Dad's sane approach to things. Anyway, Hoban had done the investigator job and showed me the ropes. The routine was to get a pile of disability, life insurance or suspected fraud claims each week from Hoban and hit the road. You had to visit the suspicious people "in person" and write a report about their appropriateness for benefits. Most of the "claimants" were legitimate, had sad stories and medical proof to back up their claims.

I tended toward being anally organized and worked fast. That first week, I came in two days later after doing an alleged week of work. Hoban pulled me aside for advice. "Slow down some, you're making the other investigators look bad."

But the job became mundane after a couple weeks, so I wrote elaborate reports to amuse myself. I remember visiting a woman who worked on an assembly line for Rohm and Haas. She had carpal tunnel syndrome in her wrist and was asking to extend her 13 weeks of disability pay. I knocked on her door and was greeted by a robust woman, snowy flour all over her face, apparently in the midst of a baking project. After telling her my identity, I followed her into the kitchen. Flora Burke was rolling cookie dough, which struck me odd with a wrist problem.

Had I spotted the elusive malingerer?

Flora gabbed away and answered all my questions. I finally hit the punch line and asked if her wrist was healed enough to return to work. Flora looked at me baffled.

"It's not the wrist that's the problem. That's okay now. What's bothering me is since the injury, my hair won't hold a perm anymore. How can I go to work like this?" Flora pointed at her head.

Her prodigious head of hair was rolled into an inverted cone, like a gigantic Dairy Queen.

I shrugged like I was equally baffled. After an embarrassing silence, I finally asked, "Have you thought about wearing a hat?"

Flora went back to work and my detailed report became an instant sensation in the Home Office. I was encouraged to continue my unusual style and was viewed as "an up and comer."

But I soon became bored with the tedious work and asked Hoban for advice.

He never hesitated, "Start your own investigation company. It'll take you a few weeks to get all the license work done. I've already looked into it, can give you my stuff." Then he pulled me closer and lowered his voice. "You didn't hear it from me, but I already suggested that the company discontinue using in-house investigators. We could save salary, benefits, company cars, the works. You just send the tough claims to outside firms. They bought my idea, think I'm an organizational genius. I'll feed you all our files. Plus you work faster than anyone we've ever had, even me.

I don't know how you fly through work so fast. Anyway, put that all together and you could make a killing."

And that's how I became self-employed.

Voyager let me buy the tasteless green company car for peanuts and Hoban sent me enough work to keep me busy full-time for months. Plus I instantly tripled what I was paid by Voyager. Maybe I'd buy a normal car that didn't look like an acne scarred watermelon.

Hoban was right, it was a snap getting my insurance investigator license. Made a few trips to town hall, filled out lots of inane forms and quickly got a license to start a business. To save money, I worked out of my apartment on the fringes of Upper Darby. I got into a nice routine. Never thought I'd be a natural at detective work.

But I was.

Figured I needed to look more legit, so I went to a printer and got enough business cards to hand out when asked. Funny how a stupid card gets you inside doors. The printer laughed when he saw the name of my company.

"LOOKOUT INVESTIGATIONS." I nodded to the printer, "Got a groove factor, doesn't it, kind of like the Lone Ranger's on the job." Plus it implied there was more than one employee. Like it was a serious company, not half-assed with only one snooping knucklehead.

Everything was working out except for one thing. I hadn't shaken Nam yet. Nothing in particular, just jumpy once in awhile, got some flashbacks.

Would be in the middle of work or even playing
hoops when my mind wandered to a tense situation or
something I'd wished I'd done but didn't. They never
lasted long or got predictable. Oh yea, and
sometimes I wanted to hit someone.

SYLVAN

Sylvan Skolnick ambled into his shop and plopped behind a neatly arranged desk. When you looked at Sylvan, you thought, "hulk." While not overly tall, his head, chest and shoulders were so massive you never thought about his height. Just that he was enormous. Sylvan wore his grayish black hair long, almost shoulder length. Like a veil to seal out the cruel world, his mane hid his large face most times. When the hair was pulled back, his distinct features seemed animal-like, ruddy. But he was somehow striking because his eyes were electric, gray with bits of yellow, piercing when directed your way. Sylvan had eyes like a panther--intelligent but feral.

Sylvan Skolnick's true name was Bela Dragomir but he legally changed it after his father died. His father, Dr. Bogdan Dragomir, emigrated to Philadephia with his parents at age 8. His dad led a charmed life. From wealthy parents, Bogdan graduated from The University of Pennsylvania Medical School and met his future wife, Cosmina, also of Romanian ancestry, while interning at Jefferson Hospital.

They fell madly in love, married quickly and gave birth to Bela, exactly 9 months later. Cosmina had a difficult pregnancy and was very weak afterwards. Less than 3 months old, Bela lost the mother he'd never know to pneumonia. Had his mother lived, would life have been different, would Bela have become a monster?

Dr. Dragomir blamed Bela for his beloved Cosmina's death. While not physically abusive, Bela's father ignored him, was cold, distant and treated him like an orphan he was forced to house.

The cruelty came into Bela's life when Aunt Anca moved in to raise him. In truth, Dr. Dragomir never knew his dead wife's older spinster sister was cruel and sadistic. When he noticed the bruises, he wrote it off to Bela's lumbering clumsiness. He often thought: Where did this lumpish oaf come from? His mother was so elegant.

And the neglect continued.

Aunt Anca also blamed Bela for her sister's death. Never married, Anca had her sister's angelic face, but the similarity ended there. Anca encouraged Bela to have pets, and then used them to punish him. He found his first dog, Lex, limping when he returned from school one day.

Aunt Anca came up behind him as Bela stared at the injured Lex. "See what happens when you don't eat your dinner, Bela? Maybe we'll find that you need crutches next time." She smiled and walked off. The pattern varied but no pet lasted long. Aunt Anca always said, "Accidents happen to bad boys."

15

Sylvan hadn't thought about Aunt Anca for years. He supposed he owed her. She taught him never to get emotionally attached. Pets or friends just died or turned on you. Don't get involved. Aunt Anca also taught him to love darkness. For punishment, she locked him in a cubby hole off the kitchen. It was there he learned to dream. He became an adventurer, like D'Artagnan or Tom Swift. In this fantasy world, he was tall and muscular, strikingly handsome. He always saved the damsel. But Aunt Anca showed him the cruelty of the real world.

Suddenly alert, Sylvan shook his head and returned to the present. He rose from his meticulous desk and paced aimlessly. Sometimes he'd drift awhile after terminating one of his "projects." He inherited his father's brilliant mind but had no practical interest in the medical field. His perfect college boards got him into Haverford College, despite a forgettable grade point average.

It didn't last long, too hard living in the dorm with other students and meeting a demanding curriculum. The college president, a friend of Dr Dragomir, told Bela to "try the Army." Bela remembered smiling at him, soundless but thinking: I've got other wars to fight.

The shop bell jolted Sylvan, he spied a customer entering the shop. The old man shuffled to the front counter. His eyes widened as Sylvan pulled his hair back and glared at him with those riveting eyes.

"I got a watch I wanna pawn. Been in my family 50 years. Never misses a second, if ya wind it reglar."

Sylvan was an expert on watches. He studied all the technical manuals, used his encyclopedic memory to master the most intricate repairs.

"Let me see it." Sylvan stared at the rare old Bruguet, got very excited, but showed nothing but disinterest. "This is a piece of shit. Ten bucks."

They settled on $20 and the old man started off but turned around. "I like the name of yer shop. 'Lost in Time,' catchy."

Sylvan nodded, seemed pleased. "I named it myself. Time never fails. It's perfect. Come back again if you've got more pieces of shit to sell."

The old man frowned but walked off thinking he'd put one over on this odd man. When the door shut, Sylvan made a favorite motion, the tapping of the cash register keys and slamming money into the till. He nodded: Dumb fuck, that Bruguet's worth at least a thousand dollars. Schmuck. He padded back to his desk, sat back and savored his last minutes with Crina Barbu.

And then he thought: I need to find another project.

DYLAN

I just got off the phone with Hoban. "I got a hot file for you, Dylan. Looks like a fraud. The old lady doctored her bills, made a killing. She did a pretty slick job, wouldn't have found it if the Doctor hadn't called in looking to change his billing address. The processor asked if he wanted the check for the wheel chair to go to the new address. The Doctor had paused before asking, 'What wheelchair'?"

Hoban finished with, "It turned out the old lady's been at it for almost a year." As I wheeled the drab Impala toward center city, I thought: Finally something interesting. That would turn out to be an understatement. I was stepping into the macabre world of Sylvan Skolnick.

The claim file for Crina Barbu was substantial. I reviewed it front to back, nothing remarkable or suspicious popped out until the last year. Suddenly the bills got pricey, more intensive treatment. Crina was a retiree from Container Corporation and had a series of maladies consistent for an eighty year old.

Actually, it was noteworthy because she seemed in pretty good health. Rheumatism, Coronary Artery Disease, mild Emphysema but nothing severe, just products of a long life.

Most of the bills were straightforward and consistent for her problems. However, I found many of the bills in the last year were fictitious, after visiting Dr Torme's office and comparing the claim paperwork with his records for Ms.Barbu.

Dr. Torme advised, "Whoever did this has extensive medical knowledge. Miss Barbu was still sharp, but would she know diagnosis codes and medical protocols? These bills for the wheelchair are exactly how I'd bill and code if I wanted no hassle from the Insurance Company. They're perfect."

That sparked a thought. "How'd she get these forms? Can anybody walk in and pick them up?"

Dr. Torme considered this possibility before answering. "No way. The average citizen can't get hold of these. We have special arrangements with printers. Have to order them through a medical clearinghouse." He thought some more. "Maybe she stole them while she was in here for a visit. She just snatched them when the secretary wasn't looking. That's all I can figure."

I went back to the Voyager office and tallied the fraudulent bills. Exactly $10,010.55 was bogus. My next step was to pay a visit to Miss Barbu. I thought about her colorful neighborhood as I drove there. Fishtown was a working-class neighborhood that abuts the northeast corner of Center City. It probably derived its aquatic nickname when it was the epicenter of the shad industry on the Delaware River. However, local legend said that Charles Dickens had penned the name when he visited and was struck by its similarity to a similarly named London neighborhood.

That exhausted my minutia about Fishtown, so I concentrated on the hit or miss street signs in this tattered part of town. York Street was wall to wall apartment buildings. There were almost no trees or shrubs. If a tree managed to survive, it was spindly and desolate.

It was mid afternoon but sunlight hit only the tops of the buildings. Street level was cheerless and dreary. I looked about and mused: If I lived here, I might be tempted to steal from the insurance company. There is something hopeless about this place.

Since I was a big guy--6'2'' and 200 lbs--dressed in dark clothes, and driving a dull green car, the first thought people had about me was "Cop."

Can't say that I blamed anybody for that impression; I even carried myself like somebody expecting trouble. When Hoban was training me he noticed how people reacted to me, reared back a little. "Tell them fast you got a check for them from the insurance company, that you just need a few pieces of information. Use your menacing appearance to your advantage."

That made me chuckle but I used the advice. Worked every time.

I went inside the apartment entrance and scanned the mail slots for Barbu. There was a pile of mail in her box, a stack on the floor beneath it. Did she know she was under suspicion and bolt? When I thought about an 84 year old woman on the lam, I laughed. Not likely. That made me wonder what we would do to her.

Remembering my Green Manual training, I remembered we usually turned the matter over to the police if it was a significant fraud. I thought about this old lady being thrown in the slammer and that also made me chuckle. I'd recommend getting restitution, then dropping the matter.

After a few tries, I still got no answer when I rang the bell. Finally, I began ringing other bells, hoping someone would be home.

A creaky voice came on the intercom, "Whatcha want?" Told her I was trying to contact Ms. Barbu about her insurance checks, but got no answer. Then I mentioned the overflowing mailbox, that I was worried something might be wrong.

"Ain't know her, what's her number?" I told her and she rang me in, said to go to the 3rd floor, that's where 317 was located. No elevators; how did a woman this old get in and out?

I found 317 and knocked hard enough to be heard but not to scare her. No answer. I repeated my knock but this time loud enough to rattle your teeth.

A door down the hall opened up and an old lady peaked out. "Keep the noise down, Bud. Watchin' my Soaps. Pipe down."

I waved, "Sorry, trying to see Ms. Barbu. She's not answering. There's a load of mail lying outside her box. Worried something might be wrong. Don't know her, do you?" The old lady walked inside her apartment without answering but reappeared seconds later.

She wandered down, "Shut off the tube, save electricity, ya know."

I introduced myself and met Helen Zegielski. She eyed me up and down.

"Ya look like a cop, anyone ever tell ya that?"

I nodded, "Like once a day. Is it the clothes or my dark, mysterious good looks?"

Helen grinned, "Yer funny, too." We banged on the door some more. And then we heard the mewing and scratching.

I asked Helen, "She have a cat?" Helen didn't know, said she hadn't seen Barbu for months.

"She's a nice lady. Kept to herself, ya know what I mean?" The cat began making more noise, almost desperate. Helen looked at me, "Somethin' ain't right. Better call yer buddies."

To my puzzled look she added, "Cops."

The police arrived in 15 minutes. They tried the knock routine, but then broke open the door. The angry cat tore out, sprinted down the hall. As we moved inside, it smelled like an old person's home, like the windows were kept shut.

It didn't take long to find her. Crina was lying peacefully in her bathtub, heavy nightgown scattered on the floor beside it.

The big cop looked around, "She's been dead a day or so, otherwise it would stink like hell. Lucky we found her quick or you'd be pukin' your guts out." I scanned the bathroom reflexively, neat as a pin, nothing out of place. And then I walked around her bedroom and noticed the tea cup. Empty. The covers were pulled back. I saw the yellow stain. Must have peed herself.

And then I went downstairs while the cops were busy upstairs with the body. I went in and out of each room, getting a feel. Pretty neat housekeeping for such an old lady. And then I realized she had no bric-a-brac like many older people. Most people collect something, her place was sparse. Odd.

I got back to the office and gave Hoban the bad news. "What next?" I asked.

Hoban said, "I've got no clue, that's why we pay you, to investigate, right?" He chuckled and walked off, happy with his witticism.

A couple days later, the Philadelphia Bulletin carried her obituary and I realized my job had gotten harder. "Crina Barbu, 84, died of natural causes at her apartment on York St., in Fishtown. Crina left her native Romania at age 10, went to Holy Name of Jesus grammar school and graduated from Roman Catholic High School. She rose to supervisor at Container Corporation. Never married, Crina died with no known relatives. Funeral mass will be held at Holy Name of March 30th at 9am. Friends welcome."

I let that sink in. With no heirs, how to get the money back?

So I had to get creative with my investigation. I went to Container Corporation and met with the head of Personnel, Doug Grimm. After explaining the fraud and amounts involved, I asked Doug if he wanted me to pursue reimbursement for his company, or drop it to avoid potential bad publicity.

He looked puzzled, so I clarified. "We'd be going after a dead lady's estate.

Might get messy if a newspaper or someone thought we were chasing a poor, dead old lady. That's what I mean." Grimm started rubbing his eyes and face, like he was hoping I'd be gone when he was done.

To his chagrin, I was there when the worrying stopped. While he was thinking, I asked, "By the way, did you know Ms.Barbu? Or is there anyone around who did? Maybe there are relatives somewhere."

Grimm was happy to switch topics. "As a matter of fact, I was out to visit her a few years ago. I gave her a whole life insurance check when she hit 80. Most retirees want to save it for funeral expenses. She wanted the cash. I remember her well. She was sharp as a tack. She said she'd use the money for her Hummel collection. She said they'd be worth a fortune some day. I like Hummels myself. She had quite a collection. I wonder what will happen to them. I wouldn't mind a shot at them, tell you the truth."

I didn't respond, thinking that a strange comment. I remembered the immaculate apartment. No Hummels, no nothing. When he first mentioned the collection, I thought she might have done the fraud to get money for more collecting. Like someone obsessed but lacking the cash to buy. But where did they go? Did she sell them? Have a premonition about her death and wanted the loose ends cleaned up? If so, where did she put the money? Or did she get robbed?

All that ran through my head as I turned to Grimm and asked again about relatives.

He scanned her personnel file and said the life insurance policy listed her church as beneficiary, if she died before the cash settlement was paid.

He shrugged, "No relatives, I guess."

≈

On the way home, I swung by the basketball courts in my old neighborhood. I'd played there since becoming obsessed with the game at 10. It was early April and unusually warm. I kept my hoop clothes in the car, just in case a game popped up. Was lucky today, about 8 guys were shooting mindlessly. I spotted Jimmer, a childhood friend and self appointed "commissioner of the courts." My real name was Thomas, but Jimmer nicknamed me Dylan as an ironic homage to his idol, Bob Dylan. It stuck, even my parents called me Dylan.

Jimmer spotted me, "Hey, Dylan, how come you're slumming with the low life? The elitists on the Main Line kick you out? Jimmer was a born storyteller and talked non-stop. Unlike most gabbers, Jimmer was very bright, considered himself a champion of the common man and was very funny without trying to be. He was (4) years older, lifted weights relentlessly, looked like it, and had been my protector since I could remember. He gave me shit incessantly, like no one else could. When I first met him in 6th grade, he looked at my slick pompadour and told me, "Lose the Dairy Queen swirl."

25

"Hey, Jimmer, they won't let me play on the Main Line till I lose my green Impala, say I ooze low class. Got to play somewhere, guess you losers got lucky."

Jimmer was not a good player, but he was a good shooter. He was so muscle bound, he couldn't dribble and had to be wide open or he ate his shot. Naturally, he surrounded himself with good players, so the defense would ignore him.

Jimmer looked at me, "You're on my team, Dylan, we'll give you a pass tonight." Jimmer looked down the street. "Here comes that douche Wang, that makes 10. He's on the other team." Jimmer had stocked his team with the best of the lot. Some things never changed.

After we won that game, I asked Jimmer if I could join his judo school. He worked for SEPTA , was a union rep for the trolley drivers, but had a judo school as a side business.

He looked disturbed by the notion, "I'm not sure Master Kano had you in mind when he fathered the fine art of Judo. You're more of a muscle head wrestler type. Sure you're ready for that, Dylan?"

I explained my new career; that I might get into some bad spots and wanted any edge I could get.

Jimmer nodded approvingly, "Bad shit happens." We made plans to meet for my first lessons that weekend.

We continued playing hoops and kept the same sides. This game got nasty. I guarded Jake Ryan and made it a point of roughing him up. Jake had sucker-punched me years ago and I hadn't forgotten. Since I now towered over him, it was fun getting some licks.

One time a shot went up; I boxed him out so hard he fell out of bounds.

He came up mad. "Watch it, dick head."

I just smiled. When he tried to shoot next time, I stuffed the ball so hard he fell backwards. This time he got up, cocked his fist and charged. As I was trained in the MP's, I waited till he got near, grabbed his coiled arm and flipped him hard to the ground. He laid there stunned.

Jimmer walked over, shook his head. "I'm not sure you need my judo class."

SYLVAN

After Aunt Anca died, a freak hit and run accident on her way to church, Bela had a better relationship with his father. Although he was disappointed that Bela had recently dropped out of Swarthmore, his father needed help running his office and appreciated Bela's willingness to pitch in. Anca had been his receptionist and right arm but Bela thrived in his new role and soon surpassed Anca in skill and efficiency. Dr Dragomir's practice flourished and he was surprised by his lumpish son. Had he misjudged him? He couldn't bring himself to show affection, but he was cordial to Bela.

This peaceful co-existence went on for a few years. Bela read medical journals voraciously and soon astounded his father with what he had learned.

"It's not too late for a medical career, Bela. You could probably get back in school, take pre-med and go full-time to make up for the years you lost. It would be a lot of work, but you already know more real life medicine than most interns. It's something to think about."

Bela seemed to consider the suggestion but shook his head. "I like this better."

Dr. Dragomir never brought it up again; he wouldn't know what to do if Bela left.

But Bela had not forgotten his father's years of neglect. He became fascinated with famous killers throughout history, studied and admired them. As a child, he mimicked Aunt Anca's abuse and used animals as payback punishment. If someone mocked or bullied him, Bela would trail the offender and look for pets or other points of weakness. By the time he was 10; he had battered every dog and cat of his persecutors. Baseball bats were his weapon of choice. Sometimes he hung the animals before pummeling them. Bela never felt more alive than when he was killing. He was fascinated by the idea of actually seeing or sensing "death."

By 8th grade, Bela had grown huge and was encouraged to try football. He found instant success as an offensive tackle at Our Mother of Consolation in Chestnut Hill. While not fast, he cleared out anyone in his path and the halfbacks ran crazy behind him. They still called him "Ding Dong," but not with the same mocking tone he'd endured since 1st grade. He remained a loner but was now part of the team and thus "protected" from tougher schoolmates. He grew to love the blocking. Whenever a halfback scored a touchdown, they'd pat his back and say, "Way to roll, Ding Dong. Way to roll." It was the best time of his life. Dr. Dragomir never made a game or acknowledged his play.

ॐ

When the shop bell tingled noisily, Sylvan woke from his childhood memories. An old woman entered with a large shopping bag that sagged with treasure. He looked carefully, prided himself on his ability to spot eastern Europeans. Polish? She feigned disinterest, continued to inspect the lamps, radios and clocks. She doesn't want to appear anxious, Sylvan thought. This might be fun. Finally, the old woman ambled to the counter, unloaded an ancient Austrian figurine. She looked up, startled when she saw Sylvan's hypnotic eyes. She soon recovered,

"What cha give for my figurine? Been in family since my tata be born." The woman relaxed when Sylvan smiled broadly.

He was very sure this was his next project.

DYLAN

Most of my investigations for Voyager were hum drum, so the Crina Barbu fraud file was a rare challenge. Container Corporation told us to drop the fraud case, so I had to use my own time to chase down Crina's loose ends. It bugged me, something smelled. I had some legal questions about her case so I turned to my old buddy Gator. Jimmer had named Bill Light, "Gator" because "he had a few extra layers of teeth- like an alligator." Gator was one of my favorite people; he'd also been to Nam and was the kind of friend who was there when you needed him. Plus he was funny as hell, uniquely eccentric. Despite his zany personality, Gator was a brilliant lawyer, had a budding practice in nearby Swarthmore.

I called his secretary and identified myself as "his only friend who would admit it out loud."

I heard her repeat that to Gator who laughed like a hyena and told her, "That's Dylan, he's a major asshole. Clear my calendar, finally something fun."

Gator listened to the whole Crina story, got excited and agreed something stunk.

"She probably doctored the insurance forms and ripped them off. People with a lot of Hummels are like baseball card collectors. Obsessed.

They're always looking for the next one. She probably got the cash so she could buy the next prize. Then someone cleaned out her apartment after she died, thinking no one would notice. It hangs together pretty nice. I don't think we're missing anything, do you?"

I sat silently for a minute or so. "Scares me when we start to think alike, Gator. Maybe I got a slow reaction to Agent Orange?"

Gator gave his maniacal laugh. "Dylan, you were a crazy bastard way before Charlie had a shot at you. They just freed your wild edges, is all."

I told him I wanted to search her apartment, try to find any records or bank accounts. "Collectors like to keep track of their trophies. My brother pours through his stamp books every night. Likes to touch them. That old lady must have Hummel books around. Something that would give me a tip. But how do I get in there?"

Gator gave me chuckle, "Didn't you say the cops knocked her door down? And wasn't she all alone, no kin? I bet no one went to the trouble of repairing her door yet. Let's take a spin to Fishtown. If someone arrests you, at least you'll have your lawyer with you."

When we got there, the door was ajar but there was police tape all over the entrance.

Before Gator could tell me the obvious, "I know, Gator, rip it off and put it back when we leave, right?"

He chuckled, "Maybe you should be a lawyer, you're devious enough."

I walked down to the neighbor, Helen Zegielski, and heard the soap operas booming away.

"We're all set, Helen couldn't hear us if we drilled a hole through the wall with a jackhammer. Let's hurry."

We pushed open the door and lifted enough tape away to slip under. After we got inside, I put most of the tape back and then shut the damaged door as we began our search.

Gator quipped, "Reminds me when we used to creep around those haunted mansions out by Villanova, try to scare our girls into putting out. Can you believe we did that shit? Man, those were the days."

I was trying to focus, so I let that pleasant memory drift by without answering. I went to the bedroom and sifted through the table by her bed. A fine layer of dust scattered as I pulled the drawer open. Tissues, Bible, Bobbie pins, flashlight and jar of moisturizer lay neatly within. Gator was in the living room pouring through her books.

He yelled, "There's nothing on Hummels. It doesn't make sense. It looks like there's some gaps on these shelves, I see some stains where books used to be, somebody cleared them out is my bet."

I was a puzzle and trivia nut, so I answered, "Looks like a mystery surreptitiously wrapped in a conundrum, Gator."

I heard his throaty chuckle but got no more play by play for the next few minutes. And then something popped into my head.

I walked out to ask Gator, "See any signs of a cat?"

Gator smirked, "Is this one of your weird jokes or is that a real question?"

I told him about the cat tearing out when the cops broke in. I looked at him, "I don't smell a cat or see a litter box. Any pet food around?" We poured through the small kitchen and found no signs of pet supplies. I asked the obvious, "If she didn't have a cat, how'd it get in here?"

We let that percolate as we continued our search. There was a junk drawer near the stove and I went through it slowly. Found Holy Name of Jesus collection envelopes. Looked at the dates, only a couple months old. Did she still go to church? Or did the priest visit her here? Maybe they'd know her and have some background information. That made me think about a checkbook.

"Did you see a checkbook, Gator? Any other financial records?" Before he answered, I spotted a pawn ticket. I looked at the name and date on the receipt, "The Powerful Pawn." Did she sell off her Hummels?

As we scooted under the police tape and carefully shut the door, Gator turned to me.

"That place was stripped clean. No personal records. No personal stuff. No nothing. Man, if my grandmother croaked today, they'd need a freakin' 18 wheeler to haul the shit away. There's no way that old lady lived that way, too neat. She was ripped off either before she died or afterwards. I've got no doubt."

We walked outside before I added. "Do you think the robber left the cat there on purpose or by accident?"

Gator grinned, "Only you would worry about the goddamned cat. A dead lady gets ripped off and you dwell on a cat. Who gives a shit?"

I saw his point but countered, "Loose ends, Gator. Tie up the loose ends."

∂

We got in the car and I asked if he had more time. Gator nodded, "What's up?"

I showed the pawn ticket. "Want to see what 'The Powerful Pawn' has to do with this mess. Maybe they have her Hummels. Don't know for sure, just following the trail."

Gator got real animated and started shifting in his seat. "I've got all day. This beats the shit out of fighting some guy's claim his property's located on holy Indian ground. He says he shouldn't have to pay taxes since he's on Sovereign territory. I'm not kidding, you can't make this shit up."

On our drive to the Powerful Pawn, I asked Gator. "Who's the 'Owl without a Vowel'?" I heard Gator inhale, could feel him puzzling what I was up to.

"Beside who gives a rat's ass, what are you talking about and, by the way, I'm not biting." Sometimes I did trivia when I tried to clear my mind. When I focused on something totally inane, answers about what troubled me popped up. Not always, but sometimes.

"Gator, anybody who follows Philly basketball knows that Temple's Bill Mlkvy is the greatest player in Big Five history without any vowels in his name.

What kind of lawyer are you, not knowing that? Maybe I need a brighter barrister."

We pulled up to the Powerful Pawn, I said to Gator, "Let's look around before we ask the owner any questions. If he thinks we're just there to snoop, he'll clam up."

Gator nodded and then grinned. "If he asks me, I'll tell him I'm looking for Bill Mlkvy's old uniforms. Someone said he might have them."

I was still laughing as we entered. The place gave dingy a bad name. It took awhile for my eyes to adjust. And then the smell hit me. Mold with a hefty dose of Pine sol.

Gator smelled it seconds later, turned to me, "Let's see how long I can hold my breath."

We ambled around and still hadn't seen anyone. Place empty or is someone just laying low? I was looking for Hummels or something similar for sale. There seemed to be no pattern to the shop, scattered with clothes, all types of shoes, silverware, old tools, wood cabinets etc. I saw Gator staring down at something under a glass display.

When I got close, he raised his head.

"Baseball cards. Old ones." From nowhere, a creepy voice hit us. "There's an original Mays card in there." A wispy old man floated from around a nearby dry sink. Had he been there all the time? He then went on a monologue about whether the rookie Dick Allen cards would someday be worth more than the Say Hey kid. He looked at me seriously, "It depends. That's all. Just depends."

Gator was a baseball freak and engaged this elfish gnome in arcane baseball facts.

While they went at it, I circled the shop and saw nothing resembling expensive porcelain collectibles. I had read everything I could get my hands on about Hummels. Originals were all based on the work of Maria Innocentia Hummel, a German nun who did drawings of children as a hobby. W. Goebel, who owned a renowned porcelain firm, saw her work and entered a partnership to manufacture her figurines. By the late 1930's these porcelain works became a worldwide sensation.

I interrupted the baseball argot, "Got any Hummels?" The gnome never looked at me but almost growled his answer.

"I've got no need for fancy stuff here. These people wouldn't know a Hummel from a statue of Joe Palooka."

Before he could get back to comparing the value of Jim Bunning versus Johnny Callison cards, I interjected, "Know where I can find some? Want to surprise my mom for her birthday. She's German, likes to support the homeland, you know."

The gnome never broke his verbal stride, "You ever hear of the Yellow Pages?"

Gator bought a few baseball cards, which loosened the guy some. I showed him the ticket I found in Crina's apartment and asked if he could tell what she pawned.

He frowned, seemed to debate, "It looks like a silverware sale. Not sure, though." Then he added, "What's it worth you to check?"

I smiled my friendliest, "Would my eternal gratitude and knowing you helped another human being be enough?"

The gnome stared at me without blinking, "Add 10 bucks and we got a deal. Keep your eternal whatever you said."

Gator was still laughing when we walked out with our answer. Crina had sold all her silver. Got $100 for a lifetime of special pieces. Why had she liquidated her prizes? To buy more Hummels?

꩜

That night I was back in Nam, on patrol outside Quang Tri when I spotted papa-sahn disappearing into the brush. I looked at my buddy Mac and asked if he saw it too.

Mac turned, looked at me funny, "The whole place is full of papa sahns, why worry about one sneaking around? Maybe he's taking a leak. Don't sweat it." Just then the RPG burst through the leaves; I watched the smoke trail coming at me. Was that how I died? But that's when I woke up, dripping wet. I looked around my bedroom in Philly. All alone, Mac wasn't there. I went to the bathroom and splashed cold water on my face. I looked in the mirror: It's all over, Dylan, it's all over.

꩜

I had my first judo lesson after work. Jimmer was pontificating before a bevy of young students as I entered. I was the oldest pupil, by far.

As I walked up, Jimmer turned and spoke to the class. "Judoka, welcome our newest student, Dylan. Don't let his size scare you. By using the techniques of "the gentle way," you can subdue even big lugs like him. Show no mercy, judoka."

That's how my judo lessons began. I changed into the white uniform, called a judogi, but referred to simply as "ji." Jimmer showed me a series of throws (nage-waza) and groundwork (ne-waza) and stayed with me long enough to be sure I had the right form. He called a little kid over and pointed at me, "Be easy on him." The diminutive judoka threw me around like a bag of potatoes for the next hour.

Afterwards, Jimmer wandered over with a big grin on his face. "Have fun?"

I shrugged my shoulders. "If getting my ass kicked by a pygmy troll qualifies as fun, then I guess that was a fiesta." And then we both laughed in good cheer.

And then Jimmer looked at me, "Hang in there. In all seriousness, with your foot speed and balance, you'll excel quickly. It just depends what's your goal, self-defense or mayhem? But either way, you'll get better fast."

I told Jimmer about the neighborhoods I worked in, that I wanted to be prepared; you never knew what might happen. "In that case, later on I'll mix in "Atemi-Waza," the striking techniques. With your natural aggressiveness, you'll be a bad person to piss off in no time." Then he added, "By the way, call me "Sensei" in here. Formality and discipline are the backbone of judo. Even for my friends." I bit my tongue.

Just then a woman and little kid came rushing in, making a beeline for Jimmer. The kid jumped into Jimmer's huge arms and hugged him like a long lost friend. When the kid relaxed, Jimmer spun him toward me. "Dylan, meet my son Jose." I shook Jose's hand as the attractive young woman arrived. "Dylan, this is Marisol, my wife. We were married when you were in Nam. Marisol, Dylan is one of my oldest friends. He lived across the street."

Marisol, looked at me with huge brown eyes, "You are the first of James's friends that I've met." She was clearly Puerto Rican but spoke flawless English. Before I could ask, "James and I met at Septa; I represent Hispanic members in the union. James was my boss."

Jimmer looked at me, grinned. "Now she's the boss."

SYLVAN

Bela renamed himself Sylvan Skolnick after his father's sudden, deadly heart attack. He loved pawn shops as a child, found comfort in the dark, nostalgic interiors. Every shop he visited had a Jewish owner.

"Jews know a deal, they like to haggle," his father said when Bela inquired why they dominated that business. Bela liked the sound of his new name-- Sylvan was in homage to his Pennsylvania roots and Skolnick sounded so tough, so Jewish. He was very proud of himself when he marched from court with his new identity. The judge nodded sympathetically when Bela explained his old named haunted him.

"Since Bela Lugosi got famous, everyone called me "Dracula." With his aunt and father dead, there was no one left who knew his old life.

Sylvan had been right about the woman who now frequented his shop. Polish, a widow with no children, collected porcelain figurines from Germany and Austria but had hit hard times and was selling treasures to get by. Biata Wozniak had proved to be a perfect project. She lived in Olney, had heard he was "very fair to the Polish."

Sylvan was especially courteous if he sensed a repeat customer with no knowledge of their treasures worth. His ploy was to overpay for a piece or two in the beginning, gain trust, and then screw them thereafter. But if he selected a project, he didn't quibble; he knew he'd get the money back in the end.

Biata told Sylvan, "Call me Bee, is what they called me at Rohm and Haas. My husband never liked that, said it disgraced our Polish heritage, but I say move on. We're in America now."

Sylvan looked at her with riveting eyes. "Bee suits you. Like a honeybee, sweet." Biata blushed but loved the attention from this gentle man. He scared her at first, until she found out what a kind person he was, always there to help. With her emphysema and arthritis, she needed all the help she could get. Sylvan knew so much about insurance companies and all those confusing things. What a blessing.

She beamed at Sylvan, "What did I do before you? Like a knight in shining armor you are."

DYLAN

I decided to return to Crina's apartment to see if I could get something, anything from her neighbors. Also the cat still bugged me; I had to work that out. Based on the lack of cat supplies and no mess inside, I thought the cat had just gotten in before I arrived that first day. That would mean someone was inside before me, had a cat with them. Maybe a friend checking to see why they hadn't heard from Crina? Heard me ringing the bell and bolted before I found them inside with Crina dead? I planned to start with her neighbor, Helen, who was there when we found the body. I rang her bell and she answered rapidly.

"Mrs. Zegielski, this is Dylan Frazier, we met when I came looking for your neighbor and we found her dead. Remember me?"

A pause then a raspy, "Ya, yer the funny guy but look edgy, like a beat cop, right?" I said, "You nailed me."

Helen's apartment was messy, papers scattered everywhere.

She noticed me looking, "Ain't had time fer spring cleanin'. Sorry fer the mess. Got hooked on crossword puzzles. Can't get enough of em, mostly Daily News. Want ta work my way to that New York Times one but can't make head nor tails outta it. I mean, who knows all that Broadway show trivia? Bunch a pansy shit, er sorry, pardon my language."

We traded theories on cracking puzzles before I hit her with the cat. She looked pensive. "It's like a puzzle aint it? The lady didn't have pets but we find a cat in there. Kinda funny."

Helen was in no hurry, think she enjoyed having company. To get her involved, I asked if she'd mind helping me solve this cat mystery.

"Is it possible the cat came through an open window that closed unexpectedly when the cat got inside? Is that possible? Or is there some vent the cat used but couldn't get out?"

Helen was smiling a gummy smile. "Ya got a wild imagination, don't ya? Me, I think it might be that old cat lady, mighta known the dead lady. She somehow got in. Maybe fergot she left a cat inside. It was like that, er something."

I said silently. Bingo! Helen went on to say there was, "An old coot, half crazy who lived somewhere behind her building. She has lots a cats. I sometimes saw her in the alley between the apartments, cats surrounding her, 'like flies on horseshit'."

I thanked Helen and made my way out back. The alley was dismal and overgrown, had a damp smell. A series of broken-down cyclone fences separated the once precious pieces of ground.

There were probably flower gardens or little vegetable patches when this street teamed with young families. Nothing left now, hope was gone. I walked up and down and smelled the cats before I saw them. Rank and carthy. Where was the "old coot?"

At least 30 cats roamed aimlessly, like a swarm of bees, watching and wary. There was a group of overgrown hemlock bushes that seemed to be their home. I saw water and chow bowls in neatly placed series of three. There was a strange order to the place. Interesting. Someone was feeding and caring for them. Where was she? I moved into the center of the overgrown lawn and looked up at the apartment. As my eyes neared the top floors, I saw a curtain pull shut. Got you! Top floor, corner apartment. Now I had to get in and get her talking. I made my way toward the front, fighting through the bramble of neglect. Hoped the cat lady liked edgy-looking cop types.

I guess she didn't because I got no response to my rings. The name on her box was blurred, Costas? Couldn't be sure. I tried all the other bells but no one answered. No helpful Helens in this building. I noted the street address and apartment number. Would see if I could get a name through some of Gator's cop contacts. I walked outside and decided to retrace my route, pretend to leave and watch to see if the cat lady showed. I sat hidden in the underbrush for half an hour, feeling a little foolish, nothing happened. So much for my cloak and dagger plan.

❧

The telephone was ringing as I walked into my pad. I quickly scanned my neat apartment. Compared to Helen Zegielski's place, I was looking good. Never liked mess, that way from a kid.

Picked up the phone, recognized Hoban's voice. "What's shakin' Hoban?"

He told me there was another weird claim he wanted investigated. "It's right up your alley, Dylan. The guys on disability from his roofing business. He leaves "the phone booth on 17th and Ingersoll" as his address. No real phone number, nothing else. A ragged note on the bottom says, "The mailman knows me. Ain't be no problem with delivery." I told Hoban I'd do it right away. I needed to keep him happy so the cash would flow.

It got even funnier as I picked up the file next morning. The disabled guy also ran "THE ONLY WAY TEMPLE OF OUR LORD AND SAVIOR JESUS CHRIST--TRUE LEADER OF THE APOSTOLIC FAITH," and described himself as Bishop and Director. All this was spelled out on a cheap, photocopied letterhead. In the left corner of the letterhead he added, "BISHOP WINN ROOFING COMPANY--ALL WORK GUARANTEED."

Hoban grinned as I looked up dumfounded, "It gets better." When Hoban wrote asking for more information about the unusual combination of careers, he got back the following letter:

"Dear Mr. Hoban. You all have been hesitation long enough with my money.

No more nonsense about my checks. If my money aint here by returns mail, I will have Jesus send an angel to your house and office and burn it to the ground."

The letter was signed, "The Son of the Living God."

I looked seriously at my buddy, "If I were you Hoban, I'd move." Hoban rarely laughed, but he liked that one.

I arrived at 17th and Ingersoll and sure enough there was a phone booth on the corner. This was a tough section of North Philly, so I kept my eyes open. There were a series of beat up buildings on the street. I had cruised up and down a few times but couldn't spot the legendary roofing and temple business. I parked my green clunker in a visible area so I could see if anybody screwed with it while I poked around. As I neared the corner, a mail truck pulled up and came to a stop. The mailman was black and looked surprised when he saw me hurry up to the truck.

He smiled, "You lost buddy? Aint a neighborhood to be messin' around in."

I shrugged, "My mom claims I've been lost for years, can't seem to change her mind." He looked puzzled by the quip. Doesn't get it? Doesn't want to? Discriminating sense of humor? Didn't give a shit?

Breaking the pause, I explained my mission and asked with a straight face, "You ever deliver mail to that phone booth?"

Without hesitation, "You must mean for Bishop Winn. I been leavin' stuff there for years. When I took over this route, was told that's how it was."

When I looked incredulous, he added, "Bishop Winn runs this neighborhood. Just look around, it's a bomb zone. Nobody fucks with him. Hear he's crazy ta boot. Playin' the game is all I do." I asked more questions but he clammed up. "Aint know nothin' else." He did point out the ramshackle building of the celestial roofer. I ambled over to look closer.

There was no visible sign this was the right place but I didn't think the mailman was messing with me. I banged on the only door and got nothing. Hammered some more but still got squat. As I began to leave, the door swung open and a huge man appeared. He had gray hair cropped short. Something about him screamed "be careful."

He looked at me with blurred, yellowish eyes. "What you want?" Only a few words but the tone was deep and powerful.

"I'm here to see Bishop Winn. Trying to get his claim cleared up so I can get his checks to him. There's already been too much delay."

His whole demeanor changed. Big smile, the amber eyes lit up, "Come in, my son, I'm Bishop Winn."

In the MP's I honed my knack for observation. In MP school, when we practiced reviewing crime scenes, I readily picked the one thing that seemed wrong or out of place. The oddity jumped out at me, usually in seconds. "Creepy" was how my surly MP buddy Fleming viewed my skill. Regardless, it was a useful tool in this line of work. The small warehouse was lined with chairs, pointing to a make-shift pulpit. No signs of a roofing business. No smells of tar paper or shingles.

Just looked like a broken-down meeting room. How to broach the roofing disability without getting my ass whipped?

His claim said he fell off a ladder and hurt his back. So I asked, "How's the back healing, Bishop Winn? Must have been a terrible fall you had. Hope you're feeling better. Backs are tough." Up until that moment, he had moved crisply and walked tall, like an angel entering the throne of glory.

As he responded, he hunched down and spoke weakly. "Doin' poorly, son. Right poorly."

I switched topics. "How's your church doing? Still lots of sinners, I guess. That's one business that'll never run dry, don't you think?"

Bishop Winn chuckled, "Say, amen to that, young brother. Say amen."

Then I doubled back to the punch line, "Can you show me your roofing business area? I've got to write a report showing your work environment and typical day. Just routine stuff, so I can help the paper pushers get your claim processed. Helps them if they can get a better sense of how you do your job when you aren't disabled. That kind of thing."

I could see the Bishop pondering how to explain the lack of materials and a workshop. His expression brightened. "Used it all up on my last job. Just happen'd to fall together at the right time."

I looked at him pleasantly, "Guess the Lord was looking out for you."

He beamed his best smile. "Say amen, brother. Say, amen!"

I bid him goodbye, said, "Your claim is pretty straightforward. I'll get you what you deserve."

Bishop Winn never got any disability payments. I did a neighborhood check and found a few non-believers who were more than happy to defrock the bishop. The best summary was, "That sum bitch never work a day in his life. Wouldn't know how ta roof a house if it bend over and kissed his ass. Jus' scams the old ladies. Charms 'em and filches they cash. Truth be told." Fortunately, Bishop Winn never asked for my identification or address, so the Lord's angel is still wandering aimlessly, lusting for fiery vengeance.

While I was fooling with the Bishop Winn scam, I let the Crina Barbu case run through my head. So far, nothing had popped into my subconscious. But I did hatch a new plan to trap the cat lady. My lawyer pal Gator had come through. His contact in the police confirmed that the resident's name was Mirella Costas.

Gator's secretary relayed the findings and told me, "Mirella Costas has no police record, nothing that made her noteworthy."

I let that sink in before adding, "Bet if I checked on Gator, the noteworthy comments would read, 'cloven hooves, spiky tail and strong desire to dress like Morticia Addams'."

She chuckled, "Mr. Light's clients are so boring, I can't wait to meet you." She had a sexy voice, I thought as I set down the phone. Wonder what she looks like?

❧

My scheme was to get outside Mirella's apartment early and intercept her as she gave the felines their morning chow. Most pets were fed like clockwork. Miss their schedule and they go nuts. These cats were already feral so I bet Mirella did what she needed to keep the neighbors from bringing in the SPCA. A pack of wild, smelly cats is bad enough. A pack of screaming, starving cats would create a racket. When I encountered the cats earlier, they were leery but they weren't starving. I bet Mirella was a good caretaker. So I arrived before 6 am and waited.

It was getting light as I lurked on the edge of the huge hemlock bushes they called home. The cats prowled around but didn't seem agitated by my presence. Again I noticed the sense of organization to this wild place. But the odor was almost overpowering. As I was pulling a handkerchief to stifle the stench, I heard movement in the backyard. A nice looking old lady appeared with what must have been a bag of cat food. The pack got excited and swarmed around her ankles as she poured the chow into bowls separated enough to disperse the throng of cats into smaller groups, like she intended to avoid chaos. I heard her purr, "There's my little angels."

I didn't want to scare her so I quietly watched her circling the pack, petting them and cooing in delight. As she went off to get the nearby hose, I came into the open and waited for her to return. If she saw me from a distance, maybe I wouldn't spook her too bad. She ambled back slowly, dragging a long hose dripping with water. Just as she turned around the hemlocks she spotted me and stood still.

I said softly, "Good morning, Miss Costas. I'm a friend of Crina Barbu. She told me how nice you were to the cats. Just thought I'd stop by and say hello."

She stared at me carefully before speaking. "That's a damn lie." That made me laugh hysterically. Pretty soon she added, "You're nuts, too."

That's how our relationship started. Over a series of visits, I learned Mirella Costas was a retired spinster who lived in this neighborhood her whole life. Pushing 85, she had outlived all her neighbors and never bothered meeting their replacements. Except for Crina Barbu. "Crina was good people. Old school. Worked hard, never stuck her nose in your business. She liked the cats. Helped out some till her rheumatism knocked her out a year or so ago. I checked on her once in awhile. That is till her nephew showed up."

That got my interest, since her work records showed no relatives. I asked Mirella about the nephew.

"Only saw him from my window, but it was always dark when he came. I never met him. Crina said he was shy. She called him her 'big boy.' Always talked about his beautiful long hair, like a movie star." Mirella paused, said she never saw his face. "He came mostly at night, like he was dropping in after work. You know what I mean?" I asked about the Hummel collection. She nodded, "Crina had a lot of 'em. Me, I never liked 'em. Too religious for me. I like statuary myself. How about you?"

I smiled, "Huge gnome fan. Most kids want to grow up to be cops or firemen. Me, I told the nuns I want to be a gnome maker."

That made her chuckle; Mirella was still sharp as a tack.

Over the course of a couple visits, I told Mirella I was an insurance investigator; that we were seeing if we owed Crina anything. She didn't react much when I told her the Hummels were gone.

I let it go and switched topics. "How do you stand the smell down here? I like cats but the odor is a killer."

She looked at me benignly. "What smell? Ain't smelled nothin' since I turned 80. You could shit in your pants and I'd never know. It comes in handy sometime." What do you say to that?

She seemed comfortable with me, so I hit her with the big one. "You were in Crina's apartment when I called up, weren't you?" I quickly added, "I won't tell anyone. It's just a cat was in there when we broke in. Been bugging me." I could see her weighing her answer.

She looked up and grinned. "Busted. You gonna lock me up?" I didn't say anything, wanted her to elaborate at her own pace. Finally, she added, "I was worried about Crina. She usually called to check on the cats. Didn't hear nothing for a couple weeks. Ain't seen the nephew either. I had a key she gave me years ago. She has mine too. Just in case, you know. I found her dead in the tub, then the bell started yackin' and I got out fast. I must have left ole Misty inside. She follows me sometimes."

When Mirella mentioned their phone calls, another thought popped. Maybe her phone records would show who she kept in touch with?

If she did hock her Hummels, maybe the pawn dealers name would be there. And maybe this illusive nephew had a name I could track. Keep asking and the leads will keep coming.

I turned back to Mirella, she had a funny look on her face. "I'm glad Crina went quietly. Something seemed to be buggin' her lately. Not her normal self. Maybe she just knew the end was comin'."

❧

That night I headed to the basketball courts to unwind. My conversation with Mirella had opened new doors and I wanted to stew awhile before calling Gator for help tracking telephone record.

Jimmer was there as I cruised up. "Well if it isn't my esteemed Sensei. You've bossed me around as court commissioner, now I've got to bow to you as my judo instructor. Life isn't treating me too well, Jimmer."

Without hesitation, "You know what William Jennings Bryant said, Dylan. 'Destiny is not a matter of chance. It's a matter of choice.' With your defective personality, maybe you just need me to show the way." Jimmer had a way with words.

With Laura still in Paris, I played ball 3-4 times a week. The competition helped quell my desire to smack someone. I tried to guard the toughest players and often pissed them off by being too rough.

One guy looked at me incredulously, "Who the hell blocks- out someone 30 feet from the basket in playground ball?"

Jimmer, who loved my intensity since he always picked me for his team, added immediately, "Someone with serious rage problems. Don't you know this is a jungle trained bad-ass from Nam? Just shut up and let him exorcize some demons, will you?" No one reacted, they just stood still. Pretty soon someone dribbled and the game started again.

Afterwards, as Jimmer and I walked to our cars, I asked about his wife and kid.

"We got married when you were in Nam. You met Marisol, kind of nice on the eyes and just my type. A tenacious bitch. We fought like cats and dogs at the negotiating table. She stuck up for her people like a Republican at an NRA meeting. It got so bad, my boss told me to find a way to get along with her. I asked her to have a cup of coffee, to see if we could mend fences. After a chilly beginning, we found we both were fighting for the same thing. But too bull-headed to listen. By the end of the 3rd cuppa Joe, I was in love."

Before I could ask about Jose, Jimmer added, "Jose was part of the package. Marisol got into a bad relationship and the husband split when she got pregnant. She hasn't seen or heard from him. That suits me, I love that little guy and from what I hear from Marisol, dad turned out to be a major douche bag. So, I got an instant family. Kind of like a Swanson dinner, no hassles." Jimmer seemed really happy. He was always an iconoclast. Never took the normal path in anything. Having met Marisol briefly, I could see they were a good match. Both burr-under-the-saddle types, never happy with the status quo, but solid and honest. People you could count on.

Jimmer lived across the street from me growing up, so I knew his parents well and wondered how they took this. I got an unexpected answer. "Other than telling me Marisol is a whore and that Jose is a bastard who's going to hell, they seem pretty happy with my life choice." When I looked for the next punch line, Jimmer let me off the hook. "My parents disowned me. I haven't talked to them since I told them I was getting married. My mother goes to church every day and prays for my soul to be saved from the devil. Seems kind of ironic, doesn't it? Goes to church everyday, but can't find forgiveness for a brave young girl who made a mistake, raised a kid by herself and never got any help." I didn't know what to say.

The conversation had gotten too touchy. Jimmer switched gears. "You might end up a good judoka but are probably too big to be great. What you do have that's hard to teach is focus. I can see you aren't afraid to be hit. You're willing to wait to the last second before striking. That's your gift. But even so, the smaller judoka will have an edge on speed. Ultimately, speed kills." I had already noted that after my few lessons. I had read that the founder of judo, Kano Jigoro, was a small, frail boy. He gravitated to martial arts for self-preservation and invented judo as a way for little people to gain advantage. I was a big guy. In judo, size was a disadvantage.

I looked at Jimmer, "I told you, all I want is an edge if I get in bad spots. Most of the knuckle-draggers I might encounter won't be trained fighters. Just want to put them on their ass and move on."

Jimmer eyed me for awhile. "You do seem kind of wound up since you got out of Nam. It must have been rough over there. Ever want to talk, just ask."

When I first moved to Philly before first grade, Jimmer took a liking to me, had me under his wing until I outgrew him and could fend for myself. More than once he'd kicked somebody's ass for screwing with me. I looked at him, "Got a few minutes?"

ᔈ

Without using real names, I told him the details of some rotten MP's in Nam who ran everything from stolen vehicles and prostitution to drugs and selling weapons to the enemy. The Army didn't want the facts leaked so I'd had to sign a form swearing to keep quiet about the incident.

I looked at Jimmer, "They made it clear they'd put me in prison if I talked and it got out. Said this was a military matter. This was serious business. These guys weren't kidding." Jimmer nodded so I continued, "Most of the MP's were great guys, did a tough job and were good soldiers. The crooked mastermind set me up. All the while he just played me like a fool. He killed off anyone who got too close."

Jimmer asked a few questions before I continued. "I lived for months scared I'd get fragged while I slept. Percy (I didn't use his name) was the craziest of them all. Was never sure he was part of the ring or just hated me.

He was sadistic, a trained killer, just liked hurting people, broke their legs if they looked at him funny. I made the mistake of standing up to him. He didn't like that, he almost killed me. Long story but I ended up testifying against him after he killed a harmless villager, putting him in prison. He swore he'd get me. I still get the willies thinking he's out and coming for me. If you knew him, you might not think I was paranoid."

Jimmer had listened intently. He knew me well, almost like a big brother. I wondered what he would say.

Finally, "Man, that's awful. I don't know how you handle that without being a little screwy." He stepped back a little, eyed me. "But I get the feeling you're holding something back."

That caught me off guard. "Like what?"

He shrugged, "It's not for me to guess. Most guys I know back from Nam were treated like shit. Like they were dumb-asses for going. Like they should have gone to Canada or got their rich daddy to pull strings. A guy I knew ate like a fucking pig for months, gained 100 pounds, had skyrocketing blood pressure. You know, imaginative shit like that. Guys like that are viewed as smart. Guys like you must be nuts. I mean, who in their right mind's going to go to Nam?"

That made me think back. So, I added, "The day I got back from Nam, my mom decorated our house for her conquering hero. She had American flags and banners all over the place, praising her brave son who had survived war.

But when we came from the airport, someone had torn down the banners, pelted the house with eggs and spray-painted "Baby Killer" on our front lawn. Never saw my mom so mad. I joked it off but I had to admit it bothered me. Mom wouldn't let me help clean it up. Said it would be hard for her to pray for these punks next morning at mass. Tough to turn the other cheek when family is involved." I looked at Jimmer. "That stuff bothers me some but I get it. The war was stupid. We should never have been there. I'm not particularly proud to have fought there, but I'm dumb enough to think if your country calls, you've got to answer. It was about that simple."

Jimmer smiled, "Now we're getting somewhere, what else is slogging around in that brain? It's better to get it out. When I run our union meetings, I hear the crazy trolley driver's bitch about everything from harsh toilet paper to needing ice water cushions in the summer to cool their asses. Just lay it out there, Dylan, anything else stewing?" My lifelong friend was perceptive. There was a haunting thought that kept rumbling through my head. I had watched people get killed and maimed. I always used my wit to divert the horror. Always had a quip to keep my buddies going and focused on surviving. It was hard to explain but one thing kept eating at me. Why had I survived?

But I looked at Jimmer, "Nothing else." He looked at me quizzically, sensing something, but said simply, "Fodder for another day." We both drove off and I wondered why I hadn't told Jimmer everything. Maybe I felt it would sound like whining.

We had been raised as Catholics to bear pain with stoic silence. I guess it wouldn't be normal if I went back to my old routine like nothing happened. Nam was a bad place. I got dumped from my idyllic life right into that cesspool. Then I got in the middle of some really rotten apples. Why wouldn't I be jumpy?

The drive home was peaceful; the conversation with Jimmer relaxed me. It was good to say the words out loud. I started to whistle Marty Robbins' classic, "El Paso" and drove mindlessly. But right before I got back to my apartment, it hit me that most of my flashbacks involved Mike McCarthy. Mac was my closest friend in Nam, one of those rare people you meet and right away you click. We were inseparable, almost like brothers. He was already married and did everything he could to stay out of the crooked MP fiasco. He didn't want to risk getting hurt and leaving his wife and kid alone. I understood that and only used him to test my thinking as I found incriminating evidence. Despite his reluctance to get involved, he never hesitated to help me. Eventually, he had no choice but to help, things had gotten out of control and he needed to pick sides. I almost got him killed.

SYLVAN

Sylvan sat in his cavernous pawn shop surrounded by other people's cast-offs. He pulled back his long hair and glanced proudly at his collection of radios. He was particularly proud of the old Walkie-Talkies and vintage HAM sets. He mused: They're from another era, but I can listen to conversations all over the world and no one knows. Sylvan liked being the invisible man, mostly watching, acting only when it suited himself. He shifted in his chair. It was a quiet day, so he did what he loved best- drifting into his dreams. He smiled when recalling his freshman high school football days. When he entered St Joseph's Prep, he had ballooned to 250 lbs. "A natural tackle," is what the coach told him. Despite his girth, he was nimble. "Like a dancing bear," Coach Leonard praised. But then the trouble started; his grade school nickname "Ding Dong" surfaced and the taunts started. Most of it was good natured ribbing but that didn't matter. Sylvan always got even.

With his medical upbringing, Sylvan knew the fragile parts of the human anatomy. When he blocked unwary opponents, he would wait for moments of weakness.

As practice wore on, he would ball his right hand and chop at exposed kidneys. He was careful to avoid being blatant. But as the play moved away from him, he'd move into the throng and hack invisibly. Usually, the unsuspecting victim would drop like a bag of door knobs, writhing in pain. Most targets were his taunters, ones who liked to rub in the slurs. He moved away from the injured teammate humming, "Ding Dong and you're out. Ding Dong and you're out."

But knees were saved for special occasions. Sylvan had planned ahead: Such a delicate joint, the knee; wrapped tight with anterior cruciate ligaments and that fickle meniscus. A tap here, a snap there and pow! Too bad, your career is ended. None of this was noticeable for the first few weeks of practice. But when a couple of the back-up running backs were hospitalized with torn ACL's, Coach Leonard lectured the team on, "Saving tenacity for game day." That was hard for Sylvan. He liked the "eye for an eye" principle. If you screw with me, I bust your knee.

Ronnie Silvato was the fastest and best halfback at St Joe's Prep, maybe the whole league. He was also handsome.

"Just call me the Italian Stallion, okay Ding Dong?" Sylvan also liked winning, so he ignored Ronnie's jabs. After all, with Ronnie running behind Ding Dong, the touchdowns kept piling up.

But Ronnie wasn't a good teammate. If someone on the line screwed up, he jumped up their ass. When Sylvan missed a block, Ronnie howled, "You fat, psycho fuck.

Move that pile a lard you call an asshole." Sylvan
seethed. Two plays later, Ronnie was running a
reverse when Sylvan blindsided him and almost
snapped his knee off. As Ronnie was being
stretchered off the field, Coach Leonard glared at
him, the look on his face unmistakable. That was the
end of Sylvan's football career.

DYLAN

I called Hoban next morning and asked if he had any interesting files for me. I was still waiting for the telephone records on Crina and wasn't making any money on her case anyway. The insurance company had decided to drop the fraud case. Nothing but bad publicity would come from chasing her estate for money. The missing Hummels ate at me. Something wasn't right. I drove immediately to Voyager and walked into Hoban's office.

He looked up, "Got a doosie for you, Dylan. This one rivals Bishop Winn, the roofing minister." Hoban handed me a file, told me to read it.

I paused, "Before we start, I was watching "The Munsters" last night and got caught up figuring out why Gomez is normal looking and the rest of the family looks like nuclear fall-out. It's been eating at me. Any thoughts?"

He thought a few seconds, smirked, "Just read the file."

I read the 3 pages and burst out laughing, looked at Hoban. "What do you want me to do? Arrest her for having a sense of humor? This is priceless. Maybe I just found my soul mate."

Hoban finally laughed. "I thought you would enjoy that. When I first read it, I thought you wrote it. That you were playing a joke on us. It has your style. But I checked; it's for real." I still waited for the punch line. Hoban patted me on the shoulder, "Just drop by and tell her we're paying her claim." As he walked away, he added, "And tell her that I loved her letter. It made me laugh all day."

I liked that about Hoban. Not to busy to see the absurdity in his job. Insurance companies are notorious for getting the facts. If something is vague, at least to them, there is a form letter issued to clarify. Corporations pay them to safeguard their health expenses, so nothing but certainty is allowed. That's what happened when Jean Robinson submitted her bill for a barium enema. The problem was she had no previous medical history and no diagnosis was noted as the cause for the procedure.

The following form was sent to her:

Dear Ms Robinson:

We acknowledge receipt of your above captioned claim. There was no reason or complaint mentioned on your bill. Please advise if there was a medical cause or if this was an elective procedure. If elective, this charge is not covered."

Thank you for your cooperation in this matter.

Very Truly Yours,

Ann Reese, Processor

Here is Ms.Robinson's return letter. You should note she worked for an advertising agency, so her creative gifts are evident.

Dear Ms. Reese:

This letter is in response to your inquiry about why I went to the Clinic to have a barium enema. I'll try to adequately paint the scene. It happened on a Tuesday. The day dawned bright and clear. The sky was cloudless as I stepped from bed into my fluffy pink bathroom slippers. I'm sure I heard the call of a blue bird in the distance. Or was it the spring of hope eternal?

As is my custom on Tuesdays, I lunched with my mother. We enjoyed a delicious repast starting with fruit cocktail- not from a can, mother makes her own, carefully removing the membrane from every section of orange, and never missing a grape seed. This was followed by a succulent roast duckling and sausage/apple stuffing. The secret of that stuffing is in the crumbling of the bread, not neatly cubed, as you buy in the store, but of uneven sizes.

I can remember the first time I was allowed to help with the crumbling. We were having company, distant relatives on my father's side, and I was wearing a brown dress that matched my eyes. But I am digressing from the point... let's get back to the enema!

We finished the feast and I helped to clean up- mother has no dishwasher; she says the old ways are the best ways and may be right (barium enemas are quite new).

As I departed, the sky remained blue, no hint of rain. So, I decided to walk back to my apartment. I live alone in a dear little flat with the light just right for my drawing board. I've repeatedly asked the landlord to repaint the living room... fuchsia walls and red woodwork offend the senses, but that's another story (If you write and ask about other tests, I may tell you.)

The walk back was glorious. The sun was warm on my hand, the grass was green, the sky almost cobalt blue, flowers were beginning to bloom. A yellow bellied sapsucker hopped across the lawn and cocked his head at me in a roguish way. I thought... this is good. Life is good... and full... and rich. I have happy memories, good friends, and bright prospects for the future... what more could I want?

That's when it hit me. There was something missing... had I really experienced all life had to offer? Could I look the future generations in the eye... could I hold my grandchildren in my arms and say: NO! I NEVER HAD A BARIUM ENEMA! The answer was clear. I swerved from my journey and rushed to the nearest facility and demanded admittance. "Bring on the barium," I demanded, "Enema me instantly!" So that's what happened. I hope this answers your question.

Sincerely,

Jean Robinson

So, that was my new assignment. Meet Ms. Robinson and tell her the enema is on us. But before that, I spun over to Gator's office to pick up the telephone records on Crina. I hadn't been to his office for awhile, so I was surprised when I met the new secretary Janice. The surprise was her being attractive and built like the god's intended. With Laura away, I was beyond horny.

"So, you're the funny guy on the phone. Mr. Light didn't tell me you're so handsome." Janice dipped her shoulders and gave me a full view of her massive breasts. I gulped deeply, thought: This isn't good.

But out loud I replied, "He's very reserved about praising my looks publicly, concerned with the whole homo thing. Had a man crush on me since second grade, fought it most of his life. So far, he's winning. Don't tell his wife, okay?" Her blue eyes opened wide, but then smiled.

"Why don't you drop by more often? We could use more fun in this place. I mostly just answer the phone and type briefs. I sure could use some excitement." This time I didn't gulp; this time my Adam's apple almost smacked my jaw senseless. Holy shitoly!

Gator came out and immediately sized up the situation. "Sorry to break this up, Janice, but I need you to make a few appointments for me. Leave pretty boy alone, he's already taken."

We walked into his office and shut the door. Before he could say anything, I threw up my hands.

"She started it. I'm a victim here."

Gator chuckled devilishly, "Judging by that lump in your pants, I'd say you were the happy victim."

I patted down my perky member and switched gears, "What did your buddy find? Hope something good."

Gator handed me the file. "There is nothing but calls to a few pawn shops and her neighbor you mentioned, Mirella Costas. Crina had a real thing for pawn shops. That probably explains the missing Hummels. She sold them is my bet."

I let that sink in. "But why would she suddenly sell all her treasures? I mean, she's sitting in that small apartment by herself all day. Her one source of pleasure is looking at her collection. Why give that up? I checked with her doctor and she was in decent health for her age, no imminent problems. It doesn't click."

Gator nodded, "You should go to law school. We could be partners. Your devious mind and my ruthlessness; we'd be quite a team. But back to your question, I agree, it seems odd." I scanned the pawn shop list. There were 8 pawn shops she called consistently. My plan was drop by each and see if anything clicked. I hadn't seen Mirella for a couple weeks, so I'd drop over there and see if any pawn shop name registered with her. Maybe Crina mentioned it. Worth a try.

I drove to the Garden Court section of West Philly to see if the humorous Jean Robinson was around. According to her file, she was employed by the Elliot Advertising firm and worked from her house. When I was a little kid, I came to this neighborhood for swimming lessons. It was then considered a classy city neighborhood. Now it was a prime example of white flight. Still the majestic brownstone homes but the tenants were mostly black. But there were pockets of Irish and Italian. Sadly the races didn't mix, just maintained a peaceful distance. Which ethnic group would Ms. Robinson be? I parked my ambiguous car and went up to meet the sarcastic advertising exec.

The front yard had a nice garden. I remembered her comment about blooming flowers. She had the top apartment, based on the door bell alignment in the lobby. I rang her buzzer, she answered quickly. Her voice was bright and chipper, asking what I wanted. I told her I was from the Insurance Company, which was paying her claim but that I wanted to get her mom's recipe for sausage/apple stuffing, that I was a victim of imperfect bread cube crumbling. Her laugh was even brighter. When she stopped laughing, she rang me up and gave directions to her door. I knocked and could sense her eyeing me through the peephole. Smart lady.

Jean Robinson was about 5 feet tall, weighed over 200 lbs, and was mocha brown with a huge Afro. Despite her chunkiness, she was absolutely beautiful.

She looked at me with her big brown eyes, "What can I do for you? I take it someone got my letter and realized you don't do barium enemas on a lark.

It was so absurd that I couldn't resist. I started writing a normal reply but it was a slow day creatively, so I let loose. Funny thing, after that, I came up with a few great ideas for ads. My customers thank you." We chatted for awhile; I again apologized for the bureaucracy but couldn't promise it wouldn't happen again. She grinned at me slyly, "Wait till you read my next tome."

SYLVAN

Sylvan sat in his private office and cleaned the old Baume & Mercier watch. Accuracy and precision, such beauty in these timepieces, he thought. Then he drifted back to thoughts of his first kill. Aunt Anca had persecuted him relentlessly since birth. By the time he was 10, he realized his lust for murder. Too young to act on his urges, he studied and planned. Most of the murders he read about in The Bulletin seemed emotional and disorganized. Sylvan considered himself devoid of feeling. Even through the worst beatings, he never cried. He came to believe he could withstand anything. He planned her death methodically for years by studying her routines. Let her get comfortable and relaxed. He would take her unexpectedly and lethally.

Finally at age 13, Bela was ready to act. Anca went to Our Mother of Consolation for mass every morning. He followed her for weeks, studying the timing and possibility of witnesses. That final morning, Anca walked to mass, lost in quiet thought. She loved the time by herself. She thought: Just me and my savior.

Attend the 6 am service, pray for my blessings, then get home to send Bela off to school. Too bad that oaf doesn't appreciate anything. Just sits there. Even when I discipline him, he just stares. I pray to Our Lady in thanks that my poor sister never had to see the creature she spawned. Like a dead fish, he is. Anca thoughts were disturbed by the roar of the engine behind her; she turned, was shocked by a familiar face behind the wheel, and stood paralyzed as the dark car drove her into the stately oak tree.

Bela jumped from the car and followed his escape route through the alleys, back into his cozy bed. It took exactly 26 minutes to fulfill his mission. Stealing the car was the exciting part. He drove through dark alleyways and wasn't spotted. Shields Tavern was only a mile from his house. He went there each night for weeks and found an unfortunate sot who made a habit of getting blind drunk most nights. The sot slept it off in his back seat before driving home. When the drunk climbed out of his car that fateful morning, he found himself looking at a dead woman pinned to a tree.

Later, Bela heard the police knock on the door and Dr. Dragomir shuffle to answer. No one came to question him and no one ever did. His father dealt with the loss as he did everything, with reserve. The drunk swore he'd seen a dark figure bolt from the car as he started awake from the jarring impact. As Bela had planned, no witnesses stirred at that hour to corroborate the story. Anca always wanted to be the first in church, got there well before anyone could take her place in the front pew. Habits, thought Bela, they are the building blocks for perfect crimes.

Life was much better after Anca was gone. Bela pondered: Just me and dad. Just me and dear old dad. Bela continued to study the famous killers. His favorite was Jack the Ripper. He was never caught but everyone feared him. Should I be more open when I kill or stay in the shadows? Both options appealed to him. If I keep the murders quiet, they will be mine alone to savor. He let that thought settle. But the fear, that excites me. He eventually opted for stealth. Plan carefully; never act rashly. Sometimes he had to kill ahead of schedule but he always avoided suspicion. But he did drink in the fear as he looked into his victim's terrified eyes. He loved those final minutes.

All these thoughts floated as he polished the ancient Swiss watch. He was disturbed as he heard his assistant William waiting on a noisy customer. Sylvan sat back and looked at the sparkling timepiece. He placed the watch in his drawer of treasures, lingered on the other jewelry within and finally locked it carefully. This office was his sanctum sanctorum. Memories from his kills were everywhere. When he looked at the gold hair pin, it brought back his cruel Aunt Anca. Thinking of his first kill, something popped into his mind. He remembered Crina talking about her friend across the alley. The cat lady! His animal eyes hardened.

DYLAN

On my way to visit Mirella, the cat lady, I thought
about my grandmothers. Both died when I was young
and I'd never gotten to know them. My parents raved
about their sense of humor and toughness. "They
survived The Depression with smiles on their faces,"
according to my mom and dad. I wondered if my
obsession with solving the Crina/Hummel mystery
had something to do with missing any interaction
with these grand women who somehow shaped me.
My way of paying back? Did my offbeat sense of
humor come from them? My grandfathers apparently
weren't prizes; little was ever mentioned. What did I
get from them? Were they to blame for the
eccentricities?

I got to Mirella's before her nightly feeding and
watering ritual. She answered my ring and told me,
"Can't get rid a ya, can I? Ya like old bags or are ya
getting attached to my gang?" We chatted as she
completed the feeding and ambled to the garden hose
to fill their water bowls. She noticed me watching the
routine, "Like to wet their whistles after chow.

Like a beer after pizza. It just works better." Mirella confirmed that Crina was a pawn shop junkie but didn't think any specific shop did more business with her. "She liked the hunt, ya know?" I thanked her for her time and told her I'd try to visit more often. Her wrinkled brow lit up, "People are gonna talk." And then she chuckled brightly.

SYLVAN

Across the alley, deep in a thicket of rambling rhododendron, Sylvan watched the guy chat with Mirella. Silently, he processed the scene: Maybe he's a cop? Or is he some relative of Crina? For a tall guy, he moves quickly. He looks like a fighter. What's he doing with the cat lady? Maybe this won't be so easy. Crina never mentioned the cat lady having any family. I have to plan what to do. One of Sylvan's rules was to never have too many projects at the same time, too easy to make mistakes. He thought about options. Should I just stick with my current projects or go for the cat lady and the tall guy too? I haven't killed a man for awhile. Women are easier. A cruel smile appeared. This might be fun. There's something about that tall guy. He's cocky. He likes to snoop around too much.

DYLAN

Gator had a slower week and wanted to visit the pawn shops with me. "Janice's been talking about you non-stop since your visit. I told her you had a serious girlfriend but she's in Paris. Guess what she said to that?" I shrugged, not knowing if I wanted the answer. She said, "Perfect."

I exhaled deeply, "Girl like that gives me impure thoughts. Not sure about my willpower these days. Laura's been away almost 6 months. Do me a favor, Gator, tell her I was exposed to Agent Orange. That my wiener glows."

Gator grinned, "That might not stop her, my friend. She's pretty aggressive, as you noticed. The glow stick might just make you more appealing."

I decided to switch topics. "Who's your source with the cops? Would like to meet him, would save me from bugging you."

Gator nodded, "Names Frankie Merlano. When I told him who I was getting the info for, he said he played ball against you in High School. He said you were more psycho than him, and that that took some doing. He seemed to like you; but I'm not sure why. He probably wouldn't like you now if he knew your dick was orange." He cracked up at his own jab.

I remembered Merlano. Talked non-stop, stocky but agile, antsy even on a slow day, had a lower lip that hung down like a flat bike tire, stayed in my face the whole game. Knew if he let me set my feet he'd have a long night. I had him by a couple inches, so I knew I had an edge. He wasn't a dirty player, just physical. Blocked out, pushed me whenever I got around him. If I thought about it, that's kind of how I played. We had good teams and beat Merlano's every year. Never seemed to stop him, still played like a bulldog. Not surprised he became a cop, had an edge to him. Gator gave me his number, planned to call him later that day.

Our first shop was in Manayunk, right near the Schuylkill River. It was a real hilly area. Streets were so steep cars had to be parked with wheels to the curb. Lots of cars found their way into the river when someone got careless. Laura's dad always joked that people from Manayunk walked with a limp when they hit flat streets. Not sure why, but that always made me laugh. My future father-in-law was a great guy.

Gator shattered my reverie, "What's our story when we go inside?"

I shrugged, "Let's play it by ear, just say we're browsing. Ask what his specialty is."

The "Treasure Trove" was not well named. It was more a junk shop than anything else.

A squirrelly looking character approached us immediately. "Help you gentleman?"

I pointed at Gator, "My friend is looking for women's clothes. Got anything from the Elizabethan period? He's going to a costume party and wants to make a splash.

Don't worry, he's not queer or anything." Gator dropped his head, trying to shake off the grin.

The squirrel bit. "I've got a couple tasty morsels over here." Gator wandered off with him, giving me the finger as he left.

A quick sweep of the place convinced me no clues would surface here. I went to extract Gator, who was in an animated discussion with the owner. There was an old mannequin before them, dressed in a burlesque outfit. "It won't fit my breasts, too busty," was what I heard. Gator was going with the routine. Seemed into the role. "My shoulders are my best feature, that won't drape right. Don't you see?" We left the Treasure Trove and headed toward center city and our next pawn shop. Gator drove silently, and then mumbled, "My shoulders really are pretty nice."

Carter Leeds was advertised as, "The Strawbridge and Clothier of Pawn Shops." We parked on south 10th street, were struck by the dissimilarity to The Treasure Trove. Carter Leeds looked like a high-end jewelry store. We wove our way through the revolving door and hit the oriental carpet pathway to an information desk.

An officious old man asked, "Do you have an appointment?"

On the way in, I had noticed a camera in the display window, "I collect vintage cameras. Who is your best man? Wasn't expecting to have a break in my schedule today, what with court so backed up and all. Hoping an appointment can be avoided. Not sure when I'll break free again."

The old turd nodded, "That would be Hanson. Let me see if he's free."

I looked at Gator, "Don't know shit about cameras, how about you?"

He looked at me skeptically, "Nada, but I am an expert in cross dressing, if that'll help."

I was chuckling as Hanson walked up. "May I help you gentleman with our camera collection? We have some old Kodak's that might intrigue." I gestured my hand out politely, asking for him to lead the way.

Gator whispered, "I can't wait to hear what comes next."

To buy time, "Can you tell me a little about the shop, this is my first visit."

Hanson took the line. "Carter Leeds is the elusive pearl in the oyster bed of pawn dealers. We've been in business for 110 years, the same year Lincoln became president. We consider ourselves designed as the Chinese intended, when they created the pawn business 2000 years ago, long before banks existed. Bartering is as old as man; we consider it a privilege to continue the time honored ways. We believe we will be here serving long after banks disappear." I nodded knowingly, like I expected that pedigree.

We arrived at the camera section. Hanson showed us a couple dozen old cameras that were pretty cool.

I pointed at Gator, "Hanson, my friend Bill is really the camera buff. Likes candid pictures, no posing or preparation. He's a purist that way. Insists these old fold outs are the best. But before I forget, do you have Hummels I can look at before we leave?" From the corner of my eye, I saw Gator cringing.

Hanson never hesitated, "We have the finest Hummel collection in the city.

Some date back to 1935. We're convinced even Sister Maria Innocentia would approve of our provenance."

That gave Gator time to compose himself. He said to Hanson, "Why don't you show him the Hummels while I weigh my camera choices?"

We moved to another corner of the large store. Hanson passed me to a fellow named Bismarck.

I looked at him stone-faced, "Any relation?"

He looked puzzled. I added, "To Otto Von Bismarck." A look of scorn followed. "Certainly not, he was a scoundrel. Bismarck is my first name. My parents were rather exotic that way."

Since I had studied Hummels after Crina's went missing, I could kibitz with Bismarck without sounding ridiculous. I mixed in some truth. "My aunt Crina died suddenly and all her Hummels were mysteriously gone, probably sold them. I'm trying to track them down. See if I can get some back. Kind of a nice remembrance."

When I gave him the details, full name and address, Bismarck offered to see if they had purchased any of Crina's recently. He shuffled off to check. Unknown to me, Gator had ambled over and heard my salvo.

He poked me, "Pretty smooth." Then he added, "Except for the Otto Von comment."

I smiled, "Overheard that, huh? Even I don't know what I'll say next."

Gator looked at me seriously, "What happens if they say she sold all her stuff to them. Wouldn't that solve the mystery? She might have sensed her days were numbered and wanted to cash out. She might have been planning a big trip or something. Go out in style kind of thing."

But Bismarck found no record of any interactions. I asked, "Where else might my aunt have sold them? I was really hoping this would be easy."

Bismarck scoffed, "In the bartering world, there is no hurry. We consider most of our pieces as "collections." People rarely part with life treasures without great thought, and often remorse."

I looked at Gator, "Remember when you lost your Richie Ashburn card? You cried like a baby for days." I looked at Bismarck, "He was inconsolable."

Totally expressionless, Bismarck nodded, "That's exactly what I mean."

I turned to Bismarck, "Would you be so kind as to help us with a list of other brokers she might have dealt with? I wanted to start with Carter Leeds, the crème-de-la crème, but see that Aunt Crina had to stoop lower. Pity I wasn't there to advise."

Bismarck got a look on his face like I'd asked him to swallow a live pigeon, but shuffled off to jot down a few leads.

I turned to Gator, "Make any decisions about your camera?"

He didn't hesitate. "I did. I'm going to buy that big Kodak and shove it up your ass when I get outside."

Bismarck returned to find us belly laughing, grimaced uncomfortably and handed the list to me like I had rabies.

❧

Next morning, I awoke early and joined my saintly mom at 6 o'clock mass.

She smiled as I entered the pew, "I hadn't heard hell had frozen over; what's my incorrigible son doing at mass this early?" Then she kissed me and hugged me like she wouldn't let go. The time I'd been in Nam had been horrible for her, only recently had she gotten that glow back in her face. Mass started and we followed the sacred rituals, responding in Latin when the laity was called upon. No matter how many doubts I had about Catholic doctrine, I still found peace in the ceremony.

Monsignor Pugh was saying mass. He'd been at St. Tim's since I was a tyke. His full name was Seamus Pugh, and was called "Shameless Poo" or just "Stinky" by me and my buddies. The nickname was handed down to future generations. Father Pugh knew of my gift for mayhem, knew I was to blame for years of hearing "Stinky" muttered behind his back but miraculously liked me anyway. He was a major sports nut. Our 8th grade class had won football and basketball city titles, so he got bragging rights around town, top parish in the County. That was apparently a get-out-of-jail free card for me.

I watched him as I walked to communion, saw him recoil as I approached the rail. The look on his face read: Are you really in the state of grace? When was the last time you went to confession? Do I see the taint of mortal sin lurking within? When I was an altar boy and served mass for him, I'd karate chop select people with the communion plate. He caught me once, I wondered if he'd return the favor today. Instead, he looked at me, smiled as he patted my head, gave me a flawless delivery of the Holy Eucharist. Impressive, not a guy to hold grudges.

When we exited church, we stood outside the doorway and I told mom about Jimmer, how his mother had abandoned him and his new family. I wanted her advice.

She nodded, "I've known about it since day one. Mary came to mass that morning and was more dour than usual."

Just then Monsignor Pugh came out, asked my mom, "Has he called me "Shameless Poo yet or did Vietnam knock that out of him?" Before I could protest, he threw his arms around me, told me how proud he was that I served our country, was glad I had returned safely. He looked at me, "I prayed for you every day, Dylan." That caught me off guard, really touched me, my eyes welled up. He was one of the few to ever thank me.

I choked back my sudden emotion, "Sorry about the Stinky stuff. As my mom will testify, I've got a wee bit of the devil in me."

We chatted for awhile and I told Monsignor Pugh that he'd see more of me at church.

He grinned, "Should I hold my breath, Kate? When do we really expect to see your devilish Dylan again? Never mind lad, let's savor the day." He ambled off and I thought he might be right. Vietnam had shaken my faith. How could God have let that happen?

Mom interrupted, "Mary Kielmann believes that Jimmer committed mortal sin when he married a divorcee. She won't admit that being a Puerto Rican has anything to do with it, but that's a big part. She's embarrassed by it. More than once she said to me, 'How could my boy do this to me?'" I let that sink in, trying to see the sense of it.

85

As I walked home with my petite mom, I pushed further. "Mom, would you do that to me? Would you disown me for marrying a divorced Puerto Rican? Before you answer, I've met Marisol and little Jose. She's beautiful and educated. The kid's adorable. If anything, she married down. As you know, Jimmer isn't any collector's item."

That made her laugh, but she answered, "At first, it would have worried me. But if she's as nice as you say, I'd welcome her to the family. If you loved her, she had to be alright. But that's not how Mary looks at it. She thinks Jimmer did it to spite her."

As we passed Jimmer's house, I felt sad. It seemed so pointless. How could you abandon your son just because he didn't marry a lily white Catholic girl? It's funny how you grow up next to a family, but have no idea what makes them tick. Jimmer and his brothers got along well, rough-housed like regular brothers and seemed happy and normal. Was their family bond so thin that any deviation from what's considered proper was reason to throw a lifetime away?

I'd parked at mom's house and told her I couldn't stay for breakfast. "Got malingerers to chase, mom" We hugged and I watched her as she entered our house. How did I get so lucky?

❧

I drove to Voyager Insurance and met with Hoban.

He gave me a load of files, told me that after the Crina Barbu fraud, he got his office audit team to review all their Medicare files, that a list of suspects was detected.

Hoban further clarified, "We looked for older people who had normal health bills, but suddenly submitted extensive claims for medical equipment and laboratory work. I didn't think we'd have many, but out popped half a dozen. Could be nothing, could be a pattern. See what you can find, huh, Sherlock?" I asked him if this project was urgent. He thought a second, "No, might be a wild goose chase, just fit them in when you can. The other work pays the bills."

I sat in his office and organized them alphabetically while he went out and cracked the whip on the floor. Hoban was priceless; he loved being the boss and was very good at it. If I had stayed working for him, he'd probably have fired me. That made me chuckle as I got the work organized. I listed the names and wrote notes beside them if something struck me odd:

1. *Bill Bonner- why the sudden use of oxygen?*

2. *Mary Craley- why did she need a chair lift in her house?*

3. *Gus Demovick- had extensive eye surgery in China- at age 66.*

4. *Gene Larrson- sudden influx of expensive drugs.*

5. *Gertrude Rawley- had breast reduction to cure sore back- age 80.*

6. *Biata Wozniak- sudden expensive medical equipment purchases.*

Since I was no longer being paid to investigate the Crina case, I put it on the back burner. Gator liked getting out of the office, so I called to see when he'd be free that week. Janice answered the phone, very business-like.

When she recognized my voice, a breathy tone took over. "I was hoping you'd call soon. Why don't you drop by more often? Maybe we can catch a drink after work. I haven't stopped thinking about those blue eyes of yours." Despite being prepared for her, my usual wit wilted. Janice got my blood boiling.

Recovering, "Not so sure my girlfriend would like that, Janice. We're pretty serious."

She didn't hesitate. "I know she's in Paris. What she doesn't know won't hurt her. She's not going to hear anything from me, handsome." I sucked in air. Whew!!!

She finally got Gator and we traded schedules. I told him about the claim audit, that new suspects had surfaced.

He raised his voice, excited, "It sounds like job security for you, my friend. People do bad things. That keeps guys like you and me busy. Let me know if anything surfaces. Maybe it's a coincidence, but maybe it's a ring of thieves. This is interesting. Sniff it out, my friend."

SYLVAN

Sylvan sat in his shop and wondered. He didn't like having his plans altered. Biata was perfect; he could milk her for months, maybe a year. He had already started to get her checks from the Insurance Company. He smiled broadly, he was proud of himself. There is nothing like chronic, rheumatoid arthritis to run up some serious physical therapy charges. Then she'll need some durable medical equipment, wheelchairs and such. Let's not forget the costly prescriptions. Sylvan knew his way around the medical world. Getting authentic forms was all it took. He continued to renew his father's medical license after his death. He got whatever form he wanted. Plus he knew not to be too greedy. Not sticking out of the normal flow, that was the thing. That formula worked perfectly; he had lots of practice.

But the cat lady worried him. Crina might have talked to her. Maybe she mentioned my name. It didn't seem like a coincidence that the big, athletic guy was suddenly snooping around. I don't believe in coincidence.

All this swirled in Sylvan's disturbed mind. He liked having complete control and he felt his power shifting loose. I'm just ridding the world of old, useless pieces of shit. They had no one left. Just hanging on, waiting to die. I'm doing them a favor, putting them out of their misery.

That was how he viewed old woman who came to this country from Eastern Europe. Like Aunt Anca, they came here and sucked the life out of America. He never consciously thought how she abused him, how she blamed him for killing his mother. But whenever he saw an older woman, his blood boiled. Although material goods meant nothing to him, he loved the money, just having all he wanted. He thought about Biata. I can't leave her alone or I'll lose her. She needs me. She relies on me for everything. But I should watch the cat lady closely, and then decide whether to kill her and the big guy right away. He exhaled, satisfied

DYLAN

My judo lessons were fun, at least for Jimmer. He was Sensei and had to maintain decorum, but he privately roared hysterically as the younger judoka eluded me deftly, and then pulled up before delivering potentially lethal arm strikes.

He pulled me aside, trying to be careful not to be overheard and said, "It gives me great pleasure watching Mr. Athlete getting his ass kicked by children." Tears spilled over his cheeks. He was enjoying my humiliation.

I countered, "That's why I'm acting like such a dufus, Jimmer, just to give you some yucks. Wait till I get serious. These malignant dwarves are in trouble." The words just left my mouth as an unseen miniature judoka pirouetted around me, leaped like a gazelle and delivered a leg strike at my midsection. Like a panther, he pulled back at the last second, avoiding contact with my vulnerable belly.

The kid smiled at me, "That was on behalf of the other dwarfs."

But I wasn't dismayed. I'd been at it for almost 3 months and could see my progress. I was getting good at the Nage-Waza, or throwing techniques. My goal was to protect myself if I got caught off-guard.

Buy some time if someone surprised me. Most of my time was spent learning the unpronounceable ma-sutemi-waza and yoko-sutemi-waza, which were simply rolling to your back or side as someone charged you. Taking their momentum, you threw them to the ground. Now you were back in charge. Next I needed better striking skill. So far, that was going slowly. My skillful partners rolled to their feet before I could strike. Little bastards!

After the session, I jabbered with Jimmer. "Talked to my mom about Mary's Christian stance on your marriage."

I could see Jimmer tense, "Stay out of it, Dylan, my mother's a mess. Practicing what you preach isn't her forte. She'd rather embody the frozen chosen approach than accept her son married a PR." He shook his head. "I'm okay with it now. I wouldn't want Marisol and Jose exposed to that sanctimonious horseshit anyway." But he showed only anger on his face. I wondered what he really felt, hurt or just the anger.

I put up my hands. "I'll back off. Just wanted my mom's read. By the way, she thinks Mary's got it ass-backward, if that means anything to you."

His face softened, "I always liked your mom."

~

Next morning I thought about my wild goose chase. There were 3 pawn shops that might have bought Crina's Hummels, according to my buddy Bismarck at Carter Leeds.

I still chuckled when I thought of his smug face. I like that about human nature, he thought I was the odd one. Well, maybe he had a point. Anyway, since Gator wanted to be part of the hunt, I had to wait for his schedule to clear. In the meantime, I had plenty to do with the new fraud cases Hoban gave me. Like all anal types, I went alphabetically and would visit John Bonner first. He lived in West Philly, so it wasn't too far away. But since I usually made my first call of the day the farthest spot away, then worked back towards home, he was my last stop that day. Make sense? It did to me.

≈

My other investigations that day were mundane; I plowed through them almost mindlessly, so I was hoping for something more fun as I motored towards West Philly. Bonner was a retiree from Scott Paper. His file said he worked in the "Sanitary Products" section for almost 40 years. Kind of glad Gator wasn't with me. Even by myself, I would have a struggle keeping my questions straight. Things like, "Mr. Bonner, did you specialize in the ass-wipe area or were you more of a mucous man?" ran through my mind. Ah well. Glad I had time to compose myself. West Philly had changed a lot in my short life. Once teeming with Irish, German and Italian immigrants, making good after WW11, it had gone through urban change.

93

Depending on which ethnic neighborhood Bonner lived in, I might be the only white face on the street. That didn't bother me; it was just something to plan for.

I had already tried the easy route with his file, called his attending physician to confirm his diagnosis had worsened, that he'd need the expensive oxygen treatment.

Was told by a stuffy business clerk, "We don't talk to anyone without written permission from Mr. Bonner." When I pleaded my case, told her it was a potential fraud investigation, tried to charm her, she listened patiently but added. "You can talk all day and all night, but no information without Mr. Bonner's written permission. Plus based on how you're acting on the phone, I'm going to call him and verify. Got me?"

Without thinking, I responded, "Yes, Drill Sergeant!" The phone slammed down.

Hoban had given me a SEPTA map my first day on the road. "Only way you'll maneuver through Philly without getting lost. Founding fathers would cringe if they saw how Ben Franklin's sensible grid got fucked up. Most maps won't show that some asshole built row homes through what had once been a straight road. Getting to the other side of said street might take a genius in navigation. It's sad, I'm telling you, Dylan." I remember looking at him, thinking he'd exaggerated. He wasn't. The SEPTA map clearly showed the cluster fucks and was vital to getting you on your way.

Bonner lived in one such maze. Although not far from West Catholic High School, it took awhile to find the elusive entry point. I drove down Chestnut St. and made a right on 60th. That's when it got interesting. Had to make another right on Hamilton, went a couple blocks, then left on an unmarked street, followed that about 6 blocks, and was forced to make another right when a warehouse appeared from nowhere. According to the SEPTA map, I was now back on Hamilton. From there I scanned the dreary houses for numbers and stopped outside what should be #70.

I sat in the car a few minutes and watched my surroundings. A few older women stood talking on a nearby stoop. Near the corner, there were a couple old men chatting. Everybody was white. That surprised me, since most of this part of West Philly was now black. I parked close to the house, in case I had to make a rapid departure. There were no young guys loitering around. That was what I was looking for, punks skipping school looking for trouble. Didn't matter whether they were black or white, if they weren't in school, they liked to mix it up with strangers. So far, so good.

The old brick row home was showing wear, had been a stylish house in its day.

I rung the bell and a weak voice answered in a few seconds. "What ya want?"

I explained who I was, that I represented the Insurance Company, wanted to make sure everything was going okay. The buzzer clanged and I ascended the steep stairs.

95

Tough climb for a guy with breathing problems, I thought. When he opened the door, my fears were resolved. A grizzled old man, dragging an oxygen unit, ending with 2 tubes up his nose, peered at me. He looked like living death.

I asked a few inane questions, made sure he was getting his disability reimbursement okay.

He gave me a wry grin, "Wish my asshole worked that reglar'. Yer checks er like a clock." I laughed and he liked that. Probably didn't get many visitors. I commented about how difficult it was to find his house. "My idea movin' here. After I got hitched, wife's mother was drivin' us nuts visitin' all the time. I couldn't even walk around in my drawers, her always poppin' by. Anyway, had to get a place she couldn't find easy. After we moved ta this maze, rarely saw the tub-a-lard. A perfect plan." I chuckled again, wished him a good day. A blind alley but at least I met Bill Bonner. He had bad health problems, but he hung in there, still had some spunk. Admired that.

MIRELLA

Mirella, the cat lady, liked to sit at her window. WHYY blared in the background; it was good to hear some radio noise, like company for her. She kept an eye on her cats but also imagined what was going on in her neighbor's lives. Her mind was still sharp, a product of her technical training as a chemist. She liked knowing how things worked. She always had lots of questions. She thought back to her younger days. She was one of the first women chemists to be hired by Philadelphia Gas and Electric. She had done internships with PG&E while going to Drexel, had great grades, and got hired right after graduation. She mused: Had it really been 60 years ago?

Even though it was chilly out, she had the window opened, liked the sounds of the city, kind of like sitting with a friend. She was finishing her coffee; it was almost time to go out to feed her babies. From her lofty perch, she heard the cats suddenly get agitated, that drew her attention. Was someone down there, upsetting them? Her eyes were still good. Not bad for an old lady, she often thought.

Then the squealing stopped. Was that a man's shadow? She shook her head, must be seeing things. Who'd be out at this hour? The sun was just rising as she prepared her gang's breakfast. They were always so happy to see her. What would I do without them?

Mirella ambled down the steps and lugged the bag of cat chow. She was more cautious than usual. She sensed something was wrong. She grasped the bag close to her, like it was protection. But then all wariness disappeared and dread set in as she spotted the cats laying on the ground, still. The other cats huddled around the bodies, almost like pall- bearers. Her eyes darted, no one was around. She knelt to inspect the lifeless cats. There were no signs of a fight. Sometimes the boys got after each other, got clawed bad. But they never killed. Three of her babies were dead. She stroked them like any mother would do. Mirella wept.

SYLVAN

Sylvan stood in the shadows and watched Mirella cry. She was so close. I could reach out and snap the old neck. Or I could poison the cats slowly and savor the misery. I do like watching her agony. But just as fast, Sylvan's mind drifted to the past. When he poisoned his father with aconite, he did it over a prolonged period. He wanted no trail should a savvy coroner suspect foul play. His trips to Chinatown in New York were untraceable, done by train, sometimes by bus; he always paid cash for the herbs. He bought other medicinal herbs so nothing would stand out. The Chinese herbalists seemed impressed with his knowledge. As usual, he had done his homework.

He learned by practicing on animals that when you used weaker rootstock, the aconite would simply cause sweating and shortness of breath. Sylvan soon managed the dosage expertly. There were 4 trips to the emergency room over 2 years when Dad's symptoms got severe.

But after a short time in the ER, Dr Dragomir always recovered fully, no telltale signs. Like a skilled actor, Sylvan paced in the waiting area, the concerned son. But the final killing dosage was pure aconitim alkaloids, almost impossible for any hospital to detect unless they had a multi- disciplinary team, skilled in herbal medicines. None existed in Philadelphia.

Hearing the sobbing, Sylvan suddenly returned to the present. As he stared at Mirella, he got excited. Don't rush this. I like having her in my control. Sylvan smiled as he thought about killing her cats, being present as she agonized. His concern about Mirella alerting the police had passed. This useless wreck can't do anything to stop me. I can manage other projects. Biata is a gold mine. The cat lady would be my morning project, Biata the rest of the day. More pleasure than ever. He watched as Mirella left the dead cats and ambled toward the apartment. Remembering her front entrance, Hum… Those front stairs are awfully steep.

DYLAN

I decided to go to Schultz Tavern after work. It was "the" hang-out in Philly for basketball junkies. Anyone who achieved some level of fame usually drank free. The place was always jammed with ballplayers, sportswriters, fans and loads of jock-sniffers. Duke, the legendary bartender/owner, double-charged the non-players and hangers-on and made a good living. If anyone bitched about the charge, he'd glance over at his regulars, who knew what was coming from years of hearing this, and delivered his favorite line, "Do you have me mistaken for someone who gives a rat's ass?"

The place was hopping as I entered and looked for my buddies. I remembered back to my going-away party for Nam. My buddies made a big deal that I was drinking for free. When we pulled up to Schultz's, I turned to Gator. "So my night of free drinks is the place where I drink for free anyway?"

He grinned his toothy grin. "They taught me something in Law School, huh?" That long ago night had been hilarious. I got free advice from all the old guys about how to handle war. Stan Stiponovich kept telling me to manage my time. "Time, Dylan, time is your enemy.

You have to conquer time. Manage your time, Dylan." I recalled commenting, "Gee, Stan, all this time I was worried about the VC shooting a rocket up my ass. Thanks for clearing that up." My buddies roared but Stan just looked confused.

Shaking off the amusing memory, I headed to the corner where I saw Drum and Gator. Drum was a childhood friend and another nicknaming victim.

"You got a melon like a fuckin' kettle drum, James," was how Jimmer dubbed him. Kevin James was smart as hell, went to Columbia and majored in nuclear physics, a real rocket scientist. But despite that, Drum was a regular guy. Took his smarts for granted. Would have traded the brains for some great athletic genes. A great friend, an interesting guy, someone I trusted. He always felt guilty about me being in Nam. Nothing I said made him feel differently. Since I got back, he treated me like a hero. Couldn't help but like that.

Drum got a Vietnam deferment to work for the government as a think tank guy.

He was evasive about his work; all he would say about it was, "Sit around figuring out what to do if Ivan pushes the button. Shit like that." He got his PhD while I was in Nam fighting the communist menace. He wrote his thesis on "managing a nuclear event." As I said, Drum wasn't just smart, he was actually brilliant. Now he taught at U of P but still did government work on the side. As I sat down beside him, "So, Drum, come clean, what do you really do for Uncle Sam? Gator says you're trying to put Tasty Kakes on Mars. Spill it."

He frowned, "Tell me again, why are we still friends?"

Gator had been watching Duke and he pointed for us to look across the bar. We sat in anticipation as some poor slob asked Duke for a dinner menu.

Duke stared into space, then yelled, "Waitress, waitress, please escort this gentleman to the dining area overlooking the country club and get the wine steward to freshen up his Cabernet Sauvignon. Make certain he knows about the specials. Chateaubriand tonight, right? Or is it the Lobster?" Duke paused before adding, "But seriously, Mac, if ya want food, ya got the wrong place. Now why don't ya order a beer or piss off." The poor schmuck slumped lower into the bar stool.

Drum brought us back to the present. "Gator was filling me in on the fraud case, missing Hummels, huh?"

I had come full circle in my thinking and wanted Drum's opinion before I spilled mine. "Tell me what you think, Drum, you're the rocket scientist."

He didn't hesitate. "It sounds like someone either robbed her before she died, or she sensed she was dying and was cleaning things up. Or maybe she was going to leave money to the church or some charity. Something like that is most logical."

I didn't let him off the hook. "But pick one, what's your gut say? If you were Solomon, what would you choose?"

Drum grinned, "Still the same old Dylan, paranoid and looking for trouble."

But then he nodded, "But in this instance, I think you're right, she got ripped off. Most people aren't tidy enough to tie up loose ends before they die. Me, as an example, I'm going to leave things a total mess. Make the bastards earn their inheritance." The rocket scientist and I had reached the same conclusion. Who had ripped-off Crina Barbu?

Gator jumped in, "It should be easy enough to check if we can get her bank records. If she had a big influx of cash, we got our answer. That, plus what she ripped off in the insurance fraud had to be a chunk a change."

It was good to hear my next steps confirmed. "Think your cop buddy Merlano can get her bank to cooperate? I was planning to call him tomorrow." Gator grinned, "Merlano loves to rough people up. And especially rich bankers."

With that resolved, we settled into our normal sports banter. There was an open stool beside me, so I made room as Dom Corsi sidled up. Dom was pear-shaped, tiny, wore Coke bottle glasses and had receding black hair. Not a looker, but he was oddly likeable, like a pet guinea pig. Dom loved sports and wisely went the reporter route after trying out for Little League and being told by one of the teenage assistant coaches, "You're a shrimp, plus you stink. How about being the batboy?" In our neighborhood, there wasn't much effort spent finding tactful ways to avoid the truth. If you sucked, you weren't left in the dark.

But he became a good writer. His column in the Bulletin was titled, "Sports? Of Corsi!"

Obviously, a bad name but he did have a loyal following and was a Schultz's regular. He went where the ballplayers were and blended into the background, listening for material.

He punched my shoulder, "Aint' seen you since you got back from Nam, Dylan. How was it?" Most people first asked if I killed anyone, so this was at least neutral.

I was going to comment on his bad grammar but instead, "It was a blast, Dom. The war shit is exaggerated. Spent most of my time catching rays, playing hoops, some trout fishing. Life guarded in the South China Sea when things got too slow. Hope you weren't worried about me?"

He pondered that awhile. "You're kidding, right? I forgot you're such a ball buster. But seriously, did you get to play some ball there? I heard they had some mean ass hoop leagues over there."

I filled him in on some of my basketball exploits, most of which were true. "Funniest place I played was in Hue, the ancient capital of Nam. The grunts made a basketball court right beside a sacred pagoda. Had hundreds of locals watching our games. I got the biggest cheer when I clanged a missed dunk; it flew into the moat surrounding the pagoda. Got a standing O. They thought I did it on purpose."

I saw Gator eyes look behind me, like he was surprised. And then I felt a hand on my neck and a tongue rolling down my ear. Hoping it wasn't Duke, I spun and saw the Gator's sensuous secretary Janice had moved in tight.

"Mr. Light told me he was headed here tonight, not much atmosphere but I like the scenery." Now her hand was on my arm, rubbing slowly. I got shivers and she noticed. She got close and whispered, "You like that, huh? I have some tricks you'll like even more." She blew hot air in my ear. I could see Dom Corsi staring at me, wondering why I was so lucky.

Conversely, I could see that Gator was pissed. He stared at her, "I don't like you following me, Janice. Why don't you scram?"

Just then a big guy walks up, "What ya doing, Janice. I thought you went to the can. Saw ya rubbin' this jerk's neck. Let's beat it."

That wasn't what I wanted to hear. I looked at the lug, "Who are you calling a jerk, dickweed?" He turned from Janice. He was my height, 6'2, but weighed at least 250, a lineman type gone to fat.

He moved closer. "Pretty clear yer the jerk, messin' with another dude's babe. So fuck off before I hurt ya."

I smiled, exhaled, and then readied myself as the Sensei had taught. Then I told the big lug, "If she's your girl, why's she rubbing my neck and telling you she's in the can? Sounds like she made a decision but you're too stupid to get it."

His face contorted, and then he swung his meaty right. I ducked, exactly as Jimmer had trained me. He almost fell down as his punch whirled into the air. I stepped back some and waited for the next punch. His left came at me; I ducked again but I took the power of his blow and hurled him to the ground.

On his ass, the lug looked up at me furious, "What are ya, some fairy fighter?"

As he got to his feet, I warned him. "Better stay on the floor, or next time I won't play nice." Infuriated he charged and I spun to the side and swept his feet from under him. He hit hard this time, jaw first.

By then, Duke arrived and stared at the dazed oaf. "Get outta here buddy or I'll call the cops. If ya wanna fight, go to the gym." Three other tall ballplayers moseyed beside Duke and the big lug slumped out.

He turned, looking at Janice. Gator said, "Janice, scram. That's enough trouble tonight. We'll talk tomorrow." She sashayed off, looking at me the whole time.

From behind me, "Jesus, Dylan, are you some kung-fu fighter or what? Did they teach you that shit in Nam?"

Dom Corsi looked like he'd just won the lottery. "Tomorrow's story", I could almost see in his eyes.

I knew that wasn't good news for me. "Keep me out of your Column, Dom. Don't want every knucklehead in Philly seeing if they can kick my ass. Make this my coming home present, huh?"

I could see his disappointment but then he perked up. "How about I make you anonymous? I never say your name or anything. Just something like, "The Velvet Hammer. No, that's been used. I'll make something else up overnight."

I could see it was a losing battle. I eyed him intently, "Just make certain I really am anonymous, okay?" He nodded, but I wasn't sure that was in agreement.

When Dom left, Drum looked at me funny. "I've got to admit that was impressive.

That's not the Dylan I grew up with. Where'd you learn to fight like that? I remember you and Nut used to wrestle all the time, but that was a new level of hurt. Remind me not to piss you off."

Gator added, "Plus you baited that guy. It was like you wanted to rile him. I haven't seen you like that except when you played ball. Off the court you stayed pretty clean. You got some evil spirits, buddy?"

My friends knew me well. Should I tell them or not?

Before I decided, Duke walked over. "Hey, I need a bouncer some time, ya interested?" And then he laughed.

I shrugged, "Sorry about the fight, Duke, he kind of egged me on when I wasn't ready to be egged."

He shrugged, grin on his face, "It's not a problem, Dylan, sort a woke the place up some. I bet business picks up after word gets out. I like this new side a ya, used to be more a finesse guy. Man, that was some fancy foot work. It reminds me of Floyd Patterson some, kind of like dancin'." He walked away pleased with his sports reference and juiced by the violence.

The distraction helped settle me, I made up my mind. "Got time, boys? Got a long story about Nam. Might do me some good to talk it out."

We went to a corner table and I unloaded the treason story in Nam, the same version I told Jimmer. I left out the real names, afraid it might somehow get back to the Army. I added one new piece of information I just got late last night. That our Green Beret buddy Nut called to warn me that Percy (again used a fake name) hadn't forgotten me and that I better watch out.

I told them Percy had sworn to get me; that I still walked around looking over my shoulder.

Drum looked upset, "Holy shit, bad enough dealing with that in Nam, now you have to worry about it here? No wonder you're doing Ninja training. I'm getting chills just hearing it. He grabbed my shoulder, "No idea you had it so rough." Drum's eyes had actually welled-up.

Gator broke the somber mood with a classic observation. "Better not tell Janice about this. She's horny enough for you already. If there's anymore danger mixed in she'll cream her jeans."

After we stopped chuckling, "Do me a favor, Gator, keep her away from me. Not sure Laura would approve of my new fan."

He nodded, "I never realized she was that psycho. I mean, she brought that goon here on purpose. She had to know he would go after you. I'll tell her tomorrow that was her last strike. The tough thing is she does a great job. Best secretary I ever had. But the thing really pissing me off is why she hasn't gone after me!" And that made me laugh harder.

Drum brought the conversation back to me. "What are you going to do? You can't go around like this forever." He was right. Ever since I got home, I'd had a shadow following me. Was it just Percy or was it something else?"

Gator was a Navy veteran and opined, "Doesn't the Army give counseling service? You can't be the only GI having trouble adjusting. I mean, it was a fucking war!"

I had looked into that already and had ruled that out. "Pretty sure they'll do a Henny Youngman on me. Like, 'if it hurts to think about it, they'll say, don' think about it.'" I looked at my childhood friends. "Hate saying anything nice about you guys, but just telling you helps. Like taking a monster dump."

Gator roared, "That's my old Dylan."

⌒

After Schultz's, I went to my apartment, turned on the tube and watched Johnny Carson. Sometime during the monologue, I went blank. The patrol was late picking me up at sunrise. I'd had night watch in Quang Tri, guarding General Freeman. I was starving and the MP Company wasn't that far, I decided to hoof it. I'd gotten a few hundred yards when I saw movement in the perimeter wire. VC? I dropped to the ground and raised the M-16. No cover to protect me. The VC stopped moving. Did he see me? And then he started moving fast, I shot off 10 rounds before thinking. I saw him crawling out the back of the wire, moving slowly, dragging his legs. Did I hit him? Wounded bad? Was this my first kill? What if it was just some starving local looking for food? Did I kill an innocent man? When I snapped out of it, the TV was humming, showing the CBS logo. I got up and slumped off to bed.

⌒

That morning I planned to visit Mary Craley, who was next on my list from Hoban for possible insurance fraud. She recently had an expensive chair lift installed to help her move upstairs and had extensive medical back-up to get it approved. Her diagnosis was "severe spinal compression." Mary lived in Upper Darby, on the busy intersection of Township Line and Lansdowne Avenue. There were 3 small homes wedged between real estate and insurance offices. You had to park in the alleyway behind the home since the front was a bustling road with a pencil thin walkway. After parking out back and scampering along the sidewalk, I looked at the steep steps and thought this climb must be tough with a bad back. Or was she another screw off?

I scaled the steps, knocked on the door, and waited patiently. The traffic was so noisy I wondered how it sounded inside. I knocked harder and rang the bell for a few seconds. The door opened slowly and I knew instantly this was a dead end, wouldn't need to look inside. Mary was in a wheelchair and must have weighed 300 pounds.

I told her, "Just making certain your insurance payments were going well, chair lift was working out okay, just a polite service call is all."

She looked a bit puzzled but smiled, "The insurance is great. I couldn't get by without it. Thank 'em for the wheel chair. I feel like a real person again. It's tough getting' around since my husband passed." She pointed at her belly, "You think I'm fat, you shoulda seen my old man, ended up killin' him, had a stroke, just dropped dead."

I didn't know what to say to that so I asked if she needed anything. She grinned through her multiple chins, "I could use a Barbie Doll figure, but that aint likely." As I walked away, Mary Craley realized she forgot to ask what I meant by "chair lift working out okay?"

SYLVAN

Sylvan saw an ugly green car pull out as he entered the alleyway behind Craley's house. As he parked, he thought about his chance encounter with Mary Craley. When she became a steady customer, he had quickly learned that Jaro Kralzyck met Maysia Kowalski while working the late shift at Honeywell. They both shared a love for America, baseball, and eating. They married after a long courtship and shamed their families when they changed their last name to Craley. Jaro became "Joe" and his beloved was now "Mary." Ostracized from family, they moved from Frankford to Upper Darby to begin their new life. Despite years of trying, they were not blessed with children. Joe and Mary settled into a cozy lifestyle. They traveled frequently, visiting all the major cities in the land of freedom. Chicago was their favorite, especially trips to Wrigley field, the lively Cubby Bar and the ethnic restaurant scene. Life was good.

As years passed, their passion for food took its toll, they grew obese. Eventually, this restricted their travel, too much trouble. Joe got so large that he became bedridden. Health problem piled up; first phlebitis and eventually high blood pressure.

When his disability ran out, bills mounted and they had trouble making ends meet. Mary heard from a friend that a pawn shop, Lost in Time, was the place to go if you wanted to sell baseball memorabilia. That was when she first met Sylvan. He gladly bought their baseball treasures and soon became a trusted friend. When Joe fell to a massive stroke, Sylvan was there to help. Lonely, Mary ate her grief away and soon joined the ranks of the disabled. Sylvan was there to fill the void, her helper.

All this ran through his mind as Sylvan ambled up the steps and hit the door bell. Mary answered the ring, wondering if the cute insurance man was back. When she saw Sylvan, she was a little disappointed. Not that she didn't like Sylvan; it was just that the young insurance fella was something different.

But she smiled, "Hello, Sylvan, guess this is my day for visitors." She watched him stop; lifting his head and pulling his hair back as he drilled those intense eyes at her.

He asked softly, "What visitors, Mary? I thought we had an agreement that I'm your right hand man." Mary explained what the insurance man said, that it was a friendly visit.

Sylvan relaxed, pushed her toward the kitchen and heard her add, "Oh, ya, he said something about how my chair lift was working. I wonder what that meant?" Sylvan stopped dead.

Mary continued to talk about the visitor and never noticed Sylvan's silence. She watched as he moved to the stove and turned on the oven. She wondered: What's he doing? And then she realized he forgot to light the pilot.

Before she could mention this, Sylvan moved
suddenly behind her and started to pull the wheelchair
rapidly in reverse, through the door into the dining
room. When he was at the farthest end of the dining
room he stopped, leaned over closely and looked into
her worried face. Sylvan said nothing, seemed to be
memorizing her.

Mary was puzzled, "What are you doing, Sylvan?"
No words came back but he viciously slapped her
face, stunning her. He continued to study her. And
then he moved behind her, gripped the handlebars and
began pushing the chair, quickly gaining speed.
Shocked, Mary screamed as the end of the kitchen
rushed at her. Sylvan drove her into the wall beside
the oven, banging her head as she hurtled from the
seat. Dazed, she looked up from the floor as Sylvan
pulled her wheelchair away and began closing
windows and shutting the doors, enclosing the
kitchen.

She moaned, "What are you doing, Sylvan?"

As he closed the last door, he moved next to her
face, inhaled deeply and spoke without emotion,
"Sacrificing the fatted calf."

DYLAN

On my drive from Craley's, I stopped at a phone booth and called my old competitor Frankie Merlano. I got him after one ring, told him who I was.

"Remember me, Frankie, I used to rain jumpers over your outstretched hands?"

He didn't answer right away, placing me. "Think ya got that wrong Frazier. I remember smackin' your bony ass to the ground each game. Made you pay for that feathery touch, didn't I?" We reminisced some, I told him about my job as an insurance investigator since leaving the Army. And then I told him about Crina's case, that I wanted to see if she had a lot of cash when she died. Told him about the Hummels, that it didn't add up. He asked for her bank name and other minor details.

He paused, then said, "Piece a cake, Frazier, give me a ring later." I promised to call in a few days.

It was still early, so I drove to see Mirella. Seeing Mary Craley reminded me how tough it must be living alone. Thought my cat lady might like a visit. It took her awhile to answer the door; I saw her eye at the peephole, careful.

Mirella was having tea, "I always have a black tea 'round now. Those Limeys don't do much right, but they sure know their tea."

As we chatted, she told me about the dead cats. She was still upset. "I could understand one dyin', but three? I'm always careful about their diet. They must a got somethin' bad. That must be it." I told her about my progress on Crina's case.

She gave me something I hadn't heard before, "Crina liked jewelry. Maybe there was a box at the bank. I don't remember seein' any layin' around after she died. She must a put it away, huh?" That made me realize that this case just kept getting worse. No jewelry, no Hummels. I made a mental note to call Merlano and mention a bank box.

I turned to Mirella, "Want to visit the cats? Maybe we can find something the gang shouldn't be eating. Make sure it's safe."

On our way down the steps, I learned she was a chemist. "That's why I'm so careful with my boy's chow; I know what bad food can do." I tried to hold her arm but she shooed me off, "I need my exercise. Aint that old." What a character, hoped I had that spunk when I hit my 80's. The cats got excited as she neared. She nudged me, "They think a treats comin'" Sure enough, she dug into her pockets and plopped a snack into each eager mouth. I scanned the area as she fed them. Although overgrown, the place was arranged carefully. Mirella liked order. Chemists arrange things the right way.

I noticed a few pellets near one bowl. "Mirella, what are those pellets? Is that just left over chow or something else?"

She ambled over, took awhile to see what I meant, picked some up to get a better look.

"They're not from me. The boys would eat it if was any good, there must be somethin' off." I had a napkin in my pocket from lunch, so I wrapped them up, not really knowing what to do with them. Mirella pointed at me, "Any lab'll analyze em for ya. If I had my equipment, I'd do it myself." While Mirella played with the gang, I wondered why anyone would poison Mirella's cats. Made a note to visit my local hardware store, see what poisons were on the shelf to kill pests. The more I thought, the more I figured a sick neighbor was at fault.

&

I called my mother that night and warned her she would see me at church next morning, that I was taking a shot at softening Jimmer's mother. Not surprisingly, she burst into a giggle.

I liked listening to her laugh. "I never thought my Dylan had such a soft side. I remember how you used to tease your sisters and their friends. Aren't you the one who called them dorks and weirdos? Maybe all my rosaries are paying off."

I waited a second, "Mom, those girl friends were pretty weird, don't you agree?" She was still laughing as she hung up.

Next morning after mass, Mrs. Kielmann eyed me as I fell in beside her as she walked home.

My mom often walked with her after morning mass, but per our plan, mom lingered to do the Stations of the Cross, giving me some alone time with Jimmer's mom.

I gave her my friendliest smile, "How are you Mrs. Kielmann? Great sermon, huh? Monsignor Pugh was on his game today." Mary Kielmann always liked me, so it wasn't too odd for me to chat her up. She knew Jimmer protected me as a kid, so she had seen a lot of me growing up, was comfortable with me.

I continued my seemingly inane chatter. "Signed up at Jimmer's judo school, he's done a great job with those kids. I'm the biggest student but they throw me around like tinker toys. If I wasn't the one getting tossed, it might be kinda funny." She smiled politely, but I saw her recoil at Jimmer's name. That didn't daunt me. "Met Jimmer's new family. That Marisol is a doll, beautiful and smart. As you sure know, Jimmer can be a handful but he's almost polite and gentlemanly with her. At first I didn't believe it, thought it was some act. Or maybe that aliens had invaded his body." That got a full laugh from her. But she still didn't ask about Jimmer.

To fill the void, I kept the blather up, added comments about Jose. "It must be great for you having such a sharp kid like Jose around. I mean he's funny but so polite. And how great is Jimmer to treat him like his own son. Jose idolizes Jimmer. Nice thing to see. Never thought he'd be such a natural father. Did you?"

Mrs. Kielmann picked up her pace but turned to look at me, her face expressionless, and said, "Jim is living in mortal sin.

Unless he leaves that woman and her son, he'll spend the hereafter in hell. I appreciate your loyalty, but Jim is no longer part of our life. He's dead to us." She rushed ahead and never looked back.

As I was walking away, I thought how miserably I'd failed. But what Mrs. Kielmann didn't know was that I didn't give up that easy. I walked back to St. Tim's and knocked at the rectory, asked for Monsignor Pugh.

He gave me a big hug but as he backed away, asked, "How come I think there's another motive other than a love for our savior's word? What brings you back, Dylan?" I told him about Jimmer, about my failed sortie with Mrs. Kielmann, asked for his advice.

"How do we melt the iceberg, Monsignor? I know what the church teaches, but if you saw Jimmer with that family, you wouldn't forsake him. Not sure we need a miracle, just some true Christian charity. Can you help me, or at least guide me?"

I had known Monsignor Pugh most of my life. Since I was mostly responsible for his tasteless nickname, there was no reason for him to give me a hand. But Monsignor Pugh was a special person, a regular guy with a beautiful, holy spirit. He went to all my games as a kid and was around for most of our family celebrations.

It didn't surprise me when he said, "The Church makes room for sinners, not just angels. Our mission is to embrace the lost souls, to heal all God's children. The Church has room for Jim Kielmann, his wife and son.

Let me look into the details of the first marriage. Annulments aren't impossible. But let me caution you, Mary Kielmann might need a miracle. Her heart is hard."

~

Gator and I had previously agreed to resume our pawn shop search this week. He loved getting out of the office. So I called to finalize plans at lunchtime on Tuesday, when I knew Janice would be out. Gator answered on the first ring, said he was free, to drop right over. "The Gilded Age" was in Overbrook, the upscale, mostly black neighborhood on the edges of West Philly, not far from Overbrook High School, alma mater of the legendary Wilt Chamberlain. As I drove, I looked over at Gator. One of his greatest traits was his enthusiasm. He was the kind of kid that ran everywhere, even in his house. Drove his step mom crazy, "Billy, settle down," was a refrain I heard a million times. He was drumming on my dashboard as we drove along. I looked at him, "Billy, settle down!" He grinned and then used the dashboard as a drum.

The Gilded Age was on the busy Lancaster Ave., next to a State Liquor Store and a bustling steak shop.

I asked, "Should we get cheese steaks before or after the visit?"

Immediately, Gator opined, "After we're done, gives me motivation to wade through all that shit quick.

It gives me something to look forward to." That sounded good to me. There weren't too many white people in the area, so we stood out. But even more so because Gator wore a dark suit and vest which was unbuttoned, with most of his shirt hanging out. He looked like a wacko. And I looked like a cop. I was on alert but nobody paid us any interest.

As I always tried to do in unfamiliar territory, we parked right out-front. Ready to bolt fast if we got in trouble. When we entered The Gilded Age, I knew something was unusual. The place was full of Colonial furniture, with bits of Mennonite and Shaker pieces mixed in. My mom and dad loved old furniture and during my childhood we made many forays to Lancaster County Amish country in search of treasures. Not that I was ever that interested but I could tell oak or pine from tiger maple without missing a beat. Why was this pawn shop full of antique furniture? Didn't put that style with this neighborhood. Interesting.

An elderly black man walked up and saw me staring at an old hutch. "Do you like that, son? That piece has some history. I found that at a foreclosure, an old brownstone off the Penn campus. I bought the whole lot. The owners liked the simplicity of the Shaker artists. It was functional but somehow elegant. Their work speaks to me. It's a steal at $100. It will last a lifetime."

I smiled, "Grew up traipsing to antiques shops outside Reading, like the hutch but it wouldn't go with my décor. I've got going more of an upscale collegiate dorm look. Need a woman to soften my rough edges."

He chuckled, "If that's the current status, what are you looking for in here?"

I liked his manner so I spilt the story about the Hummels, leaving out the juicy parts.

He shook his head. "There's nothing like that here. We have mostly furniture, some dishware, pieces like that. Most of my customers moved to Overbrook to get a more gentrified lifestyle. Folks here like the classic furniture. It gets them closer to The American Dream." I showed him our list of other pawn shops. "I don't know them. I'm too busy to visit the competition. I guess that's good and bad, huh?" Gator was over looking at some old coffee urns.

I saw the proprietor looking at my disheveled friend. I leaned in, "He's my retarded cousin. Giving him a little outing. Know what I mean?"

He shook his head sympathetically, "Nice of you, nothing more important than family."

ॐ

As we exited the store, Gator said, "Good move having lunch afterwards, that place was a bust. Now for our reward." The cheese steak was fabulous. Dripping with thin steak meat, pulverized to tender pieces, oozing cheese, onions and ketchup sprinkled in. They let the roll lay on top of the grilling meat and onions- to get it moist and warm. I watched Gator devour his classic without saying a word.

He saw me staring. "This is fuckin' great!" Couldn't argue with that.

I wolfed down my sandwich and thought about next steps. Someone had to have the elusive Hummels. But who?

On the way back, I told Gator I'd made contact with Merlano. That he was chasing down Crina's bank records.

"That'll tell you what's next. If she died flush, then she was just cashing out. Maybe she sensed her last days and was tidying up. Some people do that. They don't want to leave a mess. That won't be my way, though. I'm going to travel. Hang out like the old losers we see at Schultz's and get wasted every night. Fuck that cleaning up shit. I mean, you're dead. Who gives a shit if they think you're a slob, right?"

I grinned at my buddy, "Settle down, Billy."

I dropped Gator at work. "I'll tell Janice you said hello. I don't like her stalking you but if I was you, I'd just tap that and be done with her. She's the kind that likes the hunt. She'll probably leave you alone if she sees what a turd you really are."

I just smiled, "Don't do me any favors, my friend. Why would I take advice from my retarded cousin?" I drove off leaving him scratching his head. I headed toward my hometown hardware store. As I walked in, I remembered we used to get spray paint here when we were young and immature. Did a little art work around town; almost got expelled from St. Tim's when we got too creative on a street sign about a mean priest.

As I entered the store, I unwrapped the napkin to look at the pellets. Thought that these would help guide my search. Went to an aisle that had mouse traps and such.

A wizened old guy came over to help. "Got a varmint problem, do you? You're in the right pew but maybe I can help you narrow it down. What are we hunting, rats or mice?" I showed him the pellet and said some cats got some by accident and died. He looked carefully, bringing them to his nose and sniffing. "This here is heavy duty rat poison. It would bring down a dog if he ate too much. Smells like mint, probably treated with something. Catnip maybe? Weren't any accident. Trying to attract the cats is what." He walked to a nearby aisle and pulled off a can of rat poison. "This is the culprit."

I wrote down the name of the poison. He twisted the nearby bottle of catnip and put it under his nose. "Yep, catnip. Smell it, just much fainter. Kind of hate cats myself. Interesting concoction."

I noted the name of the catnip, looked at the clerk and added, "Wasn't an accident. I'm going to get the guy, kick his ass, then throw his butt in jail." He recoiled a little but just stared. I thanked the creepy guy for his help and walked to my car wondering. Neighborhood kids probably wouldn't have come up with that elaborate scheme. Maybe an adult who had enough of the noise and mess? There was still time to visit Mirella and get back in time to play ball that night. I felt antsy again and needed competition. Or maybe just to bang someone.

 ॐ

Mirella answered the buzzer after a couple rings. I laughed at her greeting.

"Whatever yer sellin' I don't need it, scram." She buzzed me up when she heard it was me. I told her I liked her welcoming style. "You gotta be careful, ya' know. There's nuts everywhere." I had decided to tell her the truth about the cats. If someone was poisoning her boys, she better be aware. She took the news stone-faced.

"Sons of bitches, Sons of bitches," she said repeatedly through her set jaw.

I asked if she had any hunches about who would do this. As I listened to her list of suspects, I noticed that her grammar had suddenly gotten perfect. No Philly argot or slang. Every word was perfectly articulated and flawless. I thought back to St. Tim's when the nuns hammered us to avoid Philly dialect like "ya", "youse" and "yer" or we would be judged "uneducated."

When she finished, I asked, "What happened to the Philly accent, Mirella? Have you been fooling with me?"

She seemed to weigh the matter before commenting. "You caught me. I guess I'm getting comfortable around you. That was one of the things Crina and I had in common. We were both well taught by the nuns. And at home as a kid I'd get a blank look if I asked for "wudder." Mom would have me repeat until I said "water" properly. But when I went to work, I was the only woman chemist and learned to dumb-down my language to fit in better. The other chemist shunned me early, calling me "Miss Proper" because I spoke so well. The slang became a habit. Crina spoke beautifully.

She was really smart, could have been anything she wanted if she had the opportunity.

I didn't know how to respond. "Sad", was all I came up with. Mirella looked at me, a gleam in her eye.

"I've got an idea. Maybe we can set a trap for the punk who's poisoning my boys. Let's call the cops; see if they can stake-out the area. I've contributed to the PAL for years, they owe me." I was trying to envision the greeting she'd get when asking to assign men to watch a herd of wild cats.

"Not sure they'll be too helpful, Mirella. This is a tough neighborhood; they've got REAL mean cats to chase. I know a guy, I'll ask his advice."

She wasn't happy but I convinced her to give me a shot. Maybe Merlano would have a better idea. When I left, I circled out back and looked over the cat's terrain. The obvious offender was someone living close by who could hear and smell the feisty felines. The whole alleyway was overgrown and the backyards abutting Mirella's were so wild they seemed impenetrable. There was no sign of any comings or goings. Even across the alleyway there was no obvious candidate. Crina's apartment had a pathway from the alleyway but it was overgrown enough that you'd never notice the cats unless you went looking. I thought I'd see some clue, something to go on. But I got squat.

Next I walked to both ends of the alley, trying to imagine the best point of entry and departure. I liked the farthest end, more overgrown and the street was heavily treed, no cars lined the curb.

Not much traffic. You could walk in, drop the contaminated chow, and get out in a couple minutes. I thought about her stake-out idea; might be the only way to catch the culprit. And then I wondered if they would come at night or the morning. Probably early morning. Get in early when no one was up, no witnesses. That's how I'd do it if I was nuts.

SYLVAN

Sylvan ambled into Biata's bedroom and gave her a cup of Ceylon tea. "What would I do without you, Syl?" She sat in the corner, in her favorite chair, reading The Bulletin. Her emphysema was acting up and she didn't move around much.

Biata shook her head, "Pearl Meyer died day before yesterday. I worked with her at Rohm and Haas, next ta me on the line. She was kinda pushy, never satisfied with anythin'."

Sylvan stared at her, "Meyer, sounds Jewish. Pushy and Jew go together like Hope and Crosby." Biata laughed at his quip. Sylvan didn't joke much.

Sylvan gazed at Biata and pondered wordlessly. Things were going well. He was selling off her figurines systematically.

He never gave her full payment. "These are tough times, Bee, did the best I could for my sweet girl." Biata smiled when he said that, he was so good to her. He was systematically submitting fraudulent physical therapy visits and bills to purchase whirlpool equipment and exercise apparatus. With her diagnosis, nothing seemed out of the ordinary. He already got $10,000; he'd have to stop before anyone got suspicious.

Sylvan prided himself on being disciplined. "You get greedy, you get caught," he repeated to himself. He looked at Biata again, gave her a rare smile. He thought contentedly, just a few more months.

But he was getting impatient. He muttered to himself: It's time to kill some more cats. I'll be more hands-on this time. The rat poison, catnip and aconite mix would drop a horse. Baseball bat this time? While Sylvan was in his reverie, Biata had been looking at him, admiring his beautiful hair pulled into a ponytail. She thought: Now you can see those eyes, like a beautiful cat.

She interrupted his vision when she asked, "What are ya smiling at Sylvan? First the joking and now smilin' ta yerself. Haven't seen ya so happy in weeks."

Sylvan stopped smiling; thought how irritating her voice was. Maybe I should take the bat to her first, get some practice in. But instead, "It's just so nice being here with my Bee, like the first day of spring." Biata swooned.

DYLAN

Next morning I visited Merlano. He listened as I explained Mirella's idea about getting cops to watch for the cat killer. He smirked, "Whatta ya fuckin' kiddin'? I'd be laughed outta the precinct. I can hear it now, 'There goes Merlano, leader of the pussy patrol.' Tell me that's a joke, Frazier, will ya?"

I decided to switch topics, "How about the bank records? What did you find?"

His ball-busting look changed immediately. "I think ya might be on to somethin'. Her bank accounts were drawn done to almost nothin'. She had just enough to keep things open. Definitely fishy."

I then learned there was no safe deposit box; so no place to store jewelry. "This smells, Frank. According to her buddy Mirella, Crina collected jewelry and Hummels. Made sense to me that she used the fraud money to add to her collections. That maybe she sold the Hummels to buy some special ring or necklace. Now we find she has no money, no jewelry and no Hummels. Is it possible she horded all her treasures, then she dies and someone finds her and lifts all the goods?"

Merlano looked right at me. "Do ya think your pal Mirella's got light fingers?

You said she was in the apartment after Crina died. She's the logical culprit to me. Know ya like her but the evidence points to her."

I'd seen Mirella's apartment. No sign of Hummels, jewelry or any extravagant lifestyle. Agreed she was a likely choice. But it just didn't feel right. "Hear you, Frank, just go meet her and I think you'll rule her out. I mean, she's 80 somethin', how's she going to haul all that stuff away?"

Merlano nodded, "Hear ya, but weirder shit goes down. We should check."

I had an idea, "Why not check her bank records. See if she had any influx of cash. Might be useful info. Could rule her out at least.

Merlano grinned, "Good idea. Sure ya don't want a job? Might make a good cop. Plus we need a shooter in the PAL league. We'd mop up, you and me in the backcourt."

I smirked, "Isn't that like letting the monkeys run the zoo?"

❧

Gus Demovick was next on Hoban's possible fraud list. He had huge medical bills for some exotic eye surgery. He was an engineer for GTE, went to China for the procedure. The medical department at Voyager said the surgery was considered experimental and wasn't done in the States.

Reading on about Demovick, I learned he was apparently a wizard with telephone technology and was going blind. The documentation he provided from his eye doctor was extensive. From GTE's personnel department, one line jumped out.

It stated, "Demovick's a VIP, vital to our mission to dominate the telephone industry. Pay whatever it takes to restore his vision."

Apparently the procedure was successful, but the costs continued to pour in. For surgery alone, it was $20, 000. The bills had to be translated, gave little detail to justify that cost. The big check was sent to Demovick who was supposed to pay the Chinese surgeon. A perfect set up for fraud. I called the Personnel Department to see if there was a quick way to verify these expenses and payment procedures.

When I explained my concern about the unusual cost, I got an odd response. "I'm not at liberty to discuss the matter. Just pay the bills." Then they hung up.

When I told Hoban what happened, he groaned. "Maybe someone in Personnel is also involved? Check it out." I hadn't considered that but should have. Still had much to learn.

Demovick lived in the pricey town of Villanova, not far from where Jack Kraft's basketball team played hoops. As I drove through the tree lined streets and looked at the huge mansions approaching his house, I figured this guy was wealthy. And when I saw that his house was gated, I was even more impressed. No sneaking up on this guy. There was a bell on the stone post that anchored the gates. Surprisingly, someone answered immediately.

"What can I do for you?" came from the box. The voice was low, almost strained. Sick? I wondered. After identifying myself, a creaking noise erupted suddenly as the gates rolled back. I got in my green bomb and proceeded to the front of the magnificent house.

A small man waited by the open door. As I parked, I perused my host. Totally bald, elf-like in stature but elegantly dressed, almost foppish. Was that a silk smoking jacket? Did people really wear those?

As I exited the car, the gnome screeched at me, "Get closer, want to see if you're what I pictured by the voice. I still can't see perfectly after the surgery. It's getting better, though. I'll need glasses, but should be 20-20 after that." His glasses were enormous, like fake clown ones. They struck me funny but I controlled myself.

I came near Demovick and waited while he eyed me up and down. "I thought you were tall, could tell you were well above the gate box. Small people have to lean up, almost yell to be heard. You sounded relaxed. Kind of confident, like you knew a secret." He stared some more. "I wish I was handsome like that. You move like an athlete. Tennis?"

I laughed, "Basketball, never tried tennis." And then he switched topics. "So, you're here to see if I'm a fuck-off, right?" That made me belly laugh.

And that's how my conversation started with Gus Demovick. We went inside and sat in the library. Since I'd never been in a house with a library, I just guessed that by the cherry paneling and endless book shelves, all packed with hard covers. Nice.

Demovick noticed me studying the room.

"I read them all. That's all I do, read and work. When I got the eye problem, I got worried. What would I do if I couldn't read? When the doctors told me my condition was hopeless, I began researching. I found they had been doing the miracle procedure in China for years. So I took matters into my own hands."

I asked what he did at GTE and learned he was a think tank, researcher type.

He told me what he was working on, "A wireless telephone, almost like a walkie- talkie used by the ARMY, but on a grander scale. They're testing the prototype in Nam right now. It's saving lives is what I hear. But the big idea is to make these usable for the masses. People will never be out of touch. How does that strike you, Mr. Frazier?"

I told him the truth, "Sounds like a nightmare, Mr. Demovick. When do you get a chance to fuck-off?"

He belly-laughed, and then added, "I never thought about that angle. You might have a point, son"

I'd already gotten enough evidence to prove this claim was legit, but had one more question.

"When I called Personnel at GTE, they acted nervous, made me suspicious that your claims were funny. Why would they do that?"

Demovick thought awhile. "They're scared to death of me. I told the CEO how useless they were helping me solve my problem. All I got from them was, 'Not covered under the policy.' Now that I got this done and it's successful, they're worried about other execs bypassing them. They'd lose power, which scares them." That made sense, so I got up to leave and wished him well. Another dead end but an interesting guy. Wireless phones. Crazy.

☙

Next morning, I got up at 4 am. Thought I'd stake-out Mirella's backyard. Hadn't been up this early since the Army. On the ride there, I thought about my flashbacks. All of them were Nam situations I'd been in, some tense others just striking. Looking back now, I could evaluate how I acted under pressure. Had I done all right, or did I just rationalize my actions? Was I wrong to bring Mac into the treason fray? Even back then, involving him always made me feel guilty. I was pretty sure that guilt was driving the visions. Maybe I should talk to Mac. Would the flashbacks stop if I got his forgiveness? Before I could work that out, my thoughts shifted to the present as I approached Mirella's quiet, pitch black neighborhood.

It was just past 5am when I parked around the corner from Mirella's apartment. As I got out of the car, the stillness struck me. Even though it was a decaying neighborhood, there had always been noise, cars or horns, something. Now it was dead quiet. As I approached the alleyway, a dark figure emerged from the shadows. I stopped, exhaled to steady myself, found myself assuming a defensive position that Jimmer taught me. And then I noticed the uniform and milk cartons dangling at his side. Of course, who else would be out now but a milkman? He was a blocky man, heavy coat, wore a cap with ear-flaps pulled low over his long hair on this chilly morning. That made me realize I was cold. I shivered reflexively.

The milkman halted when he saw me. Probably wasn't used to company this early. Tough neighborhood, wise to be cautious. To break the tension, I said hello in my most cheerful voice.

"Sorry if I startled you, pretty cold out, huh?" He stared for a few seconds, nodded, and then passed by without saying anything. Guess my friendly tone didn't work. Didn't blame him, with his job you had to be cautious. I turned around to see if I should say anything else. Funny, nobody there. Where did he go?

I entered Mirella's alley from the south end. As I had determined the other day, the north side was the most likely entry point, so by starting from this side I could spot anyone entering- before they saw me. The alleyway was coal black, even the faint street sounds were muffled by the undergrowth. After a few minutes, I moved further down and waited. My eyes were now accustomed to the darkness. It was clear night but no moon to help you see. Perfect for mischief.

SYLVAN

After passing the tall stranger on the street, Sylvan slipped out the Louisville Slugger from inside his coat. He liked the feel of it. Just like Richie Allen's bat, 42 ounces. The biggest bat in baseball. He knew he couldn't be identified but the stranger's presence disturbed him. There was something familiar about him. He turned and retraced his steps. Let's see what that snoopy guy was up too. Sylvan gripped the bat tightly and thought about his favorite Phillie. Like Richie Allen said, "Time to hit some more taters." Sylvan also entered the south end and moved slowly. He couldn't see anything. Still dark. He stood still, listening. He got excited.

DYLAN

The loud moaning forced me to move quickly toward Mirella's yard. Was it human or just the cats? I slowed up before entering; making sure this wasn't a trap. My neck got goose bumps. This didn't sound good. I readied myself and whirled into the cat's area. There was Mirella kneeling down, sobbing deeply. And then I saw the cats. Scattered in front of her were three cats lying motionless. What struck me were their distorted bodies. Beaten to a pulp. Their heads were misshapen, eyes and tongue hanging out, legs bent in unnatural angles and torsos bloody red and matted. Looking at the scene, one word entered my mind. Massacre.

SYLVAN

Sylvan watched the tall stranger spring from his hiding spot and run into the cat lady's yard. Sylvan moved quietly, still alert and staying on the edges. With his dark clothes, he was impossible to spot. As he neared the cat area, he slipped into the heavy brush bordering Mirella's yard. This was the spot he cleared days ago to scout the area unobserved. He moved stealthily, using the cats noisy mewling to cover his movements. He scanned the scene from his perch. There they are. He watched the sobbing cat lady being consoled. His mind raced. Why is the tall guy here so early? He thought about that. The tall one's a problem. I have to fix the problem. He snoops too much.

DYLAN

Mirella looked at me with blurry eyes, saying nothing, just sobbing. I asked, "How long have you been here?"

She gulped in her breath, answered weakly, "I heard the boys squealing, looked from my window, thought I saw someone down here. Then I heard the screams and hurried down. I found my boys like this. What kind of monster would do this?" I looked closer. It seemed like some heavy club was used for the slaughter. This was getting much worse. Why did the murderer switch from poison? This was way beyond dealing with annoying cats. This was beginning to seem like what Mirella had said. A monster.

SYLVAN

Sylvan rubbed the bat up and down, like stroking a
pet. He thought about when he killed the cats a few
minutes ago. He had wanted to kill more but decided
on three. Odd numbers were nice. He was lucky he
got done early. That big guy came snooping around.
It was almost like he knew I was going to strike.
Sylvan let those words sink in. I don't believe in luck.
I believe in plans. Sylvan made a decision. I'm going
to do it now. Snoopy goes first. Then take my time
with the old hag. He got the bat ready. He's got his
back to me. Only about 15 feet. Two or three steps.
Then come in swinging.

Sylvan took a deep breath. Let's go. He started to
move....
But flashing lights and police cars entered from both
ends of the alley. He froze, staying still, like a Black
Panther sensing danger, deciding to hide in his lair.
And then he stooped low as the frenzied cops got out
of their cruisers. They shinned their flashlights at the
cat lady and tall guy.

The lead cop yelled, "Freeze, put your hands where
we can see them." The cops entered the yard and
surrounded them. The cat lady was talking to the
cops, pointing at the tall guy.

Sylvan shifted back. Use the confusion to get into the alley. He looked both ways. Nothing. He moved into the familiar darkness.

DYLAN

It turned out Mirella called the cops when she first saw the intruder in the yard. She told them, "Someone's killing my cats." She was smart enough to give good directions, that they should enter both sides of the alley. She told the dispatcher, "Trap the guy." So naturally, they see me and think I'm the psycho. It took Mirella's impassioned plea to keep them from cuffing me. Couldn't blame them. They get a call that some nut is killing cats in her back yard. They pull up, seeing me standing over the carcasses. After things settled down, I gave the cops my name and address, told them about the insurance investigation and my interest in Mirella. They took her back to her apartment. She smiled when I said I'd be over later.

I went to a phone booth, called Merlano and told him what happened.

"That's some sick fuck that'd do that." And then he added, "I studied up on sadistic killers when I had a crazy case last year. Found out most stone-cold killers started with animals when they were kids. My guy up in North Philly killed six whores. He said he was doing, 'God's work.' It turns out he killed dogs in his neighborhood.

He said it was 'for practice.' What I'm getting' at is we might have another crazy killer here. After this, I might be able to get some juice on this case." When I hung up I wondered what was really going on. Something was stuck in my head, something about this case wasn't adding up.

&

On the ride home, I thought more about the mess I got into in Nam. When the thieves knew we were onto them, they started killing MP's. I knew I was a target; they'd be coming for me. To survive, I learned to steel myself. Went for months without letting my guard down. Watched every movement, seeing if anything was out of the ordinary. Was my bunk rumpled? Duffel bag moved? Things like that. Learned not to trust many people, just Mac and a few others. It kept me alive. But a tense, emotionless life wasn't any way to live; it ate at your guts. Now I was in the real world and found myself with the same instincts kicking in. This was when I really missed Laura. Thinking of her got me through Nam. I really wanted her home, now. But was it fair for me to marry her until I fixed my damage? I had to work that out.

&

I got home and looked at my notes on Crina's fraud case. I decided to organize my questions into a list. Maybe a pattern would jump out. How did the cat get in? I answered that with Mirella having a key. Who stripped the apartment of Hummels? Where did she pawn the Hummels? Or did someone steal them? Why was her bank account empty? Who was the nephew or friend of Crina? And then I turned to Mirella's page and listed her questions. Who poisoned her cats? Was it an annoyed neighbor or kids? Now I entered a new question. Why would someone beat her cats to death? Thinking about what Merlano had said, I added another twist. Was this killer crazy?

I sat back and let the questions percolate. Without wanting too, I had wandered into a creepy mess. Poor Mirella. All she wanted to do was take care of those homeless cats. And then some lunatic starts murdering her pets. And then what bugged me jumped out! Looking at these series of questions jogged loose what was rolling through my subconscious. Were both cases connected? Was the thief worried that Mirella knew his identity and was trying to scare her? Maybe divert her attention from thinking about Crina. Had the thief seen me in Crina's apartment that day and saw me wander over to Mirella's cats after talking to Helen Zegielski? That was a disturbing thought. And then a worse one, were we being watched by a lunatic? I'd call Merlano in the morning and tell him my theory. Satisfied with my conclusion, I flipped on the TV and watched Captain Kirk outfox the Klingons. As they used to say in Nam, Kirk had his shit together.

SYLVAN

Sylvan was in a rage. He murmured, "I can't get caught. I can't get caught. There's too much to do. Too much to do. I can't get careless. Can't get careless." He wandered to his collection of old watches to calm himself. He looked at the Vacheron Constantin from 1805, picked it up, wound it, and listened to the faint ticking; it soothed him. After a few minutes he had a comforting thought. If they knew it was me, the police would have picked me up. Or at least come around asking questions. But nothing happened. He moseyed behind his store counter and picked up his ledger. He mindlessly scrolled through recent transactions. A smile came to his face. The big guy's just snooping. He doesn't know anything. He lumbered back to the priceless watches and suddenly glared, but maybe he does?

DYLAN

Early next morning, I called Merlano, was told he wasn't in yet. So, I called Mirella and told her I was on my way over. That I'd be looking around in the back yard, so don't worry if you see someone out there in a half hour or so. That I'd be up to visit when I got done. Traffic was light, so I made good time to Fishtown. On the ride over, I decided not to retrace my steps from yesterday, to go in the opposite way. See if I could spot some clues The street was quiet except for a couple boys at the end of the block. I could see them watching me, staring at me aggressively, not wanting to break eye contact, not backing down. Playing it tough. Boys like their games.

The north entrance was similar to the south but slightly more overgrown. I moved on the side closest to Mirella's yard. Figured that's how the nut must have approached. The alley was full of sticks and trash, hard to see any patterns or something not right. As I got near Mirella's, I noticed the path beaten through the undergrowth.

I followed the trail and saw it ended in a clump of
bushes with a bushy but clear view of the cat's lair. It
looked as if the grass had been recently stomped
down. Was this where the killer stood to make sure
the coast was clear? And then a creepy thought
occurred. Did he stand there and watch Mirella as she
discovered the slaughter? Better tell Merlano about
this, he might want to stake it out.

As I emerged from the hideout, I heard a
challenging taunt. "Fuck ya doin in there? Some
kinda pervert?" One of the punks from the street
stood before me. Without taking my eyes off him, I
wondered: Where was the other one? And then I
spotted him, not far away, trying to stay out of sight.

I was startled but quickly regrouped. "Takin' a leak,
didn't want to scare the old ladies with my big white
snake, know what I mean?" The back kid chuckled
but the front one didn't react. I sized him up. Tall but
scrawny, he looked mean. Like he hadn't eaten for
awhile. The other kid was smaller, had the same
hungry look. Trouble.

I decided to take the initiative, "Move out of the
way." I pushed past the tall kid. As I passed, he
shifted and started to swing; I leaned in and
hammered his solar plexus with the Phoenix fist,
paralyzing him, just as Jimmer had taught. Moving
swiftly to get more room, I kicked his feet from under
him; he thumped to the ground. The little guy looked
at me, big eyes, scared.

I nodded to him, "Beat it." He ran down the alley,
obviously not too loyal to his buddy. I leaned down
and picked the punk up, shook him, pulled him close
to my face. "Next time, I won't be nice.

Get lost. Follow your pissant pal. Move it, now!" He waddled off trying to catch his breath.

Entering Mirella's backyard, I thought about my judo lessons. Can't whip the little bastards in Jimmer's class, but this shit sure is useful in the real world.

I remembered Jimmer lecturing about the Phoenix Eye Fist. "It's the only martial art that exclusively uses the knuckle of the index finger to strike the enemy. Give the enemy no respite till he drops." As I smiled to myself, I spotted Mirella at her window outpost. I waved and she gave me a big greeting. Nice lady. And then I worried, did I get her involved in this mess? The cats were excited, thinking I might be there for an early feeding. Everything looked okay; the organized chaos seemingly unchanged from yesterday--except the cops took the dead cats away.

I signaled to Mirella that I was coming up. She gave me a thumbs up sign. When I got to the front door I paused. Was Mirella safe? Was this nut after her too? Or was he just having fun with the cats? Better get Merlano's advice. He did this for a living, need an expert to look at the facts. Was I right that these cases were connected? As Mirella buzzed me in, I studied the entranceway and stairs leading to her apartment. Any place to hide? When I got to her level, I noticed the hall went left and right, leading to other apartments. You couldn't see everything from Mirella's door; a couple places were out of sight. Something to think about.

After talking with Mirella for a few minutes, I realized she was a tough lady, she had already recovered.

Now she was mad. "That sicko is messing with the wrong lady. I'll be watching. Next time I'll get the cops here faster. See how he likes it when the cops kick him around. I wish I was younger. Bust him one myself."

I smiled, "My money's on you Mirella. That nut's going down next time. But do me a favor. Let the cops handle it. Promise?" And then I told her what I was thinking, that this went back to Crina. That it was connected.

She shocked me, "I thought that myself. I was going to tell you the same thing. But I started to doubt myself, wondered if I was getting wacky, senility kicking in maybe. I'm glad you think so too."

෴

I left after getting Mirella's promise to be careful, that this nut was getting aggressive. That we needed to let the cops do their work. She was a smart lady. I believed she would watch out. She had agreed that from now on she'd wait until it was light outside before doing the morning feeding. When I left Mirella, I decided to do another sweep and walked down the alley, thinking about pestering Merlano to get a stake-out until we were sure this psycho wasn't coming back. Didn't think it would be a tough sell, remembering his comments about the whore killer.

It was a gray, overcast morning as I headed toward my car, facts swirling though my head. I came out of the alley, walked across the street toward my parking spot.

151

THE ACCERATING CAR was on me before I heard the engine! It was moving fast as it swerved toward me. Instinct took over; I jumped on the hood of the rampaging car and rolled into the street. A weird thought ran through my head, if I had jumped toward the alley, the car would have crushed me into the building. But I was jolted to reality as the car screamed to a halt, barely missing the brick wall. I was dazed, lying in the middle of the street. Was the car backing up? The tires squealed as the car reversed direction, coming directly at me. Almost resigned, I'M DEAD.

But my coordination returned enough to roll away as the speeding car grazed me, but missed full impact. My shoulder hurt as I dragged myself to the curb; some of my feeling came back as I got to my feet. The car paused, engine roaring in neutral. I tried to see the driver but got nothing, just a shadow. Suddenly the car bolted at me, but seemed to change its mind, straightening out and speeding off. I just watched for a few minutes, not moving. Making sure there were no more attacks. I looked but it was too dim to see a license plate. I checked my legs and arms, some bleeding but nothing terrible. But as I moved, my hip ached, probably from hitting the hood. I limped to my car and locked the doors. I sat dazed. Safe? And then I shivered as I realized: This guy is after me.

❧

When I got home, I called Merlano. He thought I was busting his balls. "Sure, Frazier, the cat killer gets tired of killin' pussies and goes after douche bags. That makes sense." He waited for my witty retort.

I let a few seconds go by, "Merlano, for once there's no punch line. The psycho came after me. He was waiting at Mirella's house again. Not sure if he was after her or me. We need to get cops over to Mirella's fast. Now hang up and get your sorry ass in gear. Call me back when they're there and I'll fill you in on the details." He hung up and I walked to the bathroom and ran the tub. Had some blood to clean up. Plus I wanted to soak the ache out of my bones. And think.

ॐ

It took a couple weeks, but I slowly healed enough to return to judo class. "Where have you been? You're moving kind of slow, Dylan. I better tell the judoka to go easy today." Jimmer had his normal smug look, as he sized me up. When I told him what happened, he turned serious. "That's bad business. Our training probably saved your life." I had already thought the same thing. Judo taught me to focus, watch movement and go the opposite way. Before judo, I would have instinctively jumped into the line of the speeding car, rather than roll away from a threatening movement. Judo saved my life.

I looked at Jimmer. "I think you're right but don't get too smug. You're still an asshole."

☙

Merlano came through in spades. Mirella was being guarded around the clock, so I didn't have to worry. He was certain that the killer wouldn't go near her now, at least for awhile. But unknown to me, Merlano had gone to his Sergeant and told him the details of the case.

The Sergeant listened wordlessly, obviously didn't like civilians being involved in the case. "Merlano, the guy doesn't know shit. Maybe he was an MP in Nam but he's still a rookie. This smells bad."

Merlano had expected that. He looked at his boss, "Sarge, this killer knows Frazier's on to him. He went after him. If we don't catch him goin' for the cat lady, we can use Frazier as bait. Follow me?"

The savvy Sarge smiled, "I like that Merlano, like that a lot. Keep me advised. It sounds like we got another crazy fuck running around." And then he pointed at Merlano, "Don't let this get outta control."

When I briefed Merlano after the second cat killing, I mentioned the pawn shop angle. He was suddenly more interested in my results, asked for my list.

I shrugged, "Dead ends so far, Frankie. Pawn shops all over the place. Never knew the pawn shop business was so booming. Been an education."

He laughed, "Some weird fuckers in that business. No doubt." And then said, "I'm gonna start my own investigation of the pawn shops, probably expand the search." I was behind my work for Hoban and told Merlano I needed to catch up on my other cases.

"No problem, Frazier, I'll keep you advised if somethin' pops." I never realized he was gently pushing me to the side.

༄

And so I went back to my Hoban fraud cases. Gene Larrson was on the radar because of an influx of expensive drugs. The diagnosis was unusual, "Male Menopause." That perked my interest as well as my funny bone. I spoke to one of Hoban's consulting physicians, who confirmed the diagnosis was validated by new research. Dr. Zachary advised, "Males go through hormonal changes and it somctimes causes havoc. Most men aren't sensitive enough to notice. Or they're too proud to admit it. It's why men die early. They're too macho to seek help. Apparently, Mr. Larrson has a gentler side; he's going for a "curc." I met Dr. Zachary a few times when first working for Hoban. He was openly homosexual, his assistant was his boyfriend.

That explained his next comment. "Queers don't have that problem. We whine with the best of them if something bothers us." I chuckled, liking his realness.

Mr. Larrson lived in a neighborhood overlooking Fairmount Park, not far from the Schuylkill River. I studied the area as I parked my green machine. Old, but still stylish brownstones filled the block. Trees lined the street, no trash or graffiti anywhere, the people still cared. I didn't see anyone on the street, nice and quiet. I thought about the psycho's car menacing toward me and shook off a shiver.

155

That won't happen again, I'm on guard, like in Nam. But that idea didn't make me feel good. Would the flashbacks get worse?

The huge brownstone had been converted into 2 large homes. Larrson's mailbox was elaborate, polished bronze, lid shaped like a golden eagle.

He answered promptly, "Can I help you?" He had a distinct voice, educated. He listened to my pitch and rather than buzz me up, said he would come down for me. Was he being careful, or just courteous? I could see him peering at me through the stained glass. Finally, he buzzed the door and I got my first look at Mr. Larrson. Rarely am I baffled, but I was now.

Larrson was small, maybe 5'7" and slender. But he wore skin tight jeans. His shirt was open in the front, his bare chest decked with layers of gold chains. His shoes were highly polished, alligator? The belt buckle looked like a Roman gladiator shield, huge and ultra-detailed- you could use it as a small umbrella. But the beret topped the look. Was that a blue-jay feather on the side?

Larrson was smiling at me. "I'm not a homo, if that's what you're trying to decide. Trust me; wearing this outfit, I'm a poontang machine." I burst out laughing. Larrson smiled, he liked the reaction.

His home was almost as dramatic. Mostly beige leather couches and chairs, lots of chrome pieces as accents, area rugs, all Orientals.

I asked about the medicines and got a priceless explanation. "You're too young to understand this, but you lose your lumber as you get older. When I hit 65, my world-class wood got a case of the termites. My dripper got droopy.

I have lots of money but what I really like is the ladies. When I couldn't finish the swordplay, I got depressed. My physician got me into the Male Menopause trials and now I'm their guinea pig. I checked with the insurance company, as long as I have a valid diagnosis, I'm covered. Agree?"

He was right. I spent a fascinating hour discussing-- rather listening--to what works and doesn't work for a full erection.

"Don't believe the Chinese ginseng nonsense. I drank all the teas, popped vitamin supplements, ate grounded-up rhino horn, nothing. My Willy just laid there, nada. And Saw Palmetto doesn't do diddly. I gobbled that down, all that happened was I pissed like a race horse. Trust me, not a winner on date night. But these new meds are something else. FDA won't approve them yet, probably want a way to cash in. Anyway, I'm back making the old ladies scream." I sat there dumfounded.

As I was riding away, I thought: Wait till Gator hears this one. This job certainly gave me some funny material. Oddly, I started to think about Jimmer's situation with his mother. I had an idea and wanted to talk with Marisol before I did anything. I knew what Jimmer would say, "Fuck off." But I bet Marisol would be more reasonable. Had to be tough raising a kid without grandparents. Even though mine died when I was young, my grandparents didn't hate me. And then I thought, maybe they would have if they lived longer and they got to know me.

∂

I pulled up to my apartment, ready to call Gator, to see if he was playing ball tonight. He didn't have much natural talent but he made up for it with gusto. Never had to push Gator to go for a loose ball. That's when I spotted the sultry Janice.

She got out of her car as I approached my door. "Buy a girl a drink, handsome?" I thought quickly, if I let her in, something might happen that I would enjoy but would soon regret.

But I was incredibly horny and that took over. "Wait here a second, let me dump this stuff and we'll go out. Okay?"

I could see she wanted to go inside but, "If that's the only way I can get you," was her answer. I waited a few minutes inside while my wood withered.

Janice was dressed for the kill. It was late summer, already a slight chill in the air. But she wore a sleeveless top, held up by her massive breasts. I tried to watch the road but my eyes kept drifting. Been a long time, I rationalized. Her tight skirt didn't help. Long, shapely legs oozed from the skimpy material. How is that skinny waist supporting that luscious frame? Janice knew she looked great. I could see her looking at my crotch.

She purred, "Why don't we just go back to your apartment, get comfortable?"

Following my libido would get me in trouble, so I pulled into The Tavern, one of our more upscale neighborhood's tap rooms. I needed other people as buffers from Janice's lure. We sat in a cozy booth. When I went to the opposite side, Janice got up and squeezed in beside me.

"That's more comfortable." She put her hand on my thigh, squeezed it; I almost lost it.

Trying to shift gears, I asked about her boy friend. "He's just a friend. He wants more than that but he's just company for me. I don't like going out alone so he's okay for that. Sorry about the other night. Mr. Light got pretty mad at me. I like my job so I had to lay off for awhile." But she smiled coyly, "I couldn't resist anymore. I found out where you lived, hoped we'd meet." She gently massaged my thigh to finish her thought.

It's funny how the mind works. As my male member throbbed, I thought about the milkman that early morning outside Mirella's neighborhood. Would a poor area like that have milk delivered? Most of the apartments had security locks. Where would he leave the milk?

Janice sensed I was drifting off. "Hey, pretty boy, where are you?"

I shook my head to regain focus. "Sorry, just remembered something important. In fact, I have to leave and tell the cops."

She snuggled up closer, moved her hands higher up my thigh, started to rub up and down. "So, where do we go from here?"

❧

After dropping Janice off, I called Merlano but had no luck. The desk sergeant wasn't much help. "Merlano, he's a different cat, he doesn't punch the clock reglar. Kind a comes in an out.

Lucky he's good. Best bet is to come by, he'll show up sooner than later. He ain't good with messages, know what I mean?" I took his advice, drove over, and waited in the office. Got to witness some real sad sacks getting processed.

One guy yells out, "You'd a smacked her too, fuckin' whines all day and looks like a bag a door knobs. Fuck I gonna do?"

The cop looks at him and laughs. "Think yer a prize, pal?"

Finally, Merlano slumps in and looks surprised. "Change your mind about joining the cops, did ya?" I told him what I remembered about the mailman, that it didn't add up. He rubbed his chin. "Jesus, you remember what he looked like, anything unusual, you know, the way he walked, kinda car, anything?"

I nodded, "Only thing was he was big, I mean NFL lineman big. Might have been a football player, he moved easy, like an athlete. Other than that, nothing. Been racking my memory, it was dark, he had a hat on, didn't see much."

Merlano called the patrol Sergeant controlling the stake-out, told him to radio the patrol that we were coming over, had some information on the culprit. He didn't say much as we drove.

To break the tedium, I asked one of my inane word questions that amused me but few others. "Hey, Merlano, did you ever wonder about Baguette? I mean, shouldn't it be a name for a little bag, not a skinny loaf of bread?"

He turned toward me, "Fuck you talkin' about?"

I kept a straight face, "Been bugging me is all."
Merlano finally figured he was being had.

He looks over, "Maybe the cops ain't right for you. You're too fucked."

The stake-out team wasn't visible as we drove into the alley. As we stopped near the cat's den, one cop rolled out of the area I'd mentioned as the psycho's lair. And then the other cop appeared from the side of the apartment. The first cop was short but stocky, moved like a wrestler.

He came up to Merlano, "No pun intended but look what the fuckin'cat drug in, how ya doin', Frankie?"

Merlano grinned, "Surrounded by funny guys today. Least you aint asking about baguettes and shit like Frazier." He introduced me to Joe Reich.

Joe looked at me, sizing me up. "You played ball at St. Tims? I played runnin back at St. Charles. We almost upset yer asses."

I did remember Reich. He was about the same size as he was in 8th grade. "I remember you Joe; you were like tackling a bowling bowl. I ached for days after that game. You guys were tough." He grinned, liking the thought of the old days. "How come you never played football at Conner?"

He grinned again, "Coach threw me off the team sophomore year, said I was too violent, that I should try the Marines." And then he added, "Ended up takin' his advice, enlisted in the marines after school. Went to Nam, did a couple tours. Found out my violent streak worked in Nam. Joined the cops when I left; my edge works here too."

Reich introduced us to his partner, "This loopy motherfucker is John Ditmore. We call him Dick, as in Dickmore."

Dick just grinned at us, shrugged, "The name kinda stuck from the Cop Academy. I don't mind it, makes the girls think I might have a big schlong, know what I mean?" I stifled a few quips, not wanting to alienate my stake-out team. I knew I had plenty of time to piss them off later.

Instead, I asked, "You guys see any milkmen since you've been here?"

They looked at me funny. "Fuck would a milkman be doin in this shithole neighborhood? Only thing the shithooks here drink is Irish Rose. Aint thinking they get that delivered, do you?"

They listened to my replay of the stocky milkman being the only one I saw that morning and then the attack later on.

Reich rubbed his chin, "Don't believe in coincidence. Hadda be the same guy." He looked at me, "He knows what ya look like, Frazier, better watch yer ass."

And then Merlano pitches in about his serial killer case, "When the nut was offin' the whores, he started losing control. Started taking chances and that got him caught. Might be what's happening here. Guy's in what they call a 'rage state.' I agree with Reich, Frazier, keep your eyes wide open, buddy."

With that jolly news, I drove home, sat in front of the TV and reviewed the case lists. I just needed some quiet to let the facts settle, to see if I was missing something else. I added the following questions to the list. Was the milkman the killer? Was he really a milkman? Or did he just use the uniform to make himself seem part of the normal scene?

I let that sink in. After a few minutes, if he wasn't a milkman, where did he get the uniform? And then added: Knows what I look like. Why is he after me? And then I wrote other random questions: How's this guy a step ahead of us? Was he waiting for me or Mirella? Nothing else jolted me, so I switched thoughts to a more pleasant topic: How could I help Jimmer?

ॐ

Next morning, I went to mass and waited for Monsignor Pugh afterwards. As I walked to the rectory with this wise man, I told him what I had planned.

He smiled, "Does your mother know what you have cooked up? She's Mary's close friend, it might be worth getting her take."

I shrugged my shoulders. "Thought of that but dismissed it. Mrs. Heilmann might get torked off, better if my mom can truthfully say she had no idea what her knucklehead son was up to. That's how I see it."

That made the Monsignor chuckle. "Lawyers call that 'plausible deniability'; I think you have a point. This could very well backfire." I left him wondering if I'd lost my mind.

I called Marisol at work so Jimmer wouldn't overhear. Surprisingly, Marisol liked my plan, thought it might help. I could almost visualize her large intelligent eyes absorbing my plan.

163

As she put it, "How can it get any worse than being disowned by your own mother?" I asked how she'd get out on Sunday morning without alerting Jimmer.

"It won't be a problem. I've been taking Jose to mass and James wants nothing to do with it. I'll just meet you at your apartment, then ride together." Before Marisol hung up, "Dylan, even though this probably won't work, I appreciate you trying. Now I know why James thinks so much of you." I hung up, starting to blush.

We got to church nice and early Sunday morning and lingered in the rear, by the west entrance. Knowing Mrs. Keilmann would come by the eastern entrance, we were waiting until she was seated. My mother walked in shortly after and sat in her normal spot, second pew, not wanting to appear pushy by taking the first row. She didn't see us. People began to pour in but I knew it wouldn't be too crowded at the 9 o'clock mass, the congregation was mostly late risers.

Finally, I spotted Mr. and Mrs. Keilmann entering and moving toward their normal spot, near the middle. When they were seated, we made our move. I held Marisol's arm and rested my arm on Jose's shoulder as we paraded down the aisle and sat near the front, opposite my mom's side. I was a well known character in the parish, so my mystery companions caused a little stir. I saw Mrs. Keilmann watch us as we passed but intentionally made no eye contact. I looked over at my mom, she quickly dipped her head. Was she laughing?

After mass, I introduced Marisol and Jose to my mother. My angelic mom did me proud.

She hugged Marisol and kissed her on the cheek, whispering, "God always has a plan. Keep faith." Just then Monsignor Pugh wandered up and shook Jose's hand. "Welcome to St. Tim's Jose, hope to see you and your mom here more often." We got lots of interested stares but everyone smiled and walked home wondering who their new parishioners were. Mrs. Keilmann had bolted church right after communion, avoiding any chance encounter with her estranged in laws. Had I done more harm than good?

fterwards, Marisol was not discouraged. "It takes time to knock down walls, Dylan."

❧

I had caught up on my work for Hoban and was ready to snoop around Crina's case. So, next morning, I called Gator, got through to him directly, avoiding any uncomfortable dialogue with Janice. I still felt guilty about Janice and like a typical man, planned to avoid her.

Gator was his normal ebullient self when I told him my plans to hit another pawn shop. "Let's rock and roll, Dylan. It's time to nail this son-of-a-bitch! I got some time right now, where we going?" I made plans to meet him at "The Clothes Horse." Wondered what that name was all about. The Clothes Horse was in South Philly, which was heavily Italian. The locals were very aware of and wary of non-residents.

I warned Gator, "Try not to come off as a cocky jackass from the suburbs, tone your act down some, okay?" He was giggling as he hung up.

I said aloud, "Oh boy!"

I parked outside of Sal's Sandwiches and waited for Gator to show. The Clothes Horse was a few doors down, nothing unusual from the outside, just seemed to fit into this row home neighborhood like everything else. After this, only one more pawn shop was left from the list of possible places selling Hummels; at least according to our buddy Bismarck at the legendary Carter Leeds. Merlano called yesterday to say his men had already checked all the pawn shops and found nothing. But I wanted to look myself, would feel better if I had the same conclusion. My window was rolled down and I could smell Italian lunch meats. Hoagie for lunch?

Gator parked across the street, I watched him bolt from his car. He had a suit with vest on, as usual with the vest unbuttoned and white shirt and tie hanging out. It looked like he'd been in a wrestling match since he got dressed. Loved the guy, he was priceless.

I yelled, "Gator, didn't I tell you not to look like a commando? You're gonna scare the locals, think the Carpet Baggers are making a comeback." Without a blink, he tears across the street and jumps in front of my car and flexes his muscles, like he's Haystack Calhoun about to pounce on a patsy. I rolled up the window and howled.

The Clothes Horse was very neat. I scanned the interior quickly and was immediately certain we'd not find any Hummel trail here. The place was mostly loaded with clothes. Stylish stuff, like you might see in a fancy consignment shop on the Main Line. I wandered towards the rear and met a well dressed man, about 40 years old.

He looked at my decidedly un-stylish outfit, and then scanned the disheveled Gator.

He smiled, "You two I can help. My name is Salvatore; let me show you some of our latest acquisitions. It's all vintage styling but it never goes out of date. All our outer wear is timeless, that's our guarantee. Follow me."

I couldn't resist, "Salvatore, my friend Bill is a lawyer but has to deal with some unsavory sorts. As you can see, he got into a wrestling match with a client trying to welch on his bill. Do you have some trendy things that can withstand a good tussle?" Gator chuckled and Sal seemed to take this as an acknowledgement of daily fisticuffs being part of his norm. Nonplussed, Sal began showing Gator some suits hanging nearby. While they were chatting, I ambled around. As I first concluded, mostly clothes, some clocks and dishware but no Hummels. Another dead end.

I wandered back to Gator and Salvatore. I was thinking about the hoagie shop nearby as I asked, "Do you also own the hoagie shop next door? Noticed the name is Sal's, like yours."

Salvatore made a face, like he'd just sniffed a yak. "Certainly not, that's the Salducci brothers. They make a nice sandwich but they wouldn't know Hickey Freeman from the man in the moon. I would move if I could, the smell of salami is penetrating. During the summer, I keep fans blowing outward, so the meat doesn't get into the clothes. My cross to bear." He rolled his eyes like a man with an intense burden.

To keep the fun going, "But you'd recommend the hoagie? When in south Philly, so to speak, eat where the locals do, right?"

Salvatore nodded, "As I said, a decent sandwich, that I'll give them."

We were near a section of ties, so I switched gears. "Some spiffy neckwear here, Billy. Take a gander."

Sal regrouped, "These are all hand painted. Classics. I have the finest collection in Philadelphia." Gator started pawing through the rack. Sal started explaining the fine workmanship, going into immense detail.

Gator's natural curiosity took over; he got into the search for a prize.

Getting bored, I barged in. "Who painted the ties?"

Sal looked at me, befuddled. "What do you mean?"

Enjoying this, I added, "You said the ties were hand painted. Who painted them? Are we talking Claude Monet, Marc Chagall, Andrew Wyeth, people like that? Or are we talking about some amateur artist just struggling to make ends meet? Like the guys that paint the fluorescent tigers you see in gas stations. Or maybe a talented car guy at Earl Schieb."

Gator looked at me like I was a mental patient but Sal was stumped. You could see him puzzling it. And then, "You're the first person who ever asked. Now that you bring it up, I would like to know who the artists are."

We left the shop and Gator started to guffaw so hard I was worried he'd choke. He kept repeating, "Who painted the ties. Was it Marc Chagall or some schmo?

Who fuckin' painted the ties, Claude Monet or Earl
Schieb?" Fuckin' priceless, Dylan, fuckin' priceless.
Poor Sal seemed embarrassed he didn't know who
painted the God damned ties. Had no idea you were
busting his hump. God that was fun. Wish we could
pal around all day making everybody's life miserable.
Too bad I have to work for a living."

We lingered outside Sal's hoagie shop, Gator
finally composed himself.

I looked at him, "Fun aside, Gator, there is only one
more shop on my list. If that doesn't pan out, we're
back to zero. Disappointing."

He frowned, "What will you do next? You said the
cops already checked the next place and found
nothing. Maybe you ought to turn the whole thing
over to the cops. Seems like this psycho was involved
with Crina's robbery, maybe you outta back out. Even
the cops seemed worried about this guy. Merlano's
on the hunt, maybe time to ease out." I didn't answer,
had been thinking the same thing.

SYLVAN

Sylvan knew he should lay low but couldn't restrain himself. Despite his immense self discipline, the pull for a new kill was magnetic. His study of Jack the Ripper mentioned "an irresistible lust for blood." Sylvan weighed that analysis and nodded. But he quickly concluded: I am smarter than all of them. And so he had driven up and down Mirella's street every day over the past week and saw the same guys loitering around the cat lady's building. He surmised: Police. Had to be police. I guess my run-in with the tall guy got them nervous. But it won't be long till they start getting bored. And then they'll get sloppy. Sylvan had thought about nothing else but snuffing out the cat lady. He felt the hunger. I need to get close. I need to blend into the background. I need to expect the police might spot me. Details. Lots of details. He exhaled. Over the last few days a plan emerged. Dangerous. And then he finished his thought. But it is flawless.

DYLAN

I had an appointment with Merlano that morning. He scanned a file in front of him and confirmed that Mirella was not a suspect in Crina Barbu's Hummel or jewelry theft.

He shook the report, "She's got less money in the bank than me. And that's some pretty sad shit. I looked back a year, saw no changes in bank patterns. Monthly deposits of her pension and Social Security, like clockwork. Nothin' funny." I told him of my visit to The Clothes Horse, that only one shop was left. He nodded, "You won't find nothin' in the last one. We already got another list of places that might carry Hummels. I was surprised, quite a few in Philly. Lot of antique lovers in our fair city. Fuckin' stupid waste a money, you ask me."

I told Merlano about my thoughts for backing away from the case. That I wanted to make certain he was fully engaged. That Mirella would be watched. Merlano laughed, "I'll shave my balls if you can stay away more'n two days, Frazier. Remember, I'm a detective, I got instincts. A guy like you gets hooked on this and ain't ever letting go.

Dog on a bone kinda thing. Your in, baby. Your in." I just stood and looked at him, not answering. He added, "Remember when we played ball, I put some hard hits on you. Most guys got tentative. You, Frazier, just got better. You like a fight."

&

I went to the courts that night, needed a good sweat. Had thought about what Merlano said. He was right; I was in this till the finish. Kept thinking about Mirella. What if something happened to her? Probably my fault she got in the cross hairs. Wouldn't forgive myself if she got hurt. I was hoping to lose my frustration playing the game I loved. Nobody was there yet, so I shot jump shot after jump shot, finally getting relaxed, forgetting the madness. What would I do without these courts? Had played here since age 10, always found peace. My college coach used to say a great basketball game's better than sex. And then I thought about my gorgeous Laura. Well maybe that's a bit crazy. Basketball versus the most beautiful girl in the city? No contest.

My random thoughts were broken as Jimmer drove up and moseyed over. "I haven't seen much of you lately. You giving up on judo already? Tired of the munchkins tossing you like a rag doll?" Jimmer was in a good mood. He obviously suspected nothing about my plans to break down his stone-hearted mom. Marisol knew he'd flip out; better to find out if we could thaw the iceberg some before telling him.

I realized how much I missed the judo drills so I said, "Be back tomorrow. This case I'm on is getting dicey, need to stay sharp." I explained the latest developments,

Jimmer nodded, "See you tomorrow. We'll teach you some new moves."

We played for a couple hours. We had a good team that night so we never had to leave the court. Tony Sol had showed up after his bakery shift ended. Sol wasn't his real last name. Jimmer shortened his ethnic Italian name that started with Sol and then meandered through an endless series of vowels and consonants. Tony had emigrated from Italy years ago and made a nice life when he opened a bakery on the edge of Drexel Heights. He was a soccer player in Italy and just played basketball because there were no "football" games here. Tony was a tremendous athlete, although barely 5'8", he dominated the game by his ball handling, passing and defense. He was like a whirling dervish, if you got open for a second, the ball got to you for an easy lay-up.

As usual, Jimmer bitched and moaned to get Sol on his team. As usual, he got his way. There was always some compelling reason why Jimmer ended up with the best players. He smirked in disgust if you bitched about stacking sides.

He glared at one guy, "Fuck you moaning about? Dylan's a Nam burnout, Sol's a fuckin illegal alien; I'm the only normal motherfucker on the squad. You ought to spot us points with this group of misfits." When he finally stopped his diatribe, we walked down to our end of the court.

TOM FAUSTMAN

I said, "You ought to go to Hollywood, Jimmer,
that's Academy Award shit you're doling out.
Plus you convince yourself that you're not full of shit.
A masterpiece." Someone yelled at Jimmer and he
went to see what the problem was.

As he left, Sol wandered over. I hadn't seen Sol
since I'd gotten back from Nam. He asked how I was
doing. Sol spoke broken English and had always
called me "Dee Land." I think he was worried about
Jimmer's comment about being a burn-out, so I
assured him all was well. "Any time I feel sorry for
myself, Sol, I think about Jimmer's wife and that
makes me feel better. I mean that's what I call a
rough assignment."

He laughed, "Jeemmer is still same seence we meet.
Talks and talks till you wear out. Pretty soon you
walk away, just shake head. Like bad headache."

Jimmer walked up, "What are you talking about, I
saw you looking at me as Sol was running his gums."

Sol grinned again and looked for me to handle this
one. "Sol was just saying he would name his first son
after you. That he talks about you whenever his
relatives in Italy ask why he likes the States so much.
That he considers you the American version of
Gandhi. I was agreeing with him. That I consider you
a role model. That I pinch myself every time I come
up here, see you hop over the fence, head to the
courts."

Jimmer looked at me, turned to Sol, "Sounds about
right." We all laughed.

⚘

I had to make some money so I called Hoban next morning, told him I was about to work on the Gertrude Rawley file. This was the other case that popped up as a potential fraud- an 80 year old woman getting a breast reduction.

Without any change in tone, Hoban added, "That's a perfect one for you, Dylan. I can see you handling this one with great discretion."

To bust Hoban some, I replied, "Just got a good camera. I'll bring you some nice pictures of the guns as they look today. We'll compare those with the pictures in the file; see if it hangs together so to speak, oops, sorry about the pun."

Hoban paused, thinking whether he was being had, "Just keep us from getting sued."

It had been a few weeks since Mirella's cats got slaughtered and the nut came after me. I stopped by Mirella's every few days and checked in with my old football buddy Reich.

"It's as quiet as a whorehouse on Mother's Day, Frazier. I think the fucker's gone. We'll hang in for awhile more then see what ta do next."

That worried me some, that they were thinking about leaving. "Wouldn't rush off too soon, Reich. Something tells me we haven't seen the last of this guy. Make sure you keep me in the loop, okay?"

And then I walked up to visit Mirella. I didn't tell her about Reich's comments. She kept vigil at her back window, looking for signs of the murderer's return.

"Next time, he comes, I'll be ready. I keep my favorite knife nearby.

If he tries something with me, he'll get a surprise. I might be old, but I can still get one jab in. He won't be expecting it from a helpless old lady."

I looked at this gutsy lady and admired her pluck. "Hope you never get the chance, but if you do, I like your odds." She liked that. Before I left each time, I made her promise to call the cops if anything looked odd.

She nodded, "Scouts honor." Mirella was tough. Had a feeling she wanted a shot at the nut.

≈

Gertrude Rawley lived in the pricey Rittenhouse Square area in Center City. As usual, the Personnel Department at her employer, Sonnenberg and Brickman, was useless. "Medical confidentiality prevails here, young man. All the medical documentation is in order. Mrs. Rawley is covered under our retiree plan, which is quite comprehensive. We take care of our loyal employees."

I couldn't resist, "But a boob job at 80, doesn't that strike you as odd. I mean, I get it if she's a long distance runner or tennis player. Got to be a drag having that weight holding you back. But at 80?" A dial tone was my response.

Rittenhouse Square was a bastion of wealthy respectability in Philadelphia. Lawyers, doctors, successful merchants and old money lived in this area. Nice parks, restaurants and boutique shops dotted the streets. No cheese steaks or hoagies allowed.

The streets were always crowded with well healed
residents, their nannies or dog walkers. It took me a
few spins around the block to find a place to park. I
could see shades gently pushed aside as the affluent
residents peaked out, wondered what my green
bomber was doing on their tidy street. Burglar? I
smiled at them as I sauntered by.

There was a doorman at Mrs. Rawley's building.
He looked me over carefully, wondering what this
miscreant wanted. "Here to see Mrs. Rawley, it's a
private insurance matter, can you give her a ring?" I
gave him my card, smiled, tried to look more
respectable.
"You got an appointment?"

I countered, "No, like to surprise people, know what
I mean? Makes it more fun. Like a birthday card a
month or so after the big day. An unexpected treat."
He glared at me, wondering what the hell that meant.

I gave it another shot. "Just funning with you. Just
call up to Mrs. Rawley, tell her I'm here to discuss
her medical claim with Sonnenberg and Brickman,
that there are some loose ends we need to tie.
Thanks." I could tell he was looking forward to
having Mrs. Rawley telling him to call the police but
was chagrined when she confirmed I was legit. He
buzzed me in, gave me the skunk eye, looking to see
if I had any weapons I guessed. Finally satisfied, he
told me Mrs. Rawley had the top floor, "the
Penthouse."

My next greeter was a well dressed older
gentleman, waiting as the elevator opened. "Mr.
Frazier, let me take your coat. Mrs. Rawley will be
with you shortly."

I gave him my coat, making sure I had my car keys, in case I pissed her off and they wouldn't give my coat back. Old habits never die. I followed what appeared to be the butler into a library. The mahogany wood shelves rose 12 feet and were packed with hard cover works. The Oriental carpet and Victorian furniture made the picture perfect. My first penthouse, probably my last as well, was no disappointment.

I refused the butler's offer of lemonade and asked if he minded my looking at the books. He gave me a smile, "Most are signed first editions, so be careful if you take them out. Mrs. Rawley has read them all and will like that you are interested in her collection." He bowed slightly, "I'll leave you to your reading." The entire collection of Alexander Dumas caught my attention, particularly "The Count of Montecristo." I'd read that masterpiece on my way to Nam. Somehow the story of the doomed Count caught my fancy; maybe the similarity of a hopeless future in Nam beguiled me.

My reverie was broken as I noticed an elegant older women standing in the doorway. She was beautifully dressed, almost like a duchess from another era.

"Do you like Dumas, young man? That book is a personal favorite. If you flip to the front, you'll see Mr. Dumas's scrawled signature. I get a thrill every time I touch that work. Such history, such majestic writing." Not knowing why, I told her my story about reading that book as I flew between San Francisco, Alaska and Vietnam, that it somehow absorbed my attention, making me forget what awaited me.

I think I surprised her with the coherent answer. She smiled, "And now it's even more special."

That was my introduction to the most refined person I'd ever met. Although 80, she was still beautiful, very white complexion with brilliant blue eyes. But the way she carried herself was the magic, like a queen used to being in charge, but taking that power as an obligation of trust. I sensed all this as we kibitzed about books.

Finally, she asked, "Now what can I do for you? I trust there is no trouble with my medical bills. My husband built that company from nothing and wanted to make certain all retirees never had to worry about paying for care." Her face showed concern.

Embarrassment caused me to get mildly tongue-tied. How do I ask this lovely lady why she had her giant boobs reduced at age 80? Being a chest man, I wondered why you'd ever do that, regardless of age. I felt like a fool but babbled, "Your procedure was very unusual and the Insurance Company couldn't get an adequate explanation from your Personnel Department. Can you explain the medical issues that caused the operation?"

Mrs. Rawley hesitated, paused before stating, "I lived with those immense breasts my whole life. Since when I was younger, they were vexing to me but my dear husband loved full-figured women. So when he passed last year, I had them reduced. My shoulders and back have never felt so good."

It turned out that Mr. Rawley built the law firm from nothing, named it Sonnenberg and Brickman because, "everybody wants a smart Jewish lawyer, a nice young wasp wasn't getting any business," according to Mrs. Rawley.

She liked my retort, "Like buying a hoagie from an Irishman, it doesn't feel right." I learned that her mother was still alive and alert at 102.

"I didn't want my elder years spent carrying those hideous things any longer. Now I can walk in the park without needing a good hot soak afterwards." We spent the next hour talking about books and what joy they brought. I left Mrs. Rawley with assurances that her claims were taken care off. The butler was waiting with my coat as I emerged from the library. I guess I didn't need to worry about him lifting my car keys.

ॐ

On the ride home, I mused about Mirella, the cat lady and Mrs. Rawley, the boob lady. Two sharp, delightful ladies but in such different places. Mirella had to worry about her beloved cats getting beaten to death, and maybe getting attacked herself. Mrs. Rawley lived in a penthouse, had a butler and just had her bazookas reduced. Same world but what different circumstances! And I got involved in both. Did it make any sense? I thought about Nam and my occasional flashbacks. Maybe the world was just too complicated and I should stop trying to button it down. For some reason, I felt better.

∂

Reich and "Dickmore" took turns watching the front and rear of Mirella's house. They believed if you stood in the same spot too long, you failed to notice small changes in the environment. "Dick" was now switching to the front of Mirella's building. As he traded positions with Reich, he asked his stocky partner. "Anything interestin' out here?"

Reich shook his head. "The only thing I've seen in the past hour is the mailman. Othern' that, squat. How bout out back?"

Dick shook his head, "Othern' the fuckin' cats, diddly. Started countin' mosquitoes to keep alert. Killed 89 of the little suckers."

Reich grinned, "See ya in an hour, bet I break that mosquito record. Fuckin' cat piss attracts the blood suckers." Dick grinned, he liked Reich.

Dick settled into his look-out spot near the front door. He was watching but his mind drifted to the Phillies. Steve Carlton's having a Cy Young season. He had already won 20 games and had at least 12 more starts. Could win 30. He's king of the city. But the team's miserable. Every time Carlton took the mound, they're sold out. But no one goes to the other games. Philly loves a winner. Losers get booed, world-class booed. Dick's daydream was interrupted as the mailman ambled out of the nearby apartment. Tough job in this weather, Dick thought. Rather camp out here than trudge up and down.

Dick's mind drifted back to his Phillies recap. Mike Schmidt's becomin' a star. He strikes out a lot but the cat can field. I like that a lot.

And Bowa's got the best glove in the majors. We got that goin' for us too. Fuckin' Luzinski's pretty good too but if I was that big, I'd hit a lot more homers. Fuckin' "Bull" my ass. More like......"

SYLVAN

Dick never completed his thought. Sylvan had slipped up behind him and crushed his skull with a Billie club he'd hidden in his mailman uniform. Sylvan bent over and rolled the cop's face over. He gazed into the motionless face and exhaled, deeply satisfied. One down, the other one's out back. I want him too but I'll follow the plan.

∾

Sylvan could think of nothing else except killing the cat lady. He'd watched the cops enough to know their routine. Plus his ace card, he listened for hours to his vintage police scanner that he got from a retired cop for peanuts. And he knew when they called in to report. Like clockwork, he thought. They'd switched positions 15 minutes ago so he had time. He could get the cat lady and avoid the other cop. Unless something goes wrong. Or if he wanted more. He had noticed the cat lady's mailbox was emptied regularly. He got to her box and rang the bell.

After a few minutes he heard, "What?" Sylvan had practiced a gentle voice.

"I have a special delivery letter for you ma'am. It needs a signature. I'm happy to come up and save you the steps."

He listened to her crisp answer. "I'm not interested, can't be anything good. Just leave it."

Sylvan had anticipated this caution, figured she'd be jumpy having cops guarding her, it made you careful.

He purred, "I can't just leave it, ma'am. Have to get a signature, its postal policy. Just take a minute of your time, ma'am."

After a short delay, he heard the buzzer and then from the speaker, "Top floor, center apartment." Sylvan smiled as he adjusted the club and then trudged up the steps.

He kept muttering, "Ding dong, ding dong." He got to the cat lady's door and lowered his cap, so she wouldn't get a good look at his face if she looked out the peep hole. He put the Billie club behind his back, knocked gently and prepared to burst inside.

As he had expected, the peep hole opened, he kept his head down but showed the official cap to ease any concern. He heard her fingering the locks; he lowered his shoulder.

But then she said, "Put the letter under the door and I'll slide it out after I sign it."

That threw Sylvan off. He swallowed hard, murmured, "I can't do that, I need to witness the signature."

And then he added, "Sorry, ma'am." He could hear her walk away from the door. Sylvan backed away. What's she doing? He knocked a little harder, "Just take a minute, ma'am." No response.

DYLAN

I met Merlano at Mirella's house, found him outside with Reich. "Fucker almost killed Dick. The ambulance got here fast; they think he'll make it. Lucky he's a got a rock for a melon." Reich filled me in on what happened. "Fuckin' mailman, who'd a figured that? Lucky the old lady smelled a rat. Pretty fuckin' smart, ya ask me." Mirella had called the cops when the mailman pressed her to open the door. "Old lady said she didn't like the way he kept his head hidden. It wasn't right. I mean, what's a mailman got to hide? But the mailman was gone when we arrived. Must a missed him by minutes. We already covered the neighborhood. Found squat. He's gone." Somehow, that didn't surprise me. I asked how Mirella was doing. Merlano laughed, "I swear the old gal enjoyed it. Said next time she'd mace him."

I laughed but soon lost my sense of humor when Merlano said, "How's this guy stay a step ahead of us? He almost thinks like a cop." I thought about that as I rode home.

SYLVAN

Sylvan entered the shop through the back entrance. He went into his private office and changed the mailman outfit immediately. She figured it out. He sat brooding but finally went into the shop and told his part-time assistant William he could leave for the day. William worked about 20 hours a week, mostly early in the morning or late in the afternoon. Sylvan had scheduled him this way since he liked to do his research thoroughly before finalizing his projects. William was 68, retired from the Philadelphia Museum, was a true expert in antiquities, hardly ever asked questions and only talked to him if necessary. But to customers, William was a chatterbox. Sylvan's business picked up since William worked for him. Sylvan liked the arrangement; it gave him time to prowl. But the icing on the cake was William being a widower, with no family. No one to pry. It was perfect.

After William left, Sylvan went to his watch collection and pulled out an IWC Schaffhausen, vintage 1905. He wound the classic time piece and listened to the perfect rhythm.

He sighed aloud, "Maybe I have some Swiss blood, the love of order; it must be so." That thought comforted Sylvan. But then he brooded: Something went wrong. I underestimated the cat lady. She almost tricked me. He shined the watch, pleased with the luster of the rose gold. He pondered what to do next. He couldn't let her go; it's just a matter of better planning.

Sylvan placed the Shaffhausen back in the display case and said firmly, "Perfect execution. That's the key."

As he sat back in his leather chair, his mind seamlessly drifted to his second childhood kill. At 16, he was now helping his father, taking over flawlessly when Aunt Anca met her unfortunate end. Dr. Dragomir relied on him fully to run his busy practice. Everything ran like clockwork until Sylvan noticed that one patient, Alenka Korzha, seemed to be coming for weekly visits and was lingering for mindless chatter with his usually taciturn father. One day while arranging the office calendar, Sylvan heard odd noises and giggling, so he drifted to the closed door, peeked through the key hole. Shocked, Sylvan watched as Dr. Dragomir kissed and fondled Alenka's ample breasts. What surprised Sylvan most was how angry that made him. He still hated his father but this dalliance seemed an insult to his dead mother. Sylvan slipped away and planned.

Alenka Korzha was widowed and lived in a fine home near Chestnut Hill College, on busy Germantown Avenue. Sylvan perused her medical records and began stalking her at night.

It was easy to find her spare key, hidden unimaginatively beside her front door flower box. After a few weeks he had her daily schedule down pat. While off on her weekly trip to the movies, Sylvan slipped inside and studied her house. When he entered her parlor, he noticed the old typewriter, Victorian desk and immense chandelier overhead, just a few feet away. On his next visit, he wandered to the musty basement and found the rest of his equipment. The old rope would do just fine, still strong.

Alenka always left lights on before going to Chestnut Hill College for their weekly movie. She had already seen "Love Story" three times but never tired of it. As she approached her house, she stooped to pull out the key and thought pleasantly of Dr Dragomir as she opened the door. He had been on her mind during the love scenes by Ryan O'Neal. She mused: Maybe Mrs. Alenka Dragomir isn't such a pipe dream after all. Just then Sylvan came from behind the door, threw the noose around her plump neck and yanked violently backward. Alenka's breath expelled rapidly as her eyes bulged in horror. Sylvan pulled her to the ground and continued to strangle her till she lay still, helpless.

He rolled her over, came near her face, sniffed deeply, whispered, "I smell whore." All Alenka could do was close her eyes, her throat too raw to utter a sound. And then he dragged her limp body towards the parlor.

While Alenka moaned in agony, Sylvan typed her final letter professing a life weariness that had become unbearable. "No family, no friends, no passion…"

The hard part was dragging the corpulent Alenka up on the desk, pulling the noose tight to the chandelier and shoving her away. Fortunately, at 350 lbs, Sylvan was freakishly strong. He watched as Alenka thrashed. Her face almost exploded from strain. She finally went still, her bowels opened and dripped to the floor.

Satisfied, Sylvan looked at his handiwork, said, as if to an audience, "If she hadn't shit herself, some smart cop might have suspected foul play. The cop might ask himself, 'Maybe she was dead before she was hung.'" He walked around to make sure nothing was amiss. He hummed to himself, "Ding Dong, Ding Dong." Next evening Sylvan watched as his father read in the Bulletin about the gruesome death of his favorite patient. Are those tears in good old Dad's eyes?

DYLAN

After the attempt on Mirella, I had agreed to follow Merlano back to his office. As soon as I walked in, I saw that he was very nervous. "This guy's getting out of control. I mean attacking a cop on a stake-out. That's nuts. What if Reich just happened to walk out front when the guy's wackin' Ditmore? No way he's takin' down two cops. What worries me more is he's getting' to be unpredictable." As I listened to the rant, I realized I'd been thinking about that too. But I had a different conclusion.

So, I added, "He must have been watching Reich and Dick, knew their routine. According to Reich, he'd seen the mailman a couple times before, so he wasn't suspicious. Guy planned it carefully. This isn't some psycho going crazy, this guy works everything out beforehand. But what he couldn't plan for was how cagey Mirella was." I looked at Merlano. "But now he will."

Reich had joined the meeting but hadn't said anything. But then he jumped in, said he wanted to stay on the stake out. "I want a piece a this fucker," was how he put it.

"Gonna make the fucker pay for what he did to Dick. Ain't losing another partner." And then Merlano surprised me, said he wanted to put a stake-out team on me.

I didn't like that. "No way, Frankie, the guy couldn't know where I live. Might know my face, but he doesn't know my name. If he did, he'd have come after me already. He keeps going back to Mirella's because that's all he knows. Waste a time following me. We can trap him at Mirella's. Bet he isn't giving up yet."

Merlano didn't react, just sat quietly. Finally he added, "That's what really makes me nervous."

❧

I went to Jimmer's judo class that night. He listened attentively as I explained the latest events in my crazy case. He frowned, "Are you ready for some serious techniques? What you've learned so far is what most students will ever learn. I don't really teach in depth the Atemi- Wazi- the striking techniques. They're used only to seriously injure or kill. When I got my training, I had to wait years before the sensei would work with me. He made me promise to share the art wisely, only with someone I "trusted fully."

He smiled for the first time since I'd walked in. "Dylan, get ready to work your ass off."

That first session was the most physical exercise I'd ever had. I was taught unarmed defense as an MP.

The training was tough but nothing I hadn't done with my child-hood buddy Nut, who was three-time State wrestling champion in high school. Nut was a beast, but Jimmer was an artist. He walked through the ude-waza arm strikes and ashi-ate leg strikes. Depending on where you hit, you could paralyze or potentially kill your opponent. He explained that the nose, throat, kidneys and solar plexus were popular targets. He made me do the moves in slow motion first, working up to full speed.

But then he showed me a spot on the shoulder that could sink a guy like a sack of potatoes. He pressed it gently and I almost passed out.

"Holy shit," was all I could say. Again he looked stern.

"If you get a clear shot at that sweet spot, use it and game's over." He shrugged, "The other moves are almost as good, the ude-waza to the nose is your most likely opening. We'll work on that a lot. Make it second nature. After that, the throat is probable. If you get really good, the ashi-ate kick to the throat can bring down a bull." We worked for a couple hours and I limped home.

I didn't play any basketball that week, as Jimmer drilled me relentlessly. But I also got really busy at work. Hoban had flooded me with disability claims that had to be investigated quickly. The economy was lousy and companies were talking about lay-offs. When that happened, "workers suddenly got sick" according to the Personnel Departments. Shifty employees tried to time their "complete inability to perform any or all the requirements of my job" till moments before a lay-off period.

The skilled malingerers usually had an in with a doctor who would verify their sudden injury.

My job was to visit the fakers unannounced, catch them doing something inconsistent with their disability claim. Most disability programs gave you 6 months of benefits with about 70% of normal pay. Some generous employers didn't tax the sick benefits, so the employee almost had full pay. Victims of their generosity, employers figured out they were getting hosed by too many fakers.

When I first started this work, I asked Hoban what a malingerer looked like. "If you visit a guy out sick with lumbar strain who's chopping wood in his backyard, that's a malingerer."

Over the next few weeks, I learned he wasn't far off. Most of the disabled workers had assembly line jobs requiring them to be on their feet all shift. So, most of the alleged problems prohibited them from being up and about for lengthy periods. I always came unannounced so I could watch how they answered the door. Since it was still warm, most people had their screen door open. Without fail, they walked briskly to my knock or door bell ring. But by the time I identified myself, they suddenly turned into Quasimodo, limping and shuffling like they carried the weight of the world. Their pained looked said, "Woe is me."

If I spotted that, I'd order an IME, an Independent Medical Exam. We used our guy, Dr. Wendell Wingate, to conduct a physical and get him to render a true opinion. Dr Wingate was a funny character. He was actually a great doctor, but it pissed him off when people ripped-off their employers.

"This country was built on hard work, not goldbrickers. Bums need to toe the line." One of his tricks was to appear very sympathetic, get them to trust him. When he noticed someone faking pain by contorting their body and hunching over, he'd leave the room, asking them to relax.

After a short while he returned and asked them to stand up, so he could check their back pain. He'd ask them to lift their shirts, exposing the sore area. While he was out of the room, he dunked his hand in a pail of ice water. And then he put his hands on their bare skin and watched them jump like jackrabbits from the icy shock. He said that a true lumbar strain wouldn't allow them to straighten up. After apologizing to the horrified malingerer for his cold hands, he noted the file "Back to work." He explained this to me with a straight face.

I asked, "What if they're really hurt?"

He gave a wry smile, "Well then they're really pissed off."

While I was hunting down these great unwashed for Hoban, I religiously went to Jimmer each night for training. He told me from the beginning that it took years to perfect these techniques. We used life-sized dummies after Jimmer walked repeatedly through the correct technique. He was meticulous with how and where to hit.

"Every opponent is a different size; you have to quickly sense where the vulnerable point will be on them. Almost isn't good enough. If you miss the first time, adjust and do it again. You won't have to guess if you're right, they'll be on the floor."

I thought I was doing okay, especially with the hand strikes. The feet were trickier. You had to do it perfectly to leap, lash out and then land in balance. Some time I did it right, most times I landed on my ass. But day after day, I improved. By the 3rd week, I got the foot work down and started making heavy contact without sprawling to the ground. And on the 4th week, I nailed the dummy almost every time.

Proud of myself, I said to Jimmer, "I think I've got it."

He nodded thoughtfully, "What you've got is a major dose of delusion. You still suck." We kept practicing.

⋘

My mass routine with Marisol and Jose was now into its second month. We marched in as a trio and always sat in the same area. They were always well dressed and followed the religious service with interest and passion. Jose belted out the hymns, drawing smiles from everyone. Marisol had a quiet dignity, and her stunning Latina looks didn't hurt. We always stopped outside and chatted with my mother and Monsignor Pugh. Each week another parishioner would wander up to introduce themselves and say hello. They were no longer an oddity; they were part of the parish community.

The plan was to make them such a routine part of St Tim's that Mrs. Keilmann would lose her embarrassment. I wanted her to see that no one thought she was a Scarlet Woman.

Maybe if Marisol and Jose seemed like normal Catholics, she would reconcile. I did feel guilty for going behind Jimmer's back. But he inherited his mother's stubbornness; I knew this was a lengthy journey, maybe with no outcome. But this week something happened that gave me hope. The Keilmann's always scooted out the farthest church door to assure no contact. This time they came out our side and Mr. Keilmann smiled and nodded at Marisol as he passed. Finally a breakthrough?

As I walked to their car, Marisol gave me a big hug. "Bless you, Dylan." For the first time, I started to think this had a chance.

∂

After a great Sunday breakfast at my mom and dad's, I drove to my apartment, went to my notebook and updated the recent patterns in the case. My list was getting long. On the bottom, I wrote: The killer wears different uniforms to blend into the background. That told me that the guy was careful, that he planned ahead. He may be a nut but he wasn't running amok. And then I added: What does he think Mirella knows? It all tied back to Crina's death. The psycho thought she knew something that would lead to him. But what was it? Mirella said Crina never mentioned names. I sat there awhile and randomly looked at the other notes. Nothing came to me.

I turned on the TV and watched the Eagles playing the Redskins in the season opener.

The Birds sucked last season and with Pete Liske the starting QB this year, they promised to be worse. As the game went on, I let my mind drift. During my furious malingerer investigations and crazy judo schedule, I'd hatched a plan for my cat lady that was probably crazy but oddly felt right. All I had to do was talk the wealthy Mrs. Rawley into agreeing to my scheme. Not a procrastinator, I called her that afternoon and told her I wanted to speak about someone she'd enjoy meeting. I gave her a brief summary of my perplexing case and outlined my worries and my idea to help Mirella.

To my surprise she said, "Come over and give me more detail. Sounds like an interesting adventure. Are we ever too old for intrigue?"

I enjoyed my second visit to Rittenhouse Square. Although early September, the leaves were turning yellow as intense city heat reflected on this center city enclave. I was early so I had lunch at a local "bistro" and had the Provencal salad, the only thing on the menu I could afford. Sun-dried tomatoes and Nicoise olives were mentioned on the menu. I thought back to my numerous French courses, remembered they were olives from Nice. The waiter had been condescending when bringing my order; obviously thinking I didn't belong because I ordered so little.

So I commented when paying the check. "Are you sure they were Nicoise olives? Not quite as crisp as others I've had from Nice. You might want to check. It was somewhat off-putting."

Caught off guard, he murmured, "Ah, not really sure." I had a bounce in my step as I exited.

Mrs. Rawley had apparently warned the doorman I was coming. He eyed me in a friendlier manner this time.

"Belden will greet you at the elevator, Mrs. Rawley is expecting you." The butler, Belden, was standing at attention as the elevator opened. Trying to lighten the moment, I gave him a crisp salute. To my surprised, he clicked his heels together and returned my salute. I noticed his crossed pistol cufflinks as he lowered his arm.

I asked, "Were you an MP, Mr.Belden? Noticed your cufflinks."

He lifted his brow, "I was, served with the 101st in WW II. That's when I met Mr. Rawley. We served together in France. We were part of the second wave on Omaha Beach. "

I told him my Vietnam background, for some reason opened up about the treason mess I'd gotten into.

And then I asked, "Did you get flashbacks when you got back?"

That caught him by surprise, "How did you know that? Mr. Rawley was the only one I ever mentioned that to." He had the same problem. "It stayed with us for years. Even now, I can picture landing on that beach, how terrified I was. It's not something you shake easily." He looked at me kindly, "Don't worry, they soften with time. They just become part of who you are. By the way, just call me Belden."

Mrs. Rawley listened to my story of innocently stumbling into the path of a deranged killer. That I was worried about Mirella, that I wanted to get her out of the apartment into somewhere safe.

She smiled when I was finished. "So what you're asking is would I mind if Mirella moved in with me for awhile. That it might be nice for me to have some company. After meeting me once, you sized me up as someone that would be willing to take this leap of faith." She watched me carefully as I delayed before answering.

I finally smiled. "Guilty as charged." She broke into a full grin; her hearty laugh told me my crazy plan was halfway there. Now onto Mirella.

That proved more difficult. Mirella eyed me after I drove over and explained my plan. "There is no way I'm leaving. What about the cats? What about luring this killer into showing up again? If he knows I'm gone, what chance do we have to catch him?" I told her that I'd feed the cats morning and night. That if I couldn't make it, we'd have the cops do it. We would whisk her away late at night when it was unlikely the killer would be watching. That he'd think she was still inside, maybe under orders not to come out after his last attack. That we'd have a cop inside her apartment, waiting for him to strike again. That this was our best chance. I never mentioned trying to protect her. Mirella wouldn't buy that. But I was relentless. Finally, her shoulders slumped.

❧

Merlano walked the streets himself before taking Mirella away in an unmarked car. I was waiting at Mrs. Rawley's as he drove up around 9 pm.

200

Merlano looked at me funny. "Back to thinkin' you might be a good cop. This is pretty slick." Merlano talked to the doorman, John Sullivan, and told him to be careful. Not to let in anyone he doesn't know. That the guy might be disguised as someone harmless. That if he let his guard down he'd regret it. Sullivan nodded, eyes wide open, worried.

Merlano looked surprised as Belden saluted me. I said, "Inside joke, Frankie, Belden gets my sense of humor. He's intelligent." Belden listened attentively as Merlano went through the same litany he had with Sullivan. Belden stood a little taller as Merlano rambled.

He said simply, "No one gets in if I don't know them. I have a Colt 45 that I keep oiled. The Rawley's are wealthy people; part of my job is protection. I go to the pistol range every other week. I haven't shot at anyone for almost 35 years but it's something you don't forget." Merlano shook his head, liked the answer.

৵

When I got home, I read the material Monsignor Pugh gave me on Catholic Annulment. Divorce was serious business if you grew up in a Catholic environment. One of the girls in my grade school was noteworthy as the only kid at St. Tim's from divorced parents.

Lisa Cheval always corrected you, "My parents weren't divorced, their marriage was annulled stupid."

No one ever understood the distinction, but Monsignor Pugh gave me the rudimentary facts and then a book with gruesome detail. I wondered if the law applied to Marisol, was hoping that might give us an angle.

If I understood it correctly, divorce said you were once married but now you weren't, after you went through a civil legal proceeding. Annulment said you were never truly married in the first place; something was missing that invalidated the marriage. There were four key requirements to make a valid sacrament of marriage:

1. *Be able to exchange consent and do so freely and unconditionally.*

2. *Consent to fidelity, indissolubility and openness to children.*

3. *Not have any impediments to marriage, like being too young.*

4. *Follow the sacrament properly.*

If one of these requirements was missing, you had a strong chance to have the marriage annulled. They listed common reasons for annulment:

1. *At least one partner did not fully and freely consent*

2. *Someone wasn't mature enough to understand what they were doing.*

3. *There was never intent to be faithful.*

4. *One or both partners did not intend to have children.*

I didn't know the details of Marisol's marriage other than that he was "a deadbeat and left as soon as he knew I was pregnant." I thought we might have enough cause but wanted to get more from Marisol before I went to Monsignor Pugh for counsel. I went to sleep happy, first I had Mirella safely tucked away, now I saw an end to the Keilmann's misery. It was a good day. I drifted off easily.

৯

It was getting dark. Clardy and I had been sabotaged by a deranged MP; our jeep was out of gas on the border of Laos and Vietnam, miles from base camp in Khe Sahn. The Tet offensive had started, this was ground zero. We camped for the night about 100 yards from the dirt road, hoping Charlie wouldn't spot our tracks. The growl of the hungry tiger made us forget the VC.

Clardy looked terrified, "What the fuck'er we gonna do?" We sat back to back praying for a quick sunrise.

Clardy kept spinning his head back and forth, like the vigilance would protect us. A branch cracked overhead, the tiger leaped and raked his mighty claw, nearly decapitating Clardy. I reached to stop the bleeding ….. and woke in a sweat. Hadn't had a nightmare in weeks. Why now? Was another killer stalking me?

∽

I called Marisol at work, told her what I was thinking, that annulment might be a way out. When I went through the litany of causes she gulped, and then answered. "He played me like a fool. Had other girlfriends the whole time we went out. He only married me because I had a great job. He thought he wouldn't have to work. He quit his job after the wedding, screwed around all day. Once I got pregnant, he split. After he left, I heard from a friend that one of the other girls got knocked up while we were married, that he paid for an abortion. And he used my money. How's that for cause?"

I called Monsignor Pugh, planned to meet him after mass that morning. While he had breakfast in the rectory, I gave him Marisol's history. After I was done, he nodded thoughtfully. "It sounds like she has a good chance. Have her call me to set up a visit. Do you still want this kept from Jimmer? He'll have to get involved sometime. They are married, you know. This type of secret can cause problems. Good marriages are built on trust.

Think about that my conniving friend." I had considered that, thought we needed to get a clear signal that Marisol could get the first marriage annulled before we opened Pandora's Box.

Monsignor Pugh smiled, "I agree, let's keep this a covert mission a bit more. After I meet with her and hear the details, we'll make a decision." I had that old bounce in my step as I drove away. Now off to catch one of Hoban's malingerers.

ॐ

The file said Jimmy Laurentiwicz hurt his back lifting bales of toilet paper at the Scott Paper warehouse. What a lucky dude, what spectacular timing, he would have been laid-off that Friday. Now he had at least 6 months of full pay. Laurentiwicz lived on Olney Avenue, not far from La Salle College. I'd considered going there but wasn't keen on my chances with the Christian Brothers---they might not like my sense of humor. With that swirling in my thoughts, I cruised the street looking to see if my disabled guy was out chopping wood. The street was lined with old Sycamore trees and thick hedges so it was hard to see much from the car. I decided to park and reconnoiter by foot before hitting the doorbell.

And that's how the fun started. I strolled by Laurentiwicz's house and spotted someone on the roof banging shingles down. I noticed a tall ladder leaning against the house- a nice climb for someone disabled.

After jotting a few notes, I walked to the front door and rang the bell. The screen door was closed but I could hear the bell echoing inside. After I got no answer, I yelled loud enough to wake the eternally damned. Shortly thereafter, I heard the roofer scrambling down the ladder. Peering into the house, I saw a commotion, someone coming in the kitchen door. I watched as the roofer came toward me and stop suddenly.

"Help ya?" I identified myself, saying that I was looking for Jimmy Laurentiwicz. Through the screen door, he replied, "What for?"

Not beating around the bush, "If you're healthy enough to repair your roof, I guess you're preparing to go back to work tomorrow, huh?"

Not missing a beat, "What ya talkin' about. Weren't me on the roof. Must a been my brother ya saw."

This was getting enjoyable. "Sure looked like you. I was watching for awhile, saw you scamper down that ladder when I yelled."

He shrugged, "He's my twin, people always confuse us."

So I asked, "Can I talk to him? That will clear it up."

Out comes another brilliant answer, "He just left for the store to get some milk. He's thirsty from the roof job."

I threw my hands up, gave a big smile, "Perfect. I'll just wait. Love milk, pretty thirsty myself."
Laurentiwicz frowned, turned, slammed the door shut and walked away. He went back to work the next day.

꙰

I called Gator after I got home that night. We had tentatively planned to meet tomorrow at the last pawn shop we got as a clue. To avoid the sensuous Janice, I now called Gator at home when we needed to consult.

"Afraid of Janice, huh?" my wily friend surmised. "It's funny, she says you guys are getting chummy. I see a disconnect in viewpoints. She bite you or something?"

I let the phone hang, "Worse than that, she likes my glow stick. You were right; the Agent Orange was a magnet." He chuckled, agreed to meet next morning,

I gave Gator the details of "Lost in Time" while we drove to this older section of Chestnut Hill, right on the Germantown border. Trolley cars ran down Germantown Ave and seemed to enjoy making cars swerve out of their way. Gator gave the finger to one driver who saluted us as he narrowly missed my car. Gator's "Fucking cowboy," followed the trolley as it forced another car to do a kamikaze maneuver. Gator opined, "It's hard to believe those morons make good bucks, their unions got the city by the nads." I just nodded, agreeing with his analysis but thinking about our next stop.

The cops had already been here and found nothing odd. Or as Merlano put it, "Nothin' odd if you think collecting old shit for a living ain't weird." I parked about a block away, wanting to get a feel for the area. Parts of Chestnut Hill were beautiful, old mansions that abutted Fairmount Park.

But this street was a hodgepodge of businesses that the zoning commission clumped together rather than spoil the ambiance of the rest of their swanky neighborhood. I looked at the old brick and stone buildings, imagining how nice this street must have been 50 years ago before they jammed all the shops here.

My reminiscing was snapped as Gator started whistling and suddenly clapped his hands.

I looked over, "What's with you?"

He clapped again, "I've been thinking about what crazy things are going to pop out of your mouth in a few seconds. I tell Mary what you say and she looks at me funny, always says the same thing, 'You two are bad influences on each other'."

That made me laugh at how bright Gator's wife was. "She's got a point, Gator. Can't say that we bring out the best in each other. Funny usually, but not stuff to put on a resume." And then I looked at him seriously, "But you know what? Who gives a shit?"

"Lost in Time" was perhaps the neatest store we'd been to. There were sections of display cases with old watches and jewelry. Looked like nice stuff. Clocks were all over the walls, cuckoos everywhere. I was looking at a cabinet of old radios and what looked like HAM sets. One reminded me of the radio I used as an MP in Nam.

My concentration was shifted as Gator spotted a rack of clothes, "Look at this, old Phillies uniforms, here's a Robin Roberts. It looks authentic."

From a nearby doorway, a reply came. "It is, we got it from a relative, he drove a hard bargain but it was a must have." I looked at the old man who spoke. He was actually dressed in a Boy Scout uniform. Gave me a bad memory, I'd been booted from the scouts for calling my Scout Master "a gorp." He didn't know what it meant but guessed it was bad. What's wrong with a bicycle seat sniffer?

This Scout Master standing before us was named William. He was very helpful, explained that old uniforms were a signature of the shop, so that was why he dressed in costume. "We even have an array of religious dress, authentic Carmelite nun habits and Franciscan vestments," William volunteered.

Before I could quip, Gator said from the nearby corner, "What's this Robin Roberts go for?"

William advised, "I'll let it go for $250, you'll get twice that at a card convention next year. If I could leave the store, I'd go there every year and make a fortune."

Since I was trying to help Gator negotiate, I asked, "How do we know it's authentic?"

William looked offended, "Would a Boy Scout Master lie?"

I couldn't resist, "My old one would, he was a gorp, you know?" Gator laughed while William looked confused.

To get back on track, "I love Cuckoo Clocks, what can you tell me about that one." I pointed at an elaborate clock with a large bird on the top.

William lit up, "Excellent pick.

That's a Romba Uhren, they've been making clocks since 1894, and it plays Der Frohliche Wanderer and Edelweiss, what a magnificent piece. The songs alternate on the hour and tone can be adjusted 36 ways to keep it interesting. The Germans are genius with clocks. Did you know that despite the Swiss having the reputation, most of the great masters came from Germany? They originally trained the Swiss." I did like the clock but my eyes had glazed over at Der Frohliche.

Keeping him off track but still gabbing, I asked, "How about Hummels, like those a lot. Was told at Carter Leeds you might carry them."

William hesitated a second, seemed to consider what to say. Finally, "We used to but no longer." I waited for one of his elaborate answers but nothing else came.

Trying to pry more, I asked, "Why not? Seems like they'd be perfect with your Cuckoos, same sort of precision. German art, that sort of thing."

William paused, "Actually, I'm sorry we had to discontinue them but the market wasn't there. Fine workmanship but we need to move our pieces to stay viable. Uniforms, clocks and watches pay the bills. Frequently, we get an expert like your friend who recognizes the value in vintage baseball uniforms." I let that pass with no comment.

Finally, I added, "An old friend sold some of her collection of Hummels and since passed away. They're nice memories for me, was hoping I could track one down. Apparently sold them off before she passed, maybe needed the money. Any ideas where else they might be sold?"

He looked uncomfortable, replied, "Not any more."
Again he seemed to ponder but added nothing else. I
thanked William for his help; Gator told him he'd
think about the uniform. As we walked out, I noticed
Police and Fireman uniforms on the rack near the
baseball stuff.

Outside, I looked at Gator, "Who buys that shit?
Can you picture an adult wanting to dress up as a
fireman?" Gator didn't answer. I pictured him dressed
as Robin Roberts as we drove off.

SYLVAN

Sylvan caressed his ancient Patek Phillippe as he watched the police outside Mirella's apartment. He alternated times when he cruised her street, looking for patterns, weaknesses. Mostly, he came at sunrise or sunset, thinking people were less alert as light changed. The old police scanner had been quiet. They checked in hourly but didn't say anything useful. They seem tired, bored. He admired his old watch again, wondering why everything wasn't this precise. Short cuts, that's the American way. That's a tragedy. He needed a plan to get the cat lady outside. I haven't seen her for awhile. For the past 2 weeks, he lurked on the opposite side of her alley at 5 am, hoping to see her feeding the cats at daybreak. All he saw was the tall guy or cops feeding them. He murmured aloud, "Must be hiding her inside. Now to flush her out."

As he drove away he thought of Coach Leonard, his old football coach from St. Joe's. Coach Leonard knew he'd crushed Ronnie Silvato's knee on purpose, had kicked him off the team. Had said he was "sick." Sylvan smiled, thinking about how he had gotten even. Coach Leonard lived near Cobb's Creek Golf Course, his backyard backed up to the 10th tee box.

Sometimes the course got crowded and foursomes had to wait their turn to tee off. They killed time smoking near the fence by Coach's backyard; sometimes chucked their butts in his backyard, not far from the garden shed attached to his house. Sylvan never played golf but scouted the neighborhood carefully, hoping Leonard had pets. No such luck, Coach Leonard wasn't an animal lover.

But Sylvan noticed the cigarette butts and got a better idea. Coach Leonard wasn't much of a gardener. He left his mower and tools outside all the time. He was also careless with the gas can. After studying the routine, Sylvan crouched in the bushes one night, watched as Coach Leonard plodded upstairs to bed. After an hour, he carefully spilled gas on the shed, trickled some onto the grass near the fence, put the can back near the shed and kept the lid off. Since it was late summer, it wasn't odd that a cigarette would smolder awhile as the last foursome pinched in another nine before it got too dark. Excited, Sylvan tossed the cigarette and skulked away. From the fairway he watched Coach Leonard's cedar shakes bungalow burn like a matchbox. He hummed, "Ding Dong, ding dong," as he loped off. Next evening, The Bulletin read, "Freak Accident Leads to Disaster."

❧

Sylvan parked behind "Lost in Time", wandered in just as William was closing up.

213

William suddenly remembered, "Sylvan, I forgot to tell you, the police were in the other day asking if we sold Hummels. Naturally, I said no, just as you told me. I know you don't want the police snooping around; bad for business." William was immediately chilled as Sylvan raised his head and drilled those spell binding eyes at him. Not realizing it till the glare dropped, William had been holding his breath, standing dead still. "Are you disturbed, Sylvan? Did I do something wrong? We haven't had Hummels in the shop for months; I thought you wouldn't want things muddy." Sylvan never answered, just stood motionless. So, William nervously shut the front door, walked to his car wondering if he should mention the other guys who asked the same question about Hummels. William had never been afraid of Sylvan, despite his somewhat menacing appearance. William had always thought that his eyes saved him, that he'd almost be handsome if he lost weight and cut his hair. But tonight William was nervous.

DYLAN

Hoban continued to flood me with disability claims. Most were hum-drum but occasionally you got a prize. After reading one he sent me, I called and asked if this was serious or was he just busting me, seeing if I was actually reading these nutty files. Hoban confirmed, "That's a verbatim reply to our disability letter. Clyde Ingardo hasn't been to work for weeks. The form is supposed to be signed from a doctor, but his mother sent that back, even signed her name. We should cut him off but this stuff is too funny to pass up. Right in your wheelhouse, Dylan, give it a look. I can't wait to get your report." He was chuckling as he hung up.

Here is Mrs. Ingardo's priceless response to, CAUSE OF DISABILITY and WHEN CAN INSURED RETURN TO WORK:

Dear Mr Hoban:

I volunteer at a rescue mission in Delaware. I preach on the evils of drinking. On this current tour, I brought my son Clyde.

Clyde is a young man of good family but is a pathetic example of life ruined by excessive indulgence in whiskey and women.

During my lectures, Clyde sits on the edge of the platform, wheezing and staring at the audience through bleary, bloodshot eyes, sweating profusely, passing gas and making obscene gestures. I point out my own son as an example of what overindulgence can do to a person possessed by these demons. Here's the sad part. I married his father in 1956 and he left when Clyde was only 2 years old. I should have picked up the signals; his mother went on early dates with us as chaperone. Clyde never knew his father but maybe that was a good thing. His father, Joseph, was a baby, a real mama's boy. If mama said the horse could fly, Joseph would put a saddle on the horse, sit there waiting for the take-off. Joseph was a weak man, NOT LIKE HIS FATHER WHO RAN OFF WITH A PROSTITUTE FROM ANOTHER BOSSY WOMAN.

I think that family led to his weakness for alcohol and loose women. So Clyde SEEMED DOOMED BY THE MAMA'S BOY GENES. He slowly slipped and now remains a fallen man. But he is important to my mission but could not work on the assembly line. He might put the gaskets in backwards while in a drunken state.

He is a good son and hard worker when sober. But those days are few. He is helping me pass the word. At least he is useful.

Sincerely,

Elenore Ingardo, Help Giver

❧

On my way to Elenore Ingardo's home, I kept debating who was worse, Clyde or his mom. They lived in Upper Darby, right on the edge of 69th street, behind the Tower Theater. The streets were crowded, no garages, so people parked out front. I parked the watermelon mobile and hoofed to Ingardo's front door. The front door was open, only a screen door separating me from the living room. I heard a TV blaring and could see a younger man perched in front, staring at the screen. I knocked but got no reaction. Maybe he couldn't hear over the screaming TV? So I banged loud enough to wake the fallen angels. The young man never budged. Weird.

I continued to bang and then started yelling who I was and what I wanted. No response. Maybe he's jerking me around, not wanting his disability payments disturbed? Finally, I said, "Screw it." I opened the door and walked toward the TV. "Hey, I'm here to check on your disability payments, any problems so far?" And then I got a look at Clyde's eyes. The sad sack in front of me was expressionless, mouth open, eyes barely blinking.

I had an aunt with mental problems and had seen this
before. I wasn't a doctor but Clyde was severely
disturbed, either paranoid or schizophrenic. Booze
and women weren't a problem. He was deranged. Did
his mother know that or was she so hung up on the
father leaving that she couldn't face reality? I left
disability forms on the coffee table and drove off. I
was expecting funny but found something really sad.

 ᕗ

I went to Mirella's that night and chatted with Paul,
Reich's new partner.

"Any action?"

Paul shook his head, "Nada, I think the guy got
scared off. He'd be stupid to try the same move
twice."

I nodded, "Hope you're right but be careful, this
nut's unpredictable. Seems to be able to sneak up on
people, even if they're looking."

Paul shrugged, "Reich says the same thing. The guy
got the jump on them, feels bad about Dick gettin'
cold-cocked." He told me that Dick was doing much
better but still doesn't remember anything about what
happened. "It's like a fuckin' mystery to him. Don't
remember shit."

Paul radioed Reich, told him I was on the way up,
that I was going to feed the cats. On the walk up to
Mirella's apartment, I thought about my crazy plan to
lure the killer back, eventually getting him to follow
me when he couldn't get to Mirella.

I counted on the killer being careful, but driven. Like a wolf pack stalking prey, not able to stop the hunger. This psycho wouldn't give up, he had already taken calculated risks; he wouldn't stop now. So when he couldn't get Mirella, he'd turn to me. Because of that, I was once again nervous. I wondered what that would do to my flashbacks.

No one else knew my true plan yet. I realized I'd have to tell Merlano soon. I didn't think he'd like it if he knew what I was really trying to do. Now that Mirella was safe with Mrs. Rawley, my next step was to agree with Merlano's earlier plan of putting a tail on me; maybe catch the killer stalking me. I shook my head. What the hell am I thinking about? This is way out of my league. Or is it? Somehow I seemed attracted to these dicey situations. Maybe found this interesting? That question lingered as I knocked on the door and greeted Reich.

He grinned, "Good ta see someone besides Paul. He ain't the sharpest pencil in the pocket protector. I worry about him some. After Dick got suckered, I don't want another goin' down on my watch. Anyway, good to see ya, Frazier." He followed me into her kitchen and watched me get the cat chow. We locked her door and headed downstairs. I could tell Reich was getting squirrelly being cooped up.

I decided to test my idea on him. "Think this guy will come after me if he knows he can't get to Mirella?"

He didn't hesitate, "Fuckin' right, this prick's smart but he's still loco. Once they smell blood, they can't help themself. He tried it once, right?"

Next day I called Merlano to confirm he was at the station house. He was, so I told him I'd be over.

Merlano mumbled, "Bring some donuts, already into my third cup a coffee and my stomach's burning. Feel pissier'n normal." I hung up after promising to feed my hungry detective. Good bakeries are an art form in Philly. Everybody had their favorite, so I stopped at Kohler's and got a box of gooey donuts. Wanted Merlano happy when I unloaded my plan. An hour later, after munching on a Boston Crème, Merlano stared at me as I confessed trying to lure the killer to go after me. "You are a devious bastard, Frazier. Don't you know you don't fuck with cops? We carry guns, ain't you noticed?" And then he laughed.

Digging into his third jelly-filled, Merlano finally nodded. "We gotta play this right, Frazier. No more cowboy shit. This fucker's losing it. They all think they're geniuses, aint' gonna get caught. But when they get like this, you can't tell what's coming next. Brain's scrambled." He paused for a second. "Starting today, we cover you all day, tuck you in at night." But then he nodded, "But your instincts right, this guy's gonna go for you if he can't get Mirella. He already knows what you look like. Probably don't know where you live, but that's easy enough if he follows you. We nail the fucker when he gets too curious. Doubt the killer knows you're smart. You kinda look like a dumb jock."

In response, I shrugged my shoulders, crossed my eyes, and smacked my palm to my forehead.

☙

Later that day, Marisol filled me in on the latest developments when I called her at work. "I told James I was looking into Catholic annulment. He looked at me funny but said, 'Whatever you want. As far as I'm concerned, we are married. Screw what the Church thinks.' I just let it go at that. I have to get him involved at some point."

She had that right, Jimmer was the tricky part. "Marisol, you need to clue me to when that time is. I might as well be the one to confess, this is my idea and all. Let him fume at me first."

She was quiet a second. "I can handle James but it might go easier if you admit it." And then she giggled, "I'm kind of looking forward to that." Weirdly, that made me giggle too.

After I hung up, I got my notes out and updated the case. I added: Finished looking at pawn shops that might carry Hummels. And then I wrote: Others we missed? I liked William from the "Lost in Time" shop, he was helpful and didn't have the snooty attitude we found in other shops. Should I go to Carter Leeds again and get other names? Drop by and run some other shop names by William? I pulled out the Yellow Pages and leafed to the Pawn Broker section. Looked for the nicer ads, thinking if they spent money on advertising, they might carry high-end stuff. Carter Leeds dwarfed the other shops, but I did find a few others that weren't on my list. I looked at my notes one more time, trying to find something. What am I missing?

࿇

Merlano called early next day to say that my bodyguard was on duty. And "don't get cute, wave at him or any of your silly shit."

He hung up when I asked, "Would you frown on mooning him?" I was glad he warned me, I was watching everything carefully and might have spotted my tail and mistaken him for the killer. Since my apartment was on the top floor, the only way to get there was the front door and up the stairs. There was no rear entrance to my place. If I wanted to get to the basement, I had to downstairs, outside and through a side door. I had never seen the basement. Even knowing that, I stacked a sturdy chair against my door knob last night.

But it was time to plan my work day. I was caught up on my disability investigations so I went looking for my last potential Medicare fraud file. I read that Biata Wozniak had sudden expensive medical equipment purchases. I looked at her diagnosis, "Rheumatoid Arthritis" and "Other Degenerative Disorders." I paged through the file looking for her age. Found it, 81. I noticed she was a widow, lived on Olney Avenue, right off Chew Avenue. I had ridden though that area frequently. Not a pricey area; if she's ripping off Medicare, she isn't living high.

Knowing where I was going that day, it was time to get started. I headed to my front door, stopped after a couple steps, said out loud, "Be careful."

And then I peered under the bottom of the door to see if anyone was outside. Murmured, "All clear." I bounded down the steps but stopped to look at the front pathway before moving toward my car. The street was wide open but there were huge Maple trees lining the curb. Without being obvious, I scanned the area to see if I could spot the tail. Nothing; looks as if Merlano assigned pros. As I pulled away, I peeked in the mirror. Still no sign of a car pulling out. Where the hell are they? I made my way to Olney wondering if I had tremendously skilled guards or maybe the mopes had fallen asleep.

This section of Olney had once been an upscale neighborhood for young families. But like much of Philly, the draw of suburban life had left the neighborhood in disrepair. The houses were three story clapboards, most with elaborate moldings and windows. Although large homes, not much room separated them; hopefully you liked your neighbors. There was a mixture of white and black families, they were cordial but didn't mix much. I parked about a block away, studied my surroundings as I approached. Made another effort to spot my tail, still nothing. Mrs. Wozniak's house was slightly overgrown but neat compared to Mirella's street. If she had severe arthritis, she wouldn't be out doing the lawn or clipping bushes. Wonder who helped out? Kids? And then I spotted a group of cats under her porch. That reminded me of Mirella and that made me worry.

After pushing the doorbell repeatedly, I gave up and pounded the door. At age 81, Wozniak was probably hard of hearing and not used to visitors. On the other hand, if she had serious health problems, she was not likely to be out. I ramped up the banging and yelled in a friendly voice that I was there to make certain her claims were going okay. Although I had a pleasant tone, it was still loud enough to chip paint. That was proven when a neighbor a couple doors away, a cranky old guy, came out and told me he was calling the police. I explained what I was doing but he wasn't impressed, muttering and slamming his door.

Just as I was walking away, I heard the door knob twist; a white-haired woman answered the door. "What is it you want?" She had a distinct Polish accent. I explained that Voyager Insurance was making certain her claims were okay, that she had some large bills lately, that we wanted to make sure there were no problems. She looked confused. "What you talk about, large bills?" Since we were still standing at her door, I asked if she wanted to go in, sit down to finish the conversation. "Not yet, you explain more." Cautious, I liked that.

So, I opened my file, talked to her through the locked screen door, said there were bills for a whirlpool bath, a motorized wheelchair, weekly physical therapy treatments etc, which totaled over $10,000 in the past 6 months. Biata Wozniak smiled at me for the first time, "What you think, I'm Zsa Zsa Gabor or something?" I could see that she was frail, but she didn't seem to have much trouble standing.

I added, "So, none of these purchases are yours?" She just shook her head.

I asked her to look at the signature on the bills.
I put the bills close to the screen. "Is this your
signature?" I could see her thinking. Troubled by
something?

Finally shook her head, "Not me. Too sloppy. Nuns
teach Palmer Method. Slap fingers if no circles. Not
me."

I never did get in the house but walked away sure
there was something she hadn't told me. She didn't
seem the type to swindle Insurance Companies. She
was old enough and frail enough to be believable. She
could have faked me easily but didn't try. It was only
when she saw the signature that she hesitated. Did she
recognize the writing? Was it a relative? I didn't
want to scare her or be too pushy about coming inside
so I told her there was probably some mistake and
that I'd check and let her know.

GATOR

While I was visiting Mrs. Wozniak, Gator was thinking about the Robin Roberts uniform. I've got to have it, kept running through his head. It's a steal at that price. He's first ballot Hall of Fame, the uniform will be worth a fortune one day. And then he grinned: Plus he's my all-time favorite Phil. To distract himself, he pulled out a case he was working on, a court appearance in a few days. His thoughts wandered to Connie Mack Stadium, watching Robin wind up, getting ready to deliver the vaunted fastball. He slammed the case file down and yelled, "Janice, I'm going out for awhile. Anyone calls; tell them I'm in court." Janice was good at covering for her boss.

Gator drove back to "Lost in Time" and parked right outside. Talking to himself, "I'm not paranoid like Dylan," he mused. "Just park right out front, get in and get out. Who the hell watches pawn shops that would give a rats' ass about me?" He was dressed in his usual disheveled manner; vest with white shirt hanging amok. He started to tuck himself in but shook it off. Fuck it, it's a pawn shop not the Taj Mahal.

It was overcast, looked like rain, so as he went inside, the store was gloomier than last time. He looked at the uniform rack and then looked around. Where's William? He ambled to the uniforms and found his prize. Robin Fuckin' Roberts!

"That uniform's priceless." The deep, monotone voice startled him, but the hulking speaker was even more shocking. Gator tried to gather himself. How did he get up behind me without making any noise? A huge guy, how's he so quiet? The large man continued, "He's the best pitcher in Phillies history, better than Grover Cleveland Alexander for my money. He wore that uniform in 1950 when they beat The Dodgers."

Gator knew his Philly trivia, "I'll bet there's no way to prove that, is there?"

The hulk's expression went dead, "Are you calling me a liar?" Gator noticed the cobra-like eyes, had seen that look before from hard characters in court.

Switching the conversation back to the uniform he coveted. "I'll give you $150 for it."

The large man softened his look, still no smile but not hostile. "The Phillies retired Number 36 in 62', in a few months it will a decade old. I won't let this go for less than $500. And don't bother dickering. The price is not negotiable."

Gator looked befuddled, "I was in a few days ago and William said I could have it for $250. Now you're saying $500. What's going on here? I want to talk to William."

The feral eyes locked on Gator, "I own the shop and decide price. William was naive to quote that price. He's not a baseball man but I am."

Without his prize uniform, Gator walked back to his car and thought aloud: Now that's an strange guy.

DYLAN

I hadn't talked to Mirella for awhile, so I called
Mrs. Rawley to see if I could drop by. "We usually go
out for breakfast and then shop afterwards. After
lunch we rest and get tea later in the afternoon,
there's a nice tea parlor on this block. After dinner is
best, but don't make it too late. Early to bed, you
know."

I held back a laugh, "Sounds like you two are
having quite the time. Glad you can fit me in."

She got my joke, "Mirella has been a godsend. I
haven't had so much fun since Mr. Rawley passed.
She's a ticket, love her sense of humor." I knew what
she meant; Mirella was a piece of work. I hung up
after agreeing to pop over that night.

I parked close to the French bistro, noticed the
snooty waiter as I walked by. Couldn't resist, turned
around and walked inside. I had done some research
on Nicoise olives, was anxious to blather some
useless facts at this A-hole. He walked by, looked at
me, seemed to remember something, but not sure.

I nodded, "Came back to see if you checked out the
Nicoise olives for me. If they're authentic, they'd be
firmer, almost meaty. Plus the color's off. Not
burgundy enough.

Couldn't pick up the signature winey, licorice notes last time. Maybe they weren't brined properly? Or did someone slip some Kalamatas by the chef?"

He looked bewildered, "Uh, uh, I don't know."

I nodded, feigned mild disgust, "I'll be back to check."

Still amused with myself, I walked towards Mrs. Rawley's and soon spotted the doorman outside the beautiful, old building.

I smiled, "Staying vigilant, Sullivan?" He obviously knew I was coming, "I saw you when you entered the restaurant. I wondered what that was about. How come you park so far away?" And then I thought about my bodyguards, "Do me a favor, Sullivan, see if you can see if anyone's following me when I go upstairs. The cops are tailing me till they catch the killer. I haven't been able to spot them. Let me know what they look like, will you?" Sullivan seemed to like the new intrigue added to his daily routine.

He gave me a thumbs up, "Got it. I'm on it."

Belden was waiting for me, saluted when I ascended and exited the elevator. I saluted crisply, "At ease, Belden."

He grinned and relaxed slightly, "Not till this killer is caught, Mr. Frazier. Not till this killer is caught." And then he flipped open his jacket to reveal a shoulder holster and pistol. "I'm not taking any chances with Mrs. Rawley's well being. She and Miss Mirella are out and about a lot so I have to prepare for the unexpected. I thought the weapon might ease any worries you might have." He was right. My money's on Belden if the killer tries anything.

I found the girls giggling away in front of the TV. They were watching the Archie Bunker Show.

Mirella turned when she heard me. "Dylan, have a seat and watch Archie with us. Meathead's in trouble again. It's hysterical." Mrs. Rawley waved and they turned back as Carroll O'Connor hammered the Meathead for another bungle. The ladies howled as Archie screamed, "EDITH…!"

Mrs. Rawley turned, "Don't you just love it when he tells Meathead to dummy up?" They were having fun.

After the show ended, I assured Mirella that her cats were doing well and so far there was nothing to report on the killer.

She beamed, "I've been having so much fun with Gertrude that I almost forgot the boys. Thanks for watching out for them. The boys and I had that in common; no one else was there to take care of us."

Mrs. Rawley looked at Mirella, "That's all changed now, you're family now. I don't know what I'd do without you. I haven't laughed this much since I was in grade school." Again Mirella glowed. Watching these two was a nice way to end my day. I bid them goodnight and said I'd check back in a few days.

Sullivan was waiting for me when I descended. "I think I spotted your guards. Two big fellows drove by shortly after you went upstairs. They kept going and made a right at the end of the block. I made note of their car, a black Chevy, I think its catty corner to the French bistro you stopped in. You'll have to go past them as you leave. You don't see many burly men in this area.

If they are your guards, it looks like they picked a couple that can handle themselves. If that's any comfort." Actually, it was.

SYLVAN

Sylvan parked in the alley near Biata's house. He rotated parking spots to avoid being conspicuous. As was his custom, he arrived shortly after sunset. He got out his key and opened the back door. Bee always had the TV on, wouldn't hear a knock and most times the bell went unanswered. He scowled: Silly bitch watches Lawrence Welk, whistles the tunes when The Lennon Sister sing. Sylvan went about his routine. Biata liked tea, so he always made her a cup when he arrived. And then he got out some Lorna Doone cookies to go with the tea. Keep her happy, plus it shuts her up. After the Tetley was properly steeped, he lumbered into the living room.

BIATA

The house was a straight-through design, so she had already seen him working in the kitchen. "There's my sweet Bee, how's my girl today?" Biata beamed and asked him to lower the TV volume so they could chat. She looked forward to his weekly visits, usually on Wednesday and Sunday. But this time she was anxious. Should I tell about Insurance man? It upsets him when I ask questions. She thought back to the investigator when he put the bills to the screen. She remembered Sylvan's signature because it was so tiny, almost like a child. When I sold that clock to him, he gave a receipt; I thought to myself: The nuns didn't teach him Palmer. The signature, I think, is Sylvan's. She remembered the Insurance man talked about physical therapy and wheelchairs. Why did he say I buy it? But she worried it would ruin the night if she mentioned it. Sylvan always said, "Don't tell anyone about me. My help to you is for us only. Do not tell." So she said nothing.

She sneaked peeks at him as he checked her mail. And that started to make her wonder. Forms he make me sign. I never read. Are they from Insurance? Something else bothered her. Silver tea set. It not where it should be.

When I look I see other silver gone.

I ask Sylvan, he say, "You must have lost it Bee, I never saw any silver. Don't worry, I'll look for it." But when I ask again he get angry, say, "Forget it, Bee." But I don't forget. Mama gave to me.

But she quickly dismissed her worry and called, "Have a cup with me Sylvan, the mail you can look later."

SYLVAN

Sylvan never looked up, but responded, "Don't want to interrupt your time with Lawrence, hey, isn't that Julius La Rosa?"

Biata loved Julius, he knew that would be an irresistible draw, so Sylvan walked in and turned up the TV and returned to the kitchen. As he got near the end of the mail: Ha, that's what I'm looking for; the check from Voyager; like clockwork that company pays. He would have Biata sign it when she got sleepy. She never questioned him. Through his pawn shop, he could cash people's checks, charging a fee for the service. Always careful, he spread his booty from the Insurance checks to different Savings and Loans, never enough to draw attention. Money gave him great pleasure, not for a lavish lifestyle but just knowing he was wealthy and could do what he wanted.

Sylvan had noticed Biata sneaking peeks at him. She seemed fidgety. He remembered her question last week. Was she still worrying about that silverware? Maybe I was too quick to take it. He peered out of the corner of his eyes, found Biata staring at him.

When she noticed his glance, she dropped her gaze quickly, went back to the show. Curious, he went to the living room and sat near Biata. She usually craved his attention, now she avoided his eyes.

"Something wrong, Bee? You seem nervous. Did you get bad news?" She kept watching the Lennon Sisters as if she hadn't heard him. He walked to the TV, turned it off. "What is it, Bee? Tell me." Sylvan had an edge to his tone that made her tear up.

She turned to Sylvan, "Someone from Insurance here today, young man asking about medical payments, about things I never bought. This Insurance man show me signature, it not mine. No want trouble."

BIATA

Biata looked at Sylvan through wet eyes and saw his face undergo a frightful change. She was addicted to TV-- watched it all day and late into the night. Never had been a person who needed at lot of sleep. She especially loved scary movies, watched them all the time, except when Sylvan came to visit. Biata tried to remember the face in front of her. But then she did and her flesh crawled. Lon Chaney, in The Wolf Man, was the face before her. And then Biata shuddered and helplessly peed herself. She stopped breathing, watched as Sylvan soundlessly paced before her, wringing his hands, blinking, mouth twitching. Why is Sylvan turning into a werewolf?

∻

Sylvan turned abruptly, slamming the coffee table with his massive fist. Biata blinked nervously, wondered: Why he so upset?

And then he rushed at her, grabbed her dress, stared at her with his wolf eyes. "What did you say to the Insurance man? Tell me.

Exactly what did you say?" Still paralyzed, she gasped for air. Sylvan pushed her back, but seemed to compose himself. As her breath came back, she tried to think: What's happening? Has Sylvan lost his mind?

And finally her words came, "Nothing I said to the young man, just my nuns wouldn't like writing so poor. What is it that's wrong?" Biata watched Sylvan's heaving chest, flared nostrils and knew she was in trouble. Her only thought: Help.

But then Sylvan walked back to the kitchen, closing the doors. Biata turned back to Lawrence Welk, thinking to call police when he left. But Sylvan stormed through the door, came at her fast. "What did the Insurance man look like?" Her breath stopped again.

Biata started to cry and Sylvan slapped her viciously "Shut up, you Polish piece of shit, what did he look like?" Biata ground her fingers together, tried to speak. He slapped her harder on the back of the head. She got dizzy, almost collapsed.

Muddled, she thought Lon Chaney was asking her, "Answer me." She was too scared, couldn't talk. And then Lon Chaney picked her up, walked to the steps and carried her upstairs. They got to the top; the wolf man turned, facing her back towards the steep drop. He shuffled forward, closer to the edge. Lon Chaney bellowed, "Last time, what did he look like?"

She gulped one choked word, "Handsome." And then he turned backwards, she felt him relax, time passed slowly. Biata began to calm a little, and then thought: It's going to be okay.

As if reading her thoughts, he tilted her upwards and looked at her eyes which were still stricken with confusion. While she tried to read his expression, he moved back to the steps and lifted her higher, peered out like he was aiming at something. And then he started rocking her back and forth, like a sack of potatoes. But the rocking stopped abruptly and she hung limply in his arms. Biata was about to vomit from the violent motion, her eyes bulging, and then she went rigid as Lon Chaney abruptly awakened and tossed her violently outward. In that last moment, her first thought: He's killing me. Her last thought was about the Insurance man: He was very handsome.

SYLVAN

Sylvan watched her fly through the air, waited for a few moments to see if Biata moved. He shook his head, as if admiring his toss. Perfect, she's dead still. He descended slowly, got to the body and leaned down; put his finger on Biata's neck. No pulse. He studied the scene, mumbled, "She fell down the steps. An old lady, weak joints from arthritis, knees gave out walking downstairs." He went upstairs and inspected her room, pulled the covers aside and rumpled the sheets and pillow. Made the bed looked slept in. Did she wander to the steps while it was still dark, got disoriented? Sylvan visualized the police inspecting the house to determine cause of death. He walked slowly around to make sure there were no traces of his presence. He left what was remaining of the tea and cookics. "Her treat before bed," he could hear the police saying. He always carried Biata's treats with a napkin, no fingerprints. And then he went through the mail again, made certain there were no other checks. Clean.

As he left through the back, he thought: It was the snooper. Why would he visit Biata?

He got in his black car and drove silently, wondering. When he got to the pawn shop, he pulled out his favorite Brueget, polished it meticulously, settled into rhythmic breathing, and finally realized: Insurance.

DYLAN

The day after visiting Mrs. Wozniak, I called Hoban, told him I smelled a rat. "I looked through the file and she's right, that wasn't her signature. Her writing is flowery, like the nuns hammer into you. I wrote like that till high school, when a priest told me, 'Shrink it, you write like a sissy.' That kind of cured me."

Hoban chuckled, "You have lots of life experiences, Dylan, you ought to write them down."

I switched gears, "But the really interesting thing is I checked Crina Barbu's file and one of the signatures looks similar. Not exactly the same but close. Not a coincidence, right?"

I told Hoban I would give the signatures to Merlano, was sure they had a handwriting expert. "Plus, I'm heading back to Wozniak's house today. Catch her off guard again. I could tell she was holding something back. Saw her suck in air, like she was surprised. Bet she knew the handwriting."

All Hoban said was, "Jesus."

I hung up, called Merlano and found him in. "What's it this time, Sherlock?" I explained what I'd found, that we finally had a pattern, that we might have a cause for the murder, that I'd be right over.

All he said was, "Jesus." As I drove, I thought: More like Satan.

Merlano looked at both signatures and agreed they looked similar. "Ain't a handwriting expert but those signatures look fucked. Hard to write that small, like he's hiding something." I told him I was on my way to Wozniak's again, asked if he could come. "Can't, got a pimp went nuts, slashed a John who tried to welch on his whore. Guys okay, more embarrassed than anything. Gotta try to get him to press charges. Don't blame him, not the kinda thing you want your name in the papers." So, I told him I'd let him know what I learned, would call later.

As I was walking away, "By the way, your goon squad is good, haven't spotted them yet."

Merlano nods, "Philly's finest."

☙

After I left Merlano, I drove down Montgomery Avenue and decided to make it interesting for my bodyguards. It was a busy street so it was almost impossible to pick out a tail car. I made a sudden right, swerved into a parking spot and ducked down. A minute later, a blue Grand Prix flies by, I rose and saw two meaty heads twitching left and right, trying to find me. I pulled out and followed them, catching up quickly. When I got behind, I hit my horn and waved. The guy riding shotgun turned, whispered to his buddy and pulled over. Not wanting to get my ass kicked, I kept going and waved as I passed. When I looked in the rearview, I saw the full bird salute.

It was an overcast day, as I pulled onto Wozniak's street in Olney. The old Sycamores were shedding bark like a hibernating snake. My feet crunched the bark as I made my way to her door. I mused: Couldn't sneak up on me in this block, that bark is everywhere. I scanned the street for my tail. Nothing. Wonder if they had enough of my shit, called it a day? Couldn't blame them, I am a serial prankster. I thought back to my 6th grade nun, called her "Burping Bernard" since she belched like a locomotive. She always said, "Master Frazier, aren't you ever serious?" She nailed me, I was wacky.

I neared Wozniak's door, was prepared for the yelling routine again, knowing she seemed slightly deaf. I banged and rang, got no answer. And then I hollered as I banged. Still nothing. The door was shut this time, I tried to peer through the glass but a shade blocked out all but a crack. I could see the TV was off and no lights were on. Since it was overcast, it was dim outside. As I walked toward the rear, I heard the cats mewling before I saw them. Sounded like Mirella's crew before they got fed. Hungry? I scooted by the cats and they tagged along as I went to the back door. Nothing. Must be out?

SYLVAN

Sylvan had spent the past two weeks studying the cat lady's street and apartment. He alternated between early evening and dawn for his stakeouts. He varied his costumes and points of observation. There was only one cop outside when there used to be two. He wondered if they were starting to lose interest. Not once had he seen the Cat Lady. It was time to flush her out. Sylvan only took calculated chances but liked his odds. After finalizing his plan of assault, he planted his weapon inside a neglected trash can on the left side of her apartment. As an extra measure to assure the trash can was untouched, he had deftly wedged a twig between the can and lid. The twig remained undisturbed. No one had noticed his lethal addition, just part of the normal mess. Sylvan counted on people ignoring things that were part of the routine. He was pleased that without exception, the guard cop stayed on the right side of the apartment building because it had the only pathway from the rear alleyway to the front door. Also without fail, the cop would rotate 30 minutes between watching the rear alleyway and then the front door. The left side of the cat lady's building was overgrown and impassable.

Tonight, that seemingly harmless, impassable side was Sylvan's point of attack. He now stood intently monitoring all activity from the darkened bushes near the front of the cat lady's apartment. He breathed deeply, quietly gathered himself before removing his stare from the cat lady's front door. Just minutes ago the cop had moved toward the alleyway. He was satisfied it was safe; Sylvan moved to the trash can and took out the gasoline container he had hidden. He lifted the gas tin, inched toward the apartment, drenched the clapboard siding and methodically soaked his way toward the front door. This was the tricky part. He counted on the cop staying out back.

He quietly lurked near the left corner of the building, gas tin dangling. Looking around the edge, he saw nothing; the cop was still out back. He quietly walked to the entrance, emptied the gas tin all over the front door and then drenched the wooden porch. He let the remaining gas trail after him as he moved back to the trash can and put the gas tin inside. Then Sylvan slipped through the bushes into the next apartment building's bushy pathway. Hidden by the underbrush, he covered his hand as he struck the match, lit the cigarette. Moving farther into the neighboring apartment's front yard, he tossed the cigarette and watched the intoxicating whoosh as the gasoline went berserk. As the blaze reached full glory, he ambled back up the street and waited from a safe distance.

The fire department was there in 10 minutes. Sylvan mingled with the curious neighbors. Everyone liked a fire.

The old lady next to him chortled, "Glad it ain't my buildin'." Sylvan nodded agreement. So far, he only saw one person from the building---a guy jumped from the second floor. No cat lady. She was probably still asleep, unaware. The police got there minutes later. He watched as they talked with the cop on stakeout and then went to the guy who jumped from the second floor, asked him something. One cop went to his car, got on the radio. He came back a few minutes later and talked again to the jumper, who was now on his feet. Still no cat lady. Why aren't the firemen trying to rescue her? Again he watched the cops talking and it suddenly came to him. It was a cop inside, the jumper was a cop. Where was the cat lady?

Not wanting to appear obvious, Sylvan slowly moved within the throng. He got into the middle and stopped to think. To calm himself, he stroked the antique watch he kept in his pocket. He suddenly lifted his eyes after a revelation: They had a cop inside. They wanted him to break in. It was a trap. Sylvan's disturbed thoughts were interrupted when a cop car came roaring up. A jumpy looking guy got out of the passenger side. He looked like he was in charge, maybe a detective. Sylvan wondered if he set this up. No one appeared to be watching the crowd so Sylvan moved closer to the detective, trying to overhear something. The crowd was buzzing so it was impossible to catch what they were saying. He didn't take chances and was about to disappear when he noticed a tall stranger walking up to the cops. Sylvan smiled broadly.

DYLAN

It was my turn to feed Mirella's cats tonight but I was running late. When I got to her street, it was blocked off by cop cars. I said to myself, "Oh shit, this isn't good." I parked quickly and started to run. I could smell the fire as I darted up the street. There was total chaos at Mirella's house. I saw Merlano's animated silhouette as I got near. And then I saw Reich, stooped over with a blanket around him.

Reich spotted me, "Fucker torched the place. I was lucky ta get out, hadda jump."

Merlano joined in, "I wonder if he knew a cop was inside or just got impatient? Either way, this asshole is crazy."

I thought about that, said to Merlano, "What was he trying to do? Trying to kill Mirella or checking to make sure she was still in there?" And then I got a weird feeling, turned to Merlano. "Is he still here watching us?"

Without answering, he went to his men and sent the cops to walk through the crowd, looking for something, anything odd.

Merlano grabbed my shoulder, "Stay near me. The guy knows what you look like, might go for you. Seems like he's losin' it. You better stay put."

I thought about that, "Better idea. Let me mingle, you stay near me, watch the crowd. If someone seems too curious, we might get lucky." I could tell by his expression he wasn't wild about the idea.

He called another cop over, "Follow us. See if anybody's takin' an interest in my friend here. If you see something, go for the fucker, no hesitation. Got it?" The cop's eyes got wide, he nodded.

Not knowing what to look for, I walked toward the heart of the crowd. People were excited, talking loud. I decided to focus on anyone that was quiet, not part of a conversation. So far nothing. I reminded myself to stay sharp. I repeated something my Green Beret buddy Nut always said, "When you least expect it." Ignoring the women, I looked at the men. My only clue was the guy was stocky; at least that's what I thought from my earlier near fatal encounter. I made a full swing through the throng, still got nothing.

Merlano finally caught up, "He split. Let's wrap it up." Merlano yelled to me as I got a few steps away, "The guy beat us again, has eyes in the back of his heads." That had been bothering me too. Is he smart or lucky?

SYLVAN

Sylvan remembered the Snooper had come from the south side of the street, so he moved that way while the Snooper was circling with the cops. He went to his car, also parked in that direction and retrieved his Louisville Slugger. He might get lucky. The street was dark. Sylvan had used a Beebe rifle to shoot the lights out on the corners of the cat lady's street. In this run down area, nobody gave a damn. He moved about 20 feet from the corner and pushed inside an old yew bush. Sylvan was comfortable in the dark, he remembered back: Just like when Aunt Anca punished me.

Thoughts of his sadistic aunt triggered memories. He remembered his 8th birthday. Uncharacteristically, Aunt Anca had been in a joyous mood, asked him what kind of cake he wanted.

He recalled his answer vividly, "Chocolate cake with chocolate icing. My favorite." She patted my head and was humming as I went to school. That night, we had a feast of fried chicken, mashed potatoes, gravy, and the vegetable I loved, green beans. As usual, self-important dad was working late and Aunt Anca had prepared a large plate for his return.

And then she brought in the crowning jewel; I made a wish, blew out the 8 candles, and dug into my cake. I nearly choked as I bit into the slice made of mud and grass. Only the icing was real. Aunt Anca smiled at me, added, "Cake is for good boys, not mother killers."

DYLAN

I was antsy as I left the fire. Thought about Mirella: What if we hadn't moved her? No way she could jump from the second floor and survive. Thoughts from Nam poured into my head, I recalled the many nights lying sleepless, worried about being fragged. Shaking that bad thought off, my buddy Nut's advice popped up, "Stay alert, always plan a retreat route." As I walked down the gloomy street, I wondered: Has the killer really left? I stopped and surveyed the surroundings. Shaggy bushes, large trees, almost pitch black; where were the street lights? I moved to the center of the street, took a deep breath and broke into a slow trot, stayed vigilant.

SYLVAN

Sylvan had recovered from his birthday vision. He watched as his prey halted, and then ran into the street. What's he up to? He can't possibly see me. But he's acting like he knows I'm here. Just then Sylvan saw two other shadows farther away appear in the street, moving at a low run. Sylvan gripped the bat, thinking about what to do next. He watched the snooper get into his car and quickly turn it on. The two other burly men were apparently parked farther away and were now sprinting for their car. Sylvan then moved from his lair and got into his nearby car. As the snooper drove by, Sylvan quickly concluded: He's probably headed home. And then he whispered, "Gotcha." But then the other car roared passed. Where are they going? He followed.

DYLAN

I was still jumpy as I drove home. The distant trailing headlights gave me some comfort, glad to have my shadows. Thought to myself: Next time I see them I'll apologize for being a jackass. Wish I'd had these guys in Nam. While I was driving something came to me that had been a cloud banging around my consciousness. When I'd first searched Crina'a apartment, I had come across collection envelopes from Holy Name of Jesus church. If she had envelopes, she probably went to mass and was registered as a parishioner. Maybe the pastor knew her? Maybe he knew something about the elusive nephew? Worth checking out.

I pulled into my parking space and scanned the area before getting out of my car. There was nowhere to hide in my front yard, landscaping was not a priority with my landlord. I sprinted upstairs, locked up tight and peeked outside to see if my shadows had arrived. When I saw the headlights cut off about a 100 feet down the street, I exhaled deeply. How long had I been holding my breath? As I turned away, another set of headlights slowly worked their way down the street. This car finally picked up speed and turned left at the corner.

I turned away, thought: Just a neighbor headed off to work for the late shift. I went to bed, tossed for a long while, finally dozed off.

SYLVAN

It didn't take Sylvan long to figure that the burly guys were also following his prey. Keeping about a block distance, they mimicked the big snooper's route. Somehow this amused Sylvan. So they put bodyguards on the Snooper? They must be scared of me. And then he thought more. They moved the cat lady. They were trying to trap me. Before he finished his analysis, the cars came to a stop on a sleepy street in Upper Darby. Since he was already moving down the street, he knew he had to roll passed them. Just ride by slowly, act like you belong there. He made a note of the street name and apartment where the snooper stopped. Sylvan had a near photographic memory.

DYLAN

Before I went to Holy Name of Jesus church to see Crina Barbu's pastor, I called Marisol to check on the annulment proceedings.

"You must have read my mind, I was about to call you this morning. Monsignor Pugh wants to talk with you before approaching James. He says you can help plan the discussion, that James can be volatile, and that you have a special rapport with him."

I let that sink in before responding. "Is that a compliment or an insult?" Marisol had a nice, feminine laugh.

She added, "Probably both, can you give him a ring? Then let me know the plan." A few seconds later she added, "I'm trying not to get too excited, but I think this might work."

I called Monsignor Pugh; he was just getting back from daily mass. When I identified myself, I could tell he was in high spirits. "I just had the Lord's flesh and blood; I'm ready to fight the devil."

I chuckled, "First I hear you're maligning my good name linking me as Jimmer's lone friend and now you're equating me with attacking the devil. Still angry about the Stinky nickname, huh?"

Not to be out done, "Sorry, lad, I calls em as I sees em. But anyway, how is my favorite sinner?"

I thought about telling him I was being chased by a homicidal maniac but settled for, "Fair to midlin, Monsignor. Well actually, par to sub-middling to be honest." He let that pass, waited till I continued. "Hear you want to consult on how to deal with Jimmer. Can't say that excites me. You know he controls an army of judo-trained pygmies. They kick me around enough already; wait till he's pissed at me."

He chuckled but added seriously, "We need James to act involved and contrite. My vote won't sway the deal. He's got to face a church tribunal who are trained to be biased against him anyway. They'll make it tough under the best of circumstances. If he's rude and dismissive, he's done."

Not trying to be funny, I added, "Jimmer is rude and dismissive when he's in a good mood. Guess we need a miracle. I'll get some holy water on the way out."

Monsignor Pugh pushed on. "I contacted the first husband. When he heard what I wanted, he laughed. He said something in Spanish. I think it translated as "Pound sand, Padre' but I can't be sure. And then he slammed the phone down. I put everything to him in writing. If he doesn't respond, I need to document that I did everything possible. The good news is the first husband's cooperation isn't essential. It would have been nice but I'll work around it."

I asked more questions about the tribunal. "It's kind of like going to court; only the case is the validity of the first marriage.

I'll act as Marisol's lawyer and advise her throughout the process. The court members are trained religious from this diocese; they do this repeatedly. It's tough to put one over on them, but I think this one will pass. It isn't a hostile environment and actually Marisol's first husband's attitude works in her favor. His belligerence helps prove he was unfit to marry in the first place. If James plays his part as the devoted, beloved spouse, it's icing on the cake. That's where you come in. Make him look good."

Because I knew my involvement was coming, I'd been giving this a lot of thought. "Marisol and I will need to one/two him. First I'll admit my guilt. Tell him I did it because I want Marisol and Jose to be happy, to have a normal relationship with his family. And then admit it will be fun watching his mother squirm. And end with I consider him like a brother and want the best for him. That, in my opinion, the best life for him is to see Marisol going to Mass Sunday morning and watching Jose sit between his doting grandparents."

Monsignor Pugh looked at me with kindly tolerance. "Say it like that and it will be a successful discussion." And then he added, "Leave out the mother squirming part, okay?'

అ

I was hungry, so I grabbed a quick hoagie at McCormick's Deli, a local hangout. I had coached the McCormick brothers, John and Kevin during my summers as a playground director.

Whenever I could, I stopped by and shot the shit with whichever brother was on duty. The deli was wall to wall basketball pictures of St. Tim ballplayers. Our grade school was a perennial powerhouse and the McCormick brothers loved to celebrate the legacy. Like everybody else, I spent most of my time looking for my own mug shots.

John was on duty and greeted me. "You were much cuter as a kid, Dylan. Got kinda rugged-looking as you aged."

I smiled at John. "And you couldn't shoot worth a shit at any age."

I ordered my Italian hoagie and kibitzed with John as he worked. "No left over rolls, John, want the fresh stuff. Save the old ones for the St. Bernie's crowd."

He chuckled as he thought about our old rival. "I hate to admit it, Dylan; those guys are about my best customers. If the St. Tim crowd doesn't pony up, might have to redecorate with St. Bernie's photos."

I laughed, "Monsignor Pugh will excommunicate you if he hears about that, just left old Stinky and he's in a foul mood. Better watch it." John grinned and passed me my to-go order. Had to fight to pay him, ended up dropping the cash in the tip jar. He had a thriving business but old friends were important. Home, it means a lot.

I munched the delicious hoagie as I drove, made sure not to drip oil on my shirt. That wasn't easy, so I blanketed myself with napkins. Everything changed as I drove into Fishtown. Joyful childhood memories were replaced with the harsh reality of a neighborhood beaten by time.

Although it bordered historic center city, Fishtown was a testimony to survival. I was in the Army with guys from here, all were tough. But all were guys you could count on. If a kid from Fishtown had your back, you were okay. I thought about one kid with the unlikely last name of Luzdgejczyk, who was quickly renamed "Alphabet." I taught him how to maneuver the monkey bars each morning before chow; you'd think I gave him a million bucks.

It still made me smile as I thought about Alphabet saying, "Aint kiddin' ya, Frazier, them monkey bars should be called gorilla bars. No fuckin' chimp can do that."

Thinking of that, I was still laughing as I pulled onto Berks Street and spotted Holy Name of Jesus on the corner of Gaul. Despite the run down area, this was a magnificent church. I'd read somewhere that the poorest towns had beautiful churches to remind people of the eternal splendor of the after-life. I liked that thought. Just then I noticed a group of older women congregating by the church door. I parked nearby but scanned the street before getting out. Still jumpy from last night, I said aloud as if to convince myself, "All clear."

Despite its size and diversity, Philly is a friendly city, people chat you up. I approached the ladies and asked who the pastor was. One looked me up and down but smiled saying, "Father Scardino, he just left. He's headed over to the rectory." She pointed, "Around the corner."

And then one of the ladies asked, "You a cop? Here to check on the break in?" I said no, that I was trying to help a former parishioner settle her insurance claim and needed to get some information from her pastor.

But then I asked, "What break-in?"

The first lady spoke up, "Some punk hit the poor box, stole some candlesticks. Sad, huh?" I nodded agreement, said thanks, made my way to the rectory.

The rectory was another nice stone building adjoining the church. A stout, dark haired priest answered the door. I identified myself, quickly summarized my interest in a former parishioner, Crina Barbu, and asked if I could speak to someone who might remember her.

Father Scardino introduced himself, said he did know Crina and invited me inside to chat. "Tea, young man? Just about to have a cup myself." He seemed pleased when I told him I loved tea, that it was my mother's afternoon ritual.

Figuring this was a priest who would be trustworthy; I unloaded the gory details of the case. That I suspected foul play, that we might have a killer loose in Fishtown. Father Scardino had a kind smile.

Almost resigned, he added, "This town has many sinners. It started as a refuge for the Eastern European immigrants. Most came here educated people but not knowing the language or customs. With time, and some education, many of the families prospered. Fishtown was a bustling place, a happy place. But today it's mostly Irish and Polish, took the parish years before they accepted an Italian pastor."

He smiled benignly, "The people are still wonderful, warm. It's just there is so little hope." I didn't know what to say.

Father Scardino seemed lost in that memory, so I interrupted, told him about the church collection envelope, about her Hummel collection and the stripped down apartment, that it didn't make sense.

The pastor nodded, "I remember Crina well. She came to church every Sunday, always went to the coffee socials afterwards, she was one of the first to make me feel at home." He thought some more. "But then she stopped coming. I asked around but no one seemed to know what happened to her. She lived at the farthest edge of the parish, near Frankford, so she had no friends close to church. Finally, I went to visit and got an answer I wasn't expecting."

He sat awhile, as if thinking of how to explain.

Finally, I asked, "So why'd she stop going to mass?"

He smiled again in his gentle way. "I thought it would be sickness. But no, she said her "big boy", that's what she called him, didn't approve of church and told her to stop going. That religion was all just a fraud, a way to get collection money. I did what I could to dissuade her but got nothing. Sad."

I asked if he noticed Hummels in her apartment. He nodded, "They were her pride and joy. Hummels were everywhere. Almost like a shrine."

And then I asked the big question, "Ever meet the big boy?"

He frowned, shook his head. "Never. She acted like he was a nephew or someone close to her, but I never laid eyes on him."

We finished our tea and I bid him farewell.

As I was leaving he said, "Let me know if you catch this person. I'll say a special prayer for you." Having met him only briefly, I believed he would.

SYLVAN

Sylvan began his study of the Snooper's apartment area. It was daylight but he wasn't concerned. His reasoning: Police won't be around during the day. The Snooper's at work, they'll be following him around. Although this area was a busy section of Upper Darby, the apartment was on a quiet street, loaded with tall trees. Sylvan was pleased, they gave cover and absorbed noise. Sylvan drove a block away and proceeded on foot. If anyone saw him, they would think he was a deliveryman by the gray uniform and large satchel hanging from his shoulder. Not someone you would remember as out of place.

There were no alleyways behind the Snooper's place, so Sylvan couldn't see the rear of the apartment without walking along a pathway by the entrance. He debated: Not yet, wait till its dark. He decided to circle the block to see if he had a better rear view from that side. Could he get in the apartment without going to the front door? As he got opposite the Snooper's apartment he saw there was no rear entrance to the top apartment.

A problem, if that's where he lives. Sylvan thought back, seemed to remember lights going on upstairs as he cruised by last night. Frontal attacks were more difficult. He let that sink in and then made a decision. Wait till he comes home after dark. Take care of the bodyguards first. He nodded, satisfied with his plan.

DYLAN

That night I watched Star Trek reruns. It was a weird day and I wanted to zone out and "boldly go where no man has gone before." Wouldn't it be great to be Captain Kirk? I mean the dude was always in control. It didn't matter whether Clingons had him trapped or if the warp speed was on the fritz, he thought of a way out. What would Kirk do with a homicidal killer? My mindless trance was broken as the phone blared.

It was Hoban. "I'm beginning to think you're jinxed, Frazier. You read the paper tonight?"

I answered honestly, "Only the sports page, Carlton smoked the Cards again. He's still pissed the dumb asses traded him."

Hoban didn't react; I learned why when he told me what was on his mind.

I was speechless. "What do you mean Biata Wozniak's dead? How do you know that?"

Hoban confessed he always read the Obituaries. "My dad did that every night, said it made him feel better that he was on the right side of the dirt. He was weird like that. I just picked up the habit.

When I read that name, I knew there couldn't be two Biata Wozniak's from Olney. I thought of you right away, called." I asked the cause of death. "Paper says she fell down the steps at night, an accident. That's all they say." I told him I'd drop over there tomorrow to see if I could get more information, that I'd call a cop I knew. I hung up, called Merlano and left a message about Wozniak. I lost interest in Star Trek and went to bed, fell into a fitful sleep.

಄

My friend McCarthy and I were playing basketball, when Lt. Clep wandered up. Till that point, Clep had seemed a buffoon, a joke as our leader. But recently he'd emerged as a commanding presence. While shooting jumpers he pulled Mac and I aside, told us he was investigating the theft of munitions, that he thought someone in the MP Company was a traitor. That was the start of our perilous partnership that almost got us killed. He wanted our help doing undercover work, reporting directly to him. Mac wanted no parts; he had a wife and young son. But I couldn't stay out of it, had gotten too curious, was pissed someone played me for a fool. Noble? Or just an idiot?

My dream moved to playing ping pong after village patrol. As usual, Mac was thrashing all comers when Percy walked in, bullied his way into the next game. Mac toyed with Percy, letting him get close but suddenly turning it on and kicking his ass.

Percy taunted him, suckered him into a fight and mercilessly decked him. Watching helplessly, I attacked Percy, got in a lucky shot, but cat-like, he reversed things, knocked me down, and was advancing on me. Percy effortlessly used his feet as lethal weapons. He always appeared to relax before striking, drawing his prey closer. Even knowing what was coming, I watched, paralyzed. And then the right leg shot out…

Dripping with sweat, I sat up in bed, got oriented. Just then it thundered outside. Another late summer thunderstorm in Philly. Biata's death had triggered the Nam flashback. And then I wondered: Was I about to meet another psychopath? I got out of bed, wandered over to the front window. I wanted to see if my bodyguards were there. Just wanted that assurance. I watched the lightning project odd shadows against the massive trees. Was that a man's shape? I waited for another burst of light. Seconds later it came; I looked but saw nothing but tree trunks. I stumbled back to a fitful sleep.

Merlano called back early, was stunned by my news. He barked, "Meet me here, get here fast. This is crazy." Soon thereafter, I walked into the police station and watched an animated Merlano holding court. He was showing a couple cops how to block-out an opponent for a rebound. "You gotta get your ass on him. Make him think your toilet paper, that close.

Then you buck your ass into him as the ball's in the air. Throws him off just enough to mess him up. That's how you do it, guys."

I continued up to his audience and shook my head in agreement. "When you have a fat ass like Merlano's, that move is deadly. Trust me guys, Merlano's as big an ass as I ever met." While his pupils chuckled, my old opponent stood looking at me with his dead pan expression.

Finally he grinned, "Let's blow this joint, funny boy."

Getting in Biata's house wasn't a problem. The ambulance crew was thoughtful enough to leave the door unlocked. Merlano told me to stay behind him as we entered. "Don't fuck-up anything, Frazier. Treat it as a crime scene, okay?"

I couldn't resist, "I'll stay on your ass like toilet paper, you know, like I'm gonna block you out."

Merlano turned to look at me. "The Tonight Show's looking for comedians, Frazier, missed your calling, maybe." The house was picked up, neat. The only clutter was a tea cup and cookies on a tray by a chair facing the TV. Merlano commented, "Good housekeeper."

I walked up closer, looked in the tea cup, noted it was half full. And there were three Lorna Doones left uneaten. "Cup's half-full, cookies untouched. That make any sense to you, Merlano? Wouldn't you finish the tea if you went to the trouble to fix it? Plus she lives by herself, why would she take more cookies than she wanted? I mean, if she wasn't that hungry, why take so many?"

Merlano spun around, looked at me but didn't say anything. He kept walking, entering the kitchen. I looked in the trash can and saw the dried tea bag.

I was poking through the trash when Merlano walked over and mumbled, "You got a point on the tea, don't make sense."

The living room had a small book cabinet, loaded with nick-knacks and books. I noticed the porcelain figures which reminded me of Crina's missing Hummels. I looked closer, could tell they weren't Hummels but they seemed nice. On the bottom I saw "Meissen" written. As I made a note of that, I wondered if she had a lot more at one time, now only seeing a couple on the shelf. A collector?

We went up the steep stairway and I thought of the poor old lady falling to her death, said, "A bad stairs to fall down." Merlano didn't respond, went in her bedroom and inspected the rumpled bed.

He said, "Looks right." And then wandered into the bathroom, looked around, opened the medicine cabinet. There were a few prescriptions in bottles, he jotted their names. "I'll check these out; she's supposed to have arthritis."

We left the house and stood outside, compared notes. "Mostly everything looked right. But the tea thing seems odd. Gotta think on that some."

We headed toward the car when I thought of something. "Merlano, last time I came here there was a neighbor who yelled when I made too much noise." I pointed his house out. "That one, maybe he noticed something. Seemed like a nosey type, I wasn't really that loud, he seemed to enjoy yelling at me. Know what I mean? Like the neighborhood know-it-all."

Merlano grinned, "Sounds like my old man. He's got Army binoculars and sits in the window all day. If a pigeon shits outta place, he knows about it."

The crotchety old coot stared at us out the second floor window as we came up the walkway. "You ought to introduce him to your Dad, Merlano. Maybe they could hang out, trade secrets on neighborhood espionage." I got no response; Merlano had his game face on. We banged on the door and waited. Nothing.

Merlano muttered, "Fuckin' A, buddy, answer the door."

I finally yelled, "Police, we're here to check on your neighbor's death."

The old man finally cracked the door, held slightly ajar by a series of chains. In a low voice, almost a growl, "Show me ID."

Merlano did, the guy agreed to talk to us but still kept the door chained. Merlano began by explaining what had happened, that at this point it seemed like accidental death, that we were asking around just to be sure. "Can't help ya. Didn't know her good. People here keep to themselves mostly." Merlano asked if he had noticed any visitors at her house recently. You could almost see the old man debating with himself before answering. "Nothin'."

Merlano gave him his card, told him to call if he thought of anything afterwards. He stared at the card, shut the door wordlessly.

Merlano drove back to his station and dropped me at my car. During the ride we compared notes. Merlano observed, "If Wozniak had visitors, you can bet that old bastard saw 'em. Fucker perches at that window dawn till dusk."

And then he added. "Guy like that ain't gonna get involved. Likes to bitch and moan about everything, but when it comes to action, he sits on his hands. A bitcher not a doer." I didn't disagree with him, we'd never hear from him. That gave me an idea, but I kept it to myself, Merlano wouldn't approve. I smiled to myself: No, he'd approve but he couldn't be involved.

～

I played ball that night, afterwards Jimmer told me I was invited for dinner. "I told Marisol you were having Nam flashbacks, that you were already unstable before that anyway and that you might be a bad influence on Jose. Still she said to invite you."

It was a bad idea to get into a word fight with Jimmer but I took a chance. "Not how I hear it. Marisol says you have no friends. That your arrogant personality is off-putting. She's thinking if neighbors see someone drop by, that might open the door."

Jimmer patted me on the shoulder. "Next time I tell the Judoka not to hold back, to use your nuts like a xylophone." I gave him the peace sign and walked to my car.

Marisol and I had rehearsed our story, so I sat with Jimmer while she made dinner. Jose was outside playing, away from the potential fight.

As he sipped a beer, I started. "Finish your brew, got something to tell you. By the way, are you in a good mood? And remember that what I'm going to say is for your wife and kid. Okay?"

I had his attention. He sat silently as I unloaded the story about annulment. That Monsignor Pugh thought she had a good chance, but that his cooperation might push it over the goal. His face got very red at first but had returned to normal as I finished. I left out the part about reconciling with his parents.

His answer was unexpected. "Fucking brilliant."

Just then Marisol walked in, "Did I hear right, James? Did you say brilliant?" Jimmer shrugged, "I know you love the church, that you feel disenfranchised being considered a sinner. Plus, even with my issues with Catholicism, I still think it's the best game in town. I would also like to see Jose go to Catholic school, might toughen him up some. There's nothing like a nun smacking your hand for writing like a mental patient." Marisol ran and hugged him like a long lost soldier. And that was that. We had a great dinner, talked about the hapless Phillies and afterwards Jimmer walked with me to my car.

He eyed me, "I wouldn't have done it myself, too proud. Thanks."

෧

Next morning, I drove back to Biata's house. I walked to the crusty neighbor's house, saw him perched at his look-out station, waved and banged on the door.

He took his sweet time and cracked the door ajar, growled, "Whatcha want?' I told him I was following up, seeing if he remembered anything overnight. His response was slamming the door shut.

Expecting that, I yelled, "Next time I come back it's to arrest you. Obstructing justice is good for 5 years in the slammer. I know you saw something. You got 30 seconds."

I counted off, and as I turned away heard the door open. "I don't know who it is but a big guy visited her a couple times a week. Always came at night." I asked if he could identify him, if he was someone from the neighborhood. "Na, never saw his face. Didn't look like a local guy. Mostly dark clothes. I think he had long hair, kinda covered his face. That's all I got." I asked when he first saw him. He scratched his chin. "Maybe 3-4 months, somethin' like that." He looked at me, "We done? Gotta take a piss." As I walked away, I thought that Crina had died almost 4 months ago. Coincidence?

WILLIAM

William liked it when Sylvan left the shop and he was alone with the treasures from the past. He was preparing to close up but was troubled with the Hummel matter. Unknown to Sylvan, William knew where the key was hidden to Sylvan's private office. He had seen Sylvan retrieve it from under the edge of the estate jewelry case when he left the keys in his car and didn't want to walk back outside. He usually snuck peeks in Sylvan's lair when Sylvan was out. That was when he first noticed the collection of Hummels. Now there was only one left. He wondered what Sylvan had done with the others and why were the cops looking for Hummels? He remembered the icy look he'd gotten when he mentioned it to Sylvan.

Sylvan was out and had been gone everyday this week. That puzzled William. Where was he going? Most times he spent all day at the shop and only went out early morning or after dark. Odd. William moseyed over to the estate jewelry case and found the office key. He walked to the rear and made certain Sylvan hadn't returned. Satisfied, he ambled to the office and entered the hallowed ground.

Sylvan was meticulously neat. He turned on the light and walked inside. Oh, my God! He saw the two porcelain figurines arranged neatly on his desk. Mesmerized by their beauty, he lifted one, confirming his guess, he murmured, "A Meissen crinoline group of the Marchand de Coeurs!" And then lifting the other, he gasped, "The Meissen Loving Couple. They're beautiful!" William loved old things.

He sat staring at them, marveling at the detail. He ran his hands over the figurines. Time passed. Hearing a noise, he turned and was jolted to see Sylvan's menacing presence. William froze.

Finally, in a low, controlled tone, Sylvan hissed "Get out." Sylvan never moved from the doorway, and as William slipped by, he grabbed William, pulled him close, "How did you get in?"

Still shook, William muttered, "Aaa…, thought I heard a crash. I thought maybe a, a, a rat. Saw you put the key there before. Just, uh, uh, uh wanted to check. Sorry." Sylvan released William and closed the door behind him. Not knowing what to do, William lingered a few minutes and then left the shop quickly.

DYLAN

I hadn't visited Mirella and Gertrude Rawley for awhile, so I called and asked if they were free for lunch. I heard a giggle as Mrs. Rawley consulted with Mirella.

She came back, "I guess we can work it in, we're going to The Academy of Music for a matinee but we can still make it if we eat early. See you around 11:30?" I almost laughed at her courtesy crumbs for an audience, but just confirmed I'd come early and walk with them to the little French bistro down the street. With the doorman Sullivan and vigilant Belden on duty, I hadn't been too worried about the two octogenarian friends. I wondered what would happen when all this mess was over. Would Mirella move in?

I parked outside Mrs. Rawley's brownstone, waved to Sullivan as I walked up. "All quiet on the Western Front?"

Sullivan nodded, "I've been watching every deliveryman that comes by. If I'm not familiar with them I don't let them get too close." And then he pointed to a billy club by his doorway seat. "Got it at an Army Navy store." And then he winked at me. "Kinda hope I get to use it, between you and me."

I smiled but hoped it never happened. "Just stay sharp, this guy has an uncanny way of blending into the woodwork. Almost killed a cop, don't forget that."

Belden greeted me as I got out of the elevator. "Young Frazier, how are you this fine day? I understand you'll be joining the ladies at lunch." I asked if they were ready. He grinned, "It won't be easy pulling them away from the "Laugh In" reruns. They watch them religiously before their lunch time outings."

I followed him to the parlor and heard Mirella almost squeal in delight. "Gert, can you believe that Judy Carne? If they 'sock it to her' any harder, she's going to pass out. By the way, did you hear she's supposed to be dating Burt Reynolds?" I waited for a pause in the mirth, announced my presence. Mirella turned, "Oh, Dylan, sit down and watch with us. Arte Johnson's going after Ruth Buzzi again." Had to admit, it was pretty funny.

Belden walked with us to "The Grateful Palate" but declined to join us. "I had enough of the Frog food during the war. A good old grilled cheese sounds much better. I'll meet you back at Mrs. Rawley's in an hour and will drive the ladies to the theatre." We entered, I saw my snobby waiter friend, who recoiled when he saw me.

I yelled quickly, "Hey buddy, did you solve the olive mystery yet?"

He started to answer but thought better of it and shook his head "no."

As he spun away, I added, "Tell the owner he might want to switch to Manzanillo olives anyway, California is starting to catch up in quality and no one will notice except olive aficionados like me." Mrs. Rawley looked at me for explanation. I smiled, "Long story."

SYLVAN

Sylvan had donned his new disguise and drove
slowly past the Grateful Palate, saw the cat lady,
snooper and some old lady sitting peacefully at lunch.
He looked up to his rear view mirror, said to himself,
"Caught you." He had followed the snooper all week,
made sure he stayed a safe distance behind the
bodyguards and finally got what he wanted. It looked
like the cat lady might be staying with the other one.
Could be a relative or just a friend. Either way, she's
mine now. He drove further down the street, parked
beside a busy group of shops, mused: Hope you enjoy
your lunch, cat lady. Won't be many more. To remain
inconspicuous, he bought a newspaper, wandered in
and out of a few shops, all the while keeping an eye
on the bistro. Finally, he got his reward, watched as
the lunch ended and they walked to the elegant
brownstone. He drove around the block and then by
the brownstone, memorizing the number.

DYLAN

After my amusing lunch with Gertude and Mirella, I drove to The Voyager to discuss my proposition.

Hoban's eyes got big when I told him my belief that a killer was targeting old woman from Eastern Europe with no families. "Jesus," was his only comment. "What I want to check is a list of files over the past few years with similar patterns."

Before Hoban could answer, I added, "What I'm getting to is I want Voyager to start paying me to catch this guy. He's defrauded you for big bucks with these two; there must be other victims he's targeting right now. I mean, you guys insure most of the factory workers in Philly; this guy's costing you a fortune."

Hoban called the Home Office, explained the two frauds and got approval for me to do this fulltime. The Audit Department agreed to do an urgent review of files to identify other possible victims in the pipeline. They would look for older retired factory workers, widows from Eastern Europe, and with legitimate medical problems that suddenly got worse. I added, "Who knows how long this has gone on?" Hoban said he'd get the list for me within a couple days.

As I walked away, he added, "Be careful." That's exactly what I thought as I drove away.

~

Gator had been pestering me to update him on the investigations. I called him at home and filled him in.

When I told him about Biata, he blurted, "You've got to shitting me. Another one, just like Crina Barbu?" And then I explained about the audit Voyager was doing, that they hired me to work on the killings full time.

I finished with, "What am I missing? What should we add to the check list?"

He thought awhile, "Start reading the Obits each night, like your buddy Hoban. Another ethic name might pop out that you recognize. In fact, I'll read them too. Make sure we got a couple sets of eyes on it. Then we compare notes after you get the list from the Audit guys."

I hadn't thought of that, "Good idea." We agreed to meet in a few days.

~

It was getting dark earlier, so I made it a point to hit the courts before dinner. Playing hoops relaxed me. No matter who was there or how good or bad the competition, it was always funny. One close friend was nicknamed "Scoot," because, like an aggravating gnat, he'd pester the hell out of you on defense.

Plus he was small and used that to his advantage. He got low, smacked at your dribble relentlessly and literally bugged the hell out of you. And Scoot could dribble like a magician, was fast as a cat and could drive to the basket better than anybody on the court. I loved to play with him. That night we won every game and stayed on the court till it got too dark to see the rim.

Afterwards, we drove to the nearby deli, bought quarts of Rolling Rock, a pound of American cheese, bologna, a jar of mustard, a bag of Kaiser Rolls and then returned to the courts to solve the world's problems. If Jimmer was there, we'd just sit and laugh at his pontification. But Jimmer was a dad now, also ran the judo school, so he rarely played anymore. So without Jimmer, we jabbered aimlessly, mostly telling stories about our youth, each of us trying to top the other with absurd things we did in high school. Mostly, I sat and listened to the old tales, things I'd heard a million times but still found hysterical. It was peaceful.

But my daydreaming was broken when Scoot told his new tale about a recurring joke his friend "Cuda" played on him. They called him Cuda because he had sharp, needle teeth, like a Barracuda. Let me describe Scoot so the prank will make sense. Scoot was very short but powerfully built. But he had an unusually long upper torso, only his legs were stubby, like fireplugs. The joke was "if Scoot had normal legs, he'd be 6'4" and would have made the NBA."

Scoot explained his story further. "Cuda's been calling me once a month from different places in Philly, saying he's spotted someone that "has my legs, the long legs that would put me in the NBA." We all chuckled as he continued. "He won't quit it. Now he's sending me pictures of long, hairy legs from all over the city. The last picture was at the Zoo, he had a Kodak of a set of giraffe legs enclosed." I laughed so hard I forgot I was after a murderer.

WILLIAM

William was pleasantly surprised. Sylvan seemed to have forgotten the break-in incident and things had returned to normal. William mused: When Sylvan had a smile on his face and pulled his hair back, he looked like a different person. In fact, lately, Sylvan seemed so amiable that he even started asking him what he did after work.

William answered honestly, "Mostly I read about our trade, trying to learn more about the pieces we sell here. I don't have any family nearby, they all moved to Florida. Most of my friends from work are too feeble to travel. So, our work has become my passion. The old German and Swiss clocks and figurines are the most beautiful pieces in the world; I didn't know what I was missing till I came here." Sylvan nodded, said nothing.

Sylvan told William to close up, that he could go home early. And then he added, "Would you like to borrow my book on German figurines, William? I doubt the library has anything with this detail."

William was thrilled, "Sylvan, I'd love that." Sylvan ambled off to his office and came back with a leather bound book.

"This should keep you busy for awhile, William. The level of detail in the pictures is unmatched, plus the descriptions are perfect. They match the precision of the art. Keep it as long as you wish. I've memorized the book, have the pictures etched in my mind." William took the book, thrilled. He put on his coat and walked out marveling at Sylvan's change of heart.

DYLAN

I called Hoban to see if he had the audit list yet. He said, "The Home Office is like dealing with the Army, 'Hurry up and wait,' you know, the normal fire drill." I told him about my experience with Army stupidity that I had in MP school, when they made my MP buddy Fleming guard a building all night that was empty except for a frog. Hoban replied, "You can't be serious?"

I assured him it was true. "I told Fleming they did it because they knew he had a way with amphibians." Hoban didn't react since he never met Fleming, who was about the pissiest guy you could ever imagine. Fleming disliked everything. I decided it wasn't worth explaining and let it dangle.

It turned out that Hoban did have an interesting case that needed checking, nothing to do with the fraud but something urgent in the mean time. I agreed to drive over right away. Using this quiet driving time, I thought over the similar facts of the Crina/Biata cases. There was no doubt the MO was identical. What a heartless bastard, killing old, defenseless woman.

And then I thought about what really happened to
Crina. He drowned her. Did she know what was about
to happen? How terrified she must have been at the
end. I shook my head, getting angry as I let that
brutality sink in. As I pulled into the Voyager parking
lot I made a vow. If I caught the guy, he would regret
he missed killing me with that car.

Hoban was grinning as I walked up. "Not used to
seeing you happy, Hoban, this must be rich" He laid
out a series of letters in front of me before explaining.
"Read these after I give you the background. He went
on, "Bob Amalfitano works for Houghlin Dictionary
Company and has been out on disability for 6 months
and is now applying for LTD, which would pay him
for another 2 years at basically full pay."

I asked the obvious, "What's wrong with him?"

Hoban continues, "That's where it gets fun. The
guy claims he has eyestrain, verging on strabismus.
That he can't focus long enough to work, since he's
an editor, that's a problem."

Still not getting the point, I waved my hand for him
to continue. Hoban starts laughing but composes
himself. "While this guy's out, he's writing the other
editors and criticizing their work, offering
corrections, all the while copying in the Chief Editor
and company President. Naturally, the other editors
are going nuts, bitching that the moron is well enough
to nit-pick them and should not only be cut off from
disability, they should can him." I listened, waiting
for a punch-line but none came.

Hoban smiled, "After you read a few letters, it might make more sense. Plus the President of Houghlin thinks this is kind of funny and wants to keep the guy but needs verification from us that he's really disabled." Hoban let me use a conference room to read the file and go through the letters.

As I read, I learned Bob Amalfitano was single, lived in Wayne, a nice neighborhood on the Main Line and had worked at Houghlin his whole career. He graduated from the U of P with a degree in English. He was now 50 years old and was out with severe eyestrain that was confirmed by his physician and twice verified by Independent Medical Exams. I looked back in his file and read that this was his first time on disability, he seemed an ideal employee. And then I started reading the letters he wrote to the rival editors. There were weekly critiques of his peers with widespread copies to the brass at Houghlin. The letters were written in a serious manner but were so absurd that I could picture the other editors becoming laughing-stocks.

I sat back and read the last of the 88 letters. This letter was addressed to his peer editor at Houghlin, Bill Fosco:

Dear Mr. Fosco:

Please excuse this intrusion into your very busy schedule, but I need this matter addressed before the next printing. As Professor Emeritus of Linguini, without portfolio, I would like your comments on the following:

- *Will the superfluous "L" ever be dropped in Llama?*

- *Are colored pictures being considered in the next printing? If so, how will you represent Dalmatians and Zebras?*

- *Does your Managing Editor, Norman Hoss trace his roots to the Ponderosa?*

- *Will you add the word "Schmu" to your lexicon? It means, "Anything you want it to mean" as in, "Isn't that outfit schmu?"*

- *Do you think it worthwhile to add "Bimbo" to your re-write? If so, is "Bimbette" also needed to further refine degrees of lasciviousness?*

- *Should you add more widely used profanity like, "Shit-bird", "Ass-wipe", "Butt-munch" and the very trendy, "Mo-fo"?*

- *You should consider replacing the picture of "Lemur." You show the Philippine Flying lemur when everyone knows the Ring-tailed lemur is the dominant breed.*

- *Why did the sex of the contortionist change? I thought the original female far out-contorted the male now used. Was there a feminist back-lash?*

- *Why have you skimped on the thumb index? Your last version allowed for generously digited readers. This change is off-putting.*

- *Can you make certain that the picture of "Gargoyle" is correctly aligned with that definition? It is now beside "Gargantuan" and could confuse.*

That's it for today. Please feel free to quibble with my request. I like to banter and would welcome the verbal sword play. You may know that I have an abundance of free time and literally have nothing that interests me other than reviewing our shared mission- providing clarity in an otherwise murky world.

Sincerely,

Bob Amalfitano

I left the office and headed toward Wayne, excited to meet Bob Amalfitano. Hoban had made it clear that Houghlin liked this guy and wanted to keep him on the payroll, that he was their most talented editor and would be impossible to replace. His last instruction was, "Use that fertile mind of yours, write a highly detailed description of his eye problem."

As I was walking toward the elevator, Hoban rushed after me. "Don't make the report too good, Houghlin might try to hire you. We need you here, Frazier." I hit the ground floor button and wondered if I could resist the challenge.

Wayne was a beautiful old town, full of Philadelphia charm. Named after Mad Anthony Wayne, a legendary Revolutionary War hero, the town was a pleasant combination of large estates and middle class homes, a nice place to grow up. I made a right on Old Eagle School Road, passed under the train bridge and made a sharp right towards his home. A train was passing by and I wondered how noisy it was to live that close to the tracks. As I pulled up to his old Victorian house, I imagined his daily walk to the train station. A painless commute in a city famous for chaotic traffic.

I usually had an accurate mental picture of the people I investigated. Knocking loudly, I pictured a dwarfish man, slender but with enormous, Coke-bottled glasses. Who greeted me was a tall, bullish guy with glasses perched on his forehead, ready to be retrieved as needed.

He looked at me with tired, red-veined eyes. "Are you the super sleuth Houghlin sent to see if I was malingering?" That made me chuckle,

I responded, "You're the first person I've interviewed that actually knew what malingerer meant. I'm Dylan Frazier, and yes this is to confirm you're still unable to work."

His answer was interesting. "This should be fun, come in." His house was sparsely decorated but everything looked expensive.

Most of the furniture was leather, in different shades of brown; and dark wood furniture, oak and maple, if I had to guess. Since I was expected to write an extensive report, my eyes scanned everything I could see. We moved to the library and not surprisingly an oriental rug, mostly burgundy and gold, matched the masculine burgundy leather chairs and chocolate couch. I looked at the books and Amalfitano confirmed, "I have an extensive collection of Dictionaries, that's probably not a surprise, is it?"

I liked this guy and got quickly to the point. "Your letters have caused a stir with your coeditors. They think you're well enough to bust their balls, so you must be well enough to get back to work," And then I added, "By the way, I love the letters and it seems you have big fans at the upper levels. So, what can you give me that will convince your numb-nut peers to shut them up?" He went on to explain that he had "floaters" in his eyes, which appeared periodically and made it impossible to function. "I need to be in a contained environment when that happens. Can you picture riding the train when this occurred? I'd need to be sitting the whole ride and as you might know, people don't give up their seats, even for someone with a seeing-eye dog."

Remembering my periodic commutes, I nodded in sympathy. "Brotherly Love doesn't apply to commuting."

And then I asked what really interested me. "Why are you after the other editors? That really intrigues me."

He gave me an answer I never expected. "One of my passions is being a gadfly. Most of the large corporations in America get notes from me periodically. I have a warped sense of humor and enjoy pointing out the absurd when I see it. It's like mental exercise, a creativity relief. For years I wrote the competing dictionaries pointing out their loose ends. When I got the eye problem, I scanned our own dictionary and found my peers wanting. I hate sloppiness, it irritates me. That's the short answer. The longer answer would become apparent if you met my co-workers, a world-class gaggle of nerds, just collecting a paycheck, absolutely no interest in what they do. Is that enough or do you want me to give examples?"

Bob Amalfitano spent the next hour regaling me with one funny tale after another. I wrote a couple down afterwards in my report but changed names to protect the guilty. For example, Bob told me, "Mr. X believes that dangling participles are undoing our culture and promoting a promiscuity of language that borders the obscene. He goes through the Bulletin every night and brings the newspaper in to work with every miscue circled. He reads them to us at coffee breaks, lunch and whenever we bump into him. This has gone on daily for 20 years." But the fun part was what Amalfitano did to silently get even.

He confided, "Every day I'd send Mr. X something about internal business that had an intentional dangling participle included. It was always about something innocuous, like 'I see your point peaking through this letter.' I was never too obvious but it made me feel better."

Bob had a wry smile on his face; he enjoyed telling me about his subtle attacks on his co-workers.

I had fun that night writing a glowing report about Amalfitano's illness and total eligibility for disability pay. The sad part was Amalfitano really loved his job and was stuck in limbo waiting for his eye problems to pass. Writing the funny letters was like therapy, an outlet for his frustration. Plus he worked with the same group of nerds forever and this was his moment to lash out. I would have loved to be there when he returned to work and faced his fellow editors. One of the benefits to this case was it made me spend time figuring out dangling participles. I didn't have the nerve to tell Amalfitano I was an English major but had never got the hang of participles, even ones properly attached.

SYLVAN

For the past few weeks, Sylvan had followed William when he left the shop each night. As Sylvan became unusually friendly and chatty, William opened up about his personal life, unknowingly giving Sylvan clues to his daily routines. Sylvan had thought about the best way to kill William.

He whispered aloud, "Violent burglary, one of those terrible accidents that befall the elderly." Sylvan scanned the neighborhood, decided it was seedy enough to make a robbery plausible. He made a note to visit the library to study articles on local theft. The challenge intrigued Sylvan. He had already made plans to hire another assistant, so there wouldn't be a gap in store coverage. Sylvan walked to his car and thought wistfully: Doesn't William know that curiosity killed the cat?

DYLAN

When I called for an update, Marisol told me everything was going well with her annulment process. "Even James seems to have embraced the classes. You should hear him debating religious doctrine with Monsignor Pugh. Last session James went after him on Purgatory. James kept asking, "Do the plenary indulgences really reduce time in Purgatory? Come on Monsignor, I mean, I saw one in the missal that said you could get 75 years off your sentence if you read the prayer once. Does God really sit up there in heaven judging the value of certain prayers justifying 75 years off versus this other prayer that drops only 50 years? It sounds to me like God might be a CPA!" Marisol started laughing and told me that even the Monsignor found that funny. "They have really hit it off." I hung up, happy that at least one plan was on track.

The following morning I went to mass, arriving slightly late, so I could grab a spot near Mrs. Keilmann. She usually sat near my mom and walked home with her afterwards. My plan was to walk home with them and mention the annulment proceedings but not to make it seem too obvious.

I called my mom the night before and coached her on how to bring up the topic.

Mom had found my involvement very amusing. "What's next with my meddling son? Are you going to enroll at Arthur Murray for ballroom dancing? My Dylan is becoming a real softie." I laughed, and then thought about my search for a sadistic killer, but said nothing to ruin her moment. Let her enjoy my gentler side.

Mass ended and I waited with for my companions.

As they came down the church steps, I asked, "Can I walk you young ladies home? Lookers like you shouldn't walk around without an escort."

Mom batted me on the shoulder and Mrs. Keilmann smiled benignly. "Your Dylan does have some of the blarney in him, Kate." My mom nodded, "He's my ticket to heaven, Mary, the dues I paid raising this one." I fell in beside them and chatted amiably as we headed home. They both worked on the altar guild, washing and pressing the priest vestments. I mentioned how nice Monsignor looked that morning.

Mrs. Keilmann concluded, "I like my priest looking crisp."

We were almost home before my mom asked, "I haven't seen Marisol and Jose lately, have they found another church?"

That was my cue. "Marisol and Jimmer started taking annulment classes with Monsignor Pugh but on Sundays decided to go to a church closer to their home. Once they have the first marriage annulled, they want to get active in their church community. Although Marisol is pushing Jimmer to move here because she's so impressed with Monsignor Pugh.

She told me she wants to be part of the church family here at St. Tim's." I tried not to look at Mrs. Keilmann during my monologue, fearing she'd sense a set up.

My mom got me off the hook, "Wouldn't that be a blessing."

Per the plan, I left quickly. "Sorry mom, gotta run. Have an early appointment but wanted to go to mass and throw the devil a curve ball today. See you, later. Nice to see you again Mrs. Keilmann. Maybe see you Sunday at mass. Bye." I jumped in my car and wondered if we had pulled this off. I would call mom later that day and get her read. She was chatting amiably with Mary Keilmann as I drove off. Would the tough old lady soften? Would she find a way to let Jimmer and his new family back in their life? Had the iceberg started to melt?

⨀

I called Hoban and got word the auditors had come up with a list of 10 candidates that fit the criteria I'd given them. "The bad news, Frazier, is that all of them are dead. The Home Office files are supposed to go back 20 years but the auditors couldn't find much documentation older than 5 years.

All these paper records are microfilmed after 5 years and somehow the microfilm got misplaced. Doesn't give you much confidence in the process, does it?" I remembered back to the days I worked as an investigator, had heard stories of "Iron Mountain" being the repository for insurance records. I guess that name was invented to instill confidence with customers.

I agreed to pick up the files and ended by telling Hoban, "Tell the Home Office to rename it Misplaced Mountain."

I went to the conference room Hoban reserved for me. I used a flip chart to categorize the similarities of the 10 deceased. The list was very similar to the notes from Crina and Biata:

Victims

1. *All women*

2. *All widows or unmarried*

3. *All Eastern European*

4. *All without family*

5. *All over 80*

6. *All with extensive medical bills*

7. *All medical bills dramatically higher within the year of their death*

8. *All found dead in bed of "natural causes"-*
   except Crina. ⅃ ℬαʈα

9. *All in fairly good health before the sudden*
   death

10. *All lived in ethnic neighborhoods*

I got out my Septa map and drew circles around the victim's neighborhoods. As I looked at the map it didn't take a genius to see the pattern. I thought: Using Temple University as the hub, all the victims were within a few miles of Germantown, Fishtown, Kensington, Frankford and Olney. I let that sink in. All the victims were chosen because they had the same characteristics. All had somehow encountered the wrong person at the wrong time. Helpless woman at the end of their lives, without any family to protect them. What drew them to the killer?

Hoban wandered in and looked at my flip chart and questions. "Jesus, Frazier, that can't be coincidence, can it?"

I shook my head. "Worse yet, we've got at least 2 murders a year for the past 5 years; how long has this been going on?" And then I added, "And this is just at Voyager; how many other victims are with other insurance companies? If this is true, this guy is not only a monster, picking out the old and defenseless and killing them for money, but he's disciplined." Hoban stood there with his hands in his pockets, saying nothing, letting the horror float in his mind.

Breaking the silence, I added, "We also need to add, 'Knowledge of medicine and insurance" to the list. The killer submits fake bills that are unlikely to raise red flags. None of these victims had outrageous bills. If that Doc hadn't called about Crina we'd never have spotted this."

Hoban agreed, "Plus you're right, he's not too greedy. He must get to a certain level or time and then moves on." I showed Hoban some samples of the fraudulent bills. "Look at the handwriting on some of the bills, similar but not exactly the same. But I bet a handwriting expert would say they were the same guy. And these are all standard billing forms. Where's he get them? Aren't these only available to Doctors or Hospitals?" And then I walked to the chart and added another question to the list. Is the killer a Doctor or in the medical field?

I called Merlano and told him what I'd found. He said nothing for a few seconds but soon added, "You're full of good news, aren't you Frazier? Anybody ever tell you you'd fuck up a wet dream?"

I let that pass. "This is worse than we thought, Merlano. This guy has probably killed at least 10 people that we know of." I thought about Mirella being the next victim and got more nervous. "We've got to stop this and stop it now." He asked me to bring the evidence, so he could add it to his investigation. I gathered my notes and files, headed out to meet Merlano.

I looked for my body guards as I left Voyager. Both Merlano and I knew I was also in the killer's cross hairs. My feeling of helplessness and dread reminded me of being stalked in Vietnam.

This killer knew my face and knew I was on to him. He had methodically killed people for years without raising suspicions. At least in Nam I had faces I knew to watch for. All I knew now was "a big guy with long hair" was involved. As I neared my car, I saw a large man dressed in a rain coat lounging about 50 feet away. My arms got gooseflesh. Breathing deeply, I calmed myself, walked toward him. When I got a few feet away, I stopped, looked at him.

He suddenly turned, saw me staring. "Fuck you lookin' at, man?" I relaxed, the big guy was about 20 years old, couldn't be the psycho. I smiled, "Sorry, thought I knew you."

SULLIVAN

Sullivan stood outside the door of Mrs. Rawley's apartment and surveyed the street. There was always lots of activity on the street, it was a vibrant neighborhood. Most of the residents walked to work, shopped at the local shops and went to lunch or dinner in the myriad of fashionable restaurants. And then add in all the visitors to this historic neighborhood every day. So spotting the person that didn't fit in was harder than he'd imagined. He kept remembering what Frazier had said. "This guy seems to blend in. Even the cops didn't notice him till it was too late." Sullivan tried to make it a game each day. Who doesn't fit in?

DYLAN

Jimmer's private sessions with me were paying off. I was at the point where even the elfin experts had a hard time landing a solid kick.

When I arrived last night, he was beaming at me, clearly pleased with himself. "I've got a surprise for you, Dylan."

I bit the bait, "What is it?"

He grinned, "I have someone your own size to fight you tonight. Let's see how you do with a full grown man trying to take your head off." Just then, a huge man, at least 275 came out dressed for battle.

He walked up to me and bowed. "You must be Frazier. Good luck tonight." He smiled at Jimmer and added, "He'll need it."

Jimmer led us to the sparring area and gave us the rules. "As in any judo competition, no strikes and kicks with hands and feet are allowed. However, to simulate a life and death struggle, strikes and kicks can be performed but must be held before full contact. If I judge either of you is overzealous, the match will be over. With that said, I do want to observe technique you would use if your life was at stake.

The match is over if one of you pins the other for a full 30 second count. Questions? If not, return to your position and begin."

And that's how it started. This was like fighting a circus bear. My opponent was unbelievably agile for his size. He wanted this over fast, came right at me and seemed surprised when I rolled with his charge and threw him hard to the mat. Shaking his head he rose and charged again. This time I dove sideways, swept his left foot and quickly kicked at his unprotected kidney.

I heard Jimmer's monotone, "Potential match ender." I went back to the middle of the mat and watched. The big moose rose, turned toward Jimmer, started to bow as if in defeat, but suddenly rushed, knocking me to the ground. Caught off-guard and smothered by his weight, I listened helplessly as Jimmer counted to 30 and finally said, "Match." I lay there for a few minutes, thinking of my arrogance. It was clear I had much to learn.

Jimmer had been unusually compassionate after my screw-up. He said the obvious. "Now you know what the killer might do. No rules. No giving up. If he's what you said, he'll fight till one of you is dead. You were doing so well, had total control of the fight but lost your focus. You must squash any thought that you're winning. The best judoka act like they are losing- at all times." There wasn't much to add, I knew he was right. Just as he had done as we grew up, Jimmer had my back. As I left he said something interesting.

"I'm glad you lost tonight. If you had hammered him, you might have gotten over confident. Now you know you can lose. Keep your edge."

❦

It was dark as I parked in front of my apartment. I saw the following headlights stop farther down the street and go dark. "Goodnight buddies," I whispered to myself. Before I opened the car door, I scanned the sidewalk. To my utter surprise, there stood the voluptuous Janice. I hadn't seen her since my lapse in judgment. I had sworn off the forbidden fruit and called Gator at home if I needed him. I still didn't trust my self-control. As I opened the door, I realized I was disheveled from my judo whipping; I must have looked a mess.

Janice asked, "What happened to you?"

I told her the truth. "A large fat guy dressed in a robe beat the crap out of me." Janice looked puzzled, not getting my self-deprecation.

I was still nervous being out in the dark and definitely not trusting myself fully, so I asked, "What can I do for you?"

She got right to the point. "I've got the feeling you're avoiding me. Did I do something wrong? I thought we were starting to hit it off." I had thought about this since going to Confession and getting forgiveness. Catholic guilt still had its hold on me. I answered honestly, "Janice, what happened last time was a mistake. I don't want to mislead you; I love Laura and plan to marry her."

Without saying it, I thought to myself: If I'm not too screwed up from Nam. And then I continued, "I'm sorry if I led you on. You're a beautiful girl and deserve better."

Janice folded her arms and looked at me. "I think I get a say in this. I know about Laura and that doesn't bother me. Things change. Maybe you'll forget about her after you get to know me better." She unfolded her arms and moved closer, brushing her breasts up close. And then she lifted her hands and rubbed my shoulders.

Before my resolve melted, I took her hands and put them down as I stepped back. "Janice, it's over." She had a puzzled look again, probably not used to rejection. While she was thinking, "And Janice, it's not safe to be around me. Gator might not have told you but I'm in the midst of a bad investigation, after a cold-blooded killer. Particularly after dark, this is a dangerous place to be. Let me get you to your car."

Janice stayed quiet as I got to her car and helped her inside. She rolled down her window, "I don't give up that easy." I was going to tell her how I had chased Laura for years, never realizing that the girl of my dreams lived 4 blocks from me. That Laura and I understood our attraction but knew I had to grow up before the timing was right.

Instead I said, "Believe me, it isn't worth the effort. Once you got to know the real Dylan, you wouldn't like him. Have a good night. Drive safely." She rolled up the window and started the old Beetle. As she drove away, I realized I was jumpy.

The conversation went as I'd planned. I just hoped Janice would move on. I walked inside, still edgy.

SYLVAN

Sylvan watched the snooper's encounter with Janice from his leafy hiding place. He memorized her license plate, planning on tracing it for an address, and then wondered how the busty girl fit in. She's probably a girlfriend. He remembered her moving close to the snooper, stroking him. He concluded: They're more than friends. This was his 5th night in a row watching. The bodyguards never let the snooper out of their sight. There was never a pattern to his day. He never came directly home. He got home after dark most nights. Rather than getting discouraged, Sylvan perked up. Maybe the chaos is the weakness. I could hit him when he comes back after basketball. He left his perch, headed towards the bodyguards, thinking: But those guys are predictable.

DYLAN

Merlano looked at my evidence and grimaced. "Fuck. If the press gets wind of this, the city will go nuts. I can just see The Bulletin headline, "Is Your Grandma Next?"

I asked him something that had bothered me a lot, "How's this guy getting to meet all these people?" Merlano sat quietly, didn't respond. It was helpful having him there to react to my questions, even if he said nothing. I continued, "Thought a lot about the Doctor angle and that doesn't add up. The victims lived in different towns and probably went to a Doctor, or maybe a clinic in their own neighborhood. At their age, these people wouldn't want to travel long distances. So, what's the link?"

Merlano finally said, "Anything about pawn shops in those 10 files? I mean, Crina had some pawn slips. Wozniak had some nice old stuff. We never found any pawn slips, but who knows? It's worth checking, huh?" I remembered the note I'd made about the figurines in Wozniak's house.

Opened my notebook and paged back. "The ones in Wozniak's house were 'Meissen.' I checked that afterwards, they're just as valuable as Hummels."

But I remembered back to my German grandmother's house, chock full of porcelain figurines. "Might not be that unusual, Frankie, these woman were from Eastern Europe and they all love that stuff."

Merlano nodded, non-committal, "Keep it as a question anyway."

I then got to what was really on my mind. "Think we need to bait the trap a little better, Frankie. Chances are this guy's watching me but your bodyguards are keeping him cautious. Time to change tactics. Maybe flush him out."

Merlano reacted quickly, "That's a bad idea, Frazier. All I need is this crazy fuck killing you. I know you think you're a hot shot, but trust me, when this guy goes for you, all bets are off. He won't freeze, you might. The bodyguards stay."

I knew that would be his answer. "How about making it look like they disappeared?" Merlano smiled for the first time that day.

WILLIAM

On Thursday nights, William went to his favorite Italian restaurant. It was his one treat for the week. Del Vecchios catered to an older clientele by running mid-week specials for senior citizens. With his work schedule, it was hard to get dinner before 6 pm, so Mr. Del Vecchio made an exception and extended the pricing to accommodate him. William smiled: It's nice to be a regular customer. William rotated between his favorite entrees each week, Veal Piccata, Spaghetti with clam sauce, and Lasagna. He thought about the marinara sauces. They're better than Mama made. Luigi DelVecchio always took his order and commented, "Excellent choice, one of our specialties." William enjoyed his lasagna this night and treated himself to cappuccino for dessert. He waved goodbye to Luigi as he moved into the gray Philadelphia night.

William rounded the corner and was shocked to see Sylvan standing there, hidden by shadows.

Before he could ask, Sylvan said, "I was hoping I'd catch you coming home. I remembered you mentioned going to Del Vecchios Thursdays after work. I just found a book on the history of German pottery.

It explains how the Germans were the first Europeans to discover the Chinese secret for hard-paste porcelain. You've taken such an interest in the subject that I rushed over, hoping to see you before you got home and locked up. I know you don't answer the doorbell at night."

He handed the book to William and fell into the walk towards home.

Recovering from his shock at seeing Sylvan in his neighborhood, William gushed, "Sylvan, That's so thoughtful."

Sylvan bowed, as if dismissing the effort, and added, "This book goes into more detail on German dolls. Heinrich Hanwerck was a genius; we should look to acquire one. With the German community in Philadelphia, there must be some hidden gems available." William listened in fascination, realizing that Sylvan was a walking encyclopedia on rare porcelains. Sylvan continued the history lesson. "Heubach and Kestner are my favorites, even more than Hanwerck. The Heubach dolls are truly cherub-like, so alive. But the Kestner dolls are all about the eyes, the gray-eyed dolls are mesmerizing."

They were about two blocks from William's apartment. It was a dark, over-grown street, most of the street lights out. William never liked this part of his journey home, was grateful to have Sylvan as company.

Sylvan must have sensed his unease, "This is a dangerous street, William. You shouldn't be out here all alone." William smiled, turned to agree, when the crushing blow knocked him to the ground.

He blinked through blurry eyes, struggling to regain focus, and looked helplessly at the looming Sylvan. A tire iron hung at his side.

Sylvan had no expression on his face as he lifted the iron rod to strike again. "You're just like a Kestner doll, William, old and fragile."

DYLAN

I called my mom early, before she went to Mass.
"How do you think my performance went over with
Mrs. Keilmann? Was it Oscar worthy or more like
Oscar Wiener territory?"

Mom liked my sense of humor but didn't react, she
was too busy thinking how to answer. "I didn't say
anything to Mary after you left. I wanted to hear her
reaction. She never said anything but I think I know
what she was thinking."

There was silence, so I asked. "Okay mom, what's
your read?" Mom surprised me. "Mary had tears in
her eyes, Dylan. Mary's not a crier. I think she was
shocked by what you said. I think she's starting to
soften."

SULLIVAN

Sullivan stood at his perch. He had begun to think that the killer could have no clue Mirella was living with Mrs. Rawley. He mentioned that feeling to Belden and got a tongue-lashing. "Sullivan, I saw that attitude get people killed during the war. The minute they thought the German's left, pow, that's when they got hit. In war, the leaders count on boredom happening, soldiers letting down. A killer is patient. Killers wait and hit when they see their victim relax. Count on it, Sullivan. Based on what Dylan has told us, this killer is methodical. He'll be coming after us. Stay on guard."

But Sullivan wasn't so sure. Rittenhouse Square was a bustling neighborhood but after a few weeks of practice, visitors had become easier to spot. Shoppers usually traveled in twos or threes, talked loudly, seemed excited to be out. The delivery people were rarely changed; this area was a plum route, most of their customers were within a few miles of each other. They didn't have to ride all over kingdom come. The cops let them double park, so there was no hassle parking. Some of the people evened tipped. A great place to work.

Sullivan had gotten to know most of them. Sullivan scanned the street. Same old, same old.

Just then a priest walked by and waved to him. And then he turned back and spoke to Sullivan. "Hello, I'm Father Melzen, new priest at St. Patrick's. I'm trying to get a feel for the neighborhood. I noticed your bellman uniform and thought maybe you could give me some pointers."

Sullivan smiled, "I've been here for almost 20 years, Father. I'm Presbyterian myself, so don't know much about St. Pats. But I know the area like a local."

The large priest smiled benignly, "St. Patrick's accepts all God's sheep, my son. Stop by sometime." Sullivan liked this amiable man but wasn't much of a church goer.

He shrugged in reply, "Ya never know, Father, ya never know."

The priest looked into the lobby where Sullivan spent most of his day. "It must be pretty quiet most of the time, what, maybe 6 families live here?"

Sullivan shook his head. "Believe it or not, Father, only 3 people live here, 2 widows and 1 widower, just two apartments and the penthouse.

The kindly priest smiled, "You know what the Lord says, 'It is easier for a rich man to pass through the eye of a needle than to enter God's kingdom.' Maybe I should pay them a visit and see if I can ease their passage."

Sullivan grinned, "Mrs. Rawley lives in the penthouse but is real generous, couldn't meet a nicer person." He pointed at the far elevator. "But them other two, now they are tight with a buck. Maybe they could use your help."

The priest laughed gently, told him he'd consider a special house call, bid him goodbye and ambled down the street.

SYLVAN

Sylvan looked back and waved again to Sullivan. He thought: Next time he won't bat an eye when I walk to his door. Sylvan adjusted his fedora, liking how his new short hair-cut made him look. Gentler, no more the long-haired menace. He continued to peruse the neighborhood, acting like the rookie priest trying to gauge the new parish. When he got to The Grateful Palate and entered, he thought: I'll order a nice cup of tea. Act like a proper priest. His plan was to be seen enough that he wouldn't be noticed as out of place. What could be more harmless than a Catholic priest? The waiter came up and he asked for a list of teas. The waiter rattled off an impressive array. "I'll take the Ceylon oolong, young man. They say it's good for the soul."

DYLAN

I decided to get home early, didn't play ball or have any judo lessons. Wanted to think about the case, I felt it was about to pop. But I kept thinking about calling Mac. I had to find time to do that, I hoped it would lessen my guilt. But this killer absorbed my thoughts. So I checked in with Merlano to see if he had come up with new ideas for the killer's occupation.

He answered succinctly: "Nada." But he liked the medical connection and was running down every Doctor's office and clinic in the area of the murders. I offered to help with the canvassing but Merlano didn't like that. "I don't want it on my conscience if you get fucked up doing our job."

I quickly told him, "I'm already fucked up," which made him laugh but didn't get him to change his mind. As I hung up I looked at the Philly map on my couch for the 100th time. What aren't you telling me? All the victims were of humble means and had normal health problems of octogenarians. How did you all bump into this psycho?

I thought about what I already had done. The first thing I'd checked was if they all had a common physician but none did.

And then I looked at medical supply companies and only found one match. I planned to check that out but didn't feel optimistic. There were bills from the 3 hospitals in that part of Philly, so I was visiting each one tomorrow to see if something clicked. I also wanted to see if the other victims had figurine collections. That would be hard to pin point since there were no living relatives. But I did plan to do some neighborhood checks in case the victims had friends who might remember collections of figurines. Maybe the killer is a collector?

My phone rang which broke my concentration.

Gator was on the other end. "You won't believe this Dylan. Janice just got the shit beat out of her. If that goofy boyfriend hadn't been stalking her, she might have been killed." I let that sink in, not sure why Gator was calling me about this.

As if he read my mind, "Janice said the mugger was a big guy. That he mentioned you after knocking her down. That he called you 'snooper'." And then he filled in more details. "The jealous boyfriend surprised him and probably saved her life. The guy had a club or something and held him off before he ran away. The boyfriend stayed with Janice, never chased him or anything."

I called Merlano and luckily he was working late. I filled him in and agreed to meet him at Delaware County Hospital. Janice was being kept overnight for observation and Merlano wanted to question her while her memory was fresh. I met Merlano at the front door and we got Janice's room number.

The jealous boyfriend was seated outside and got agitated when he saw me. "Fuck you doin' here.

You the one got Janice beat up."

He started to move toward me but Merlano pushed him back in his chair. "Sit tight, cowboy. Frazier had nothing to do with this. He's working with us to catch this maniac. Your girl was in the wrong place, is all. We square?' The lug nodded, sank into his seat.

Janice was a mess. The voluptuous girl looked like she'd been beaten with a club; her whole appearance looked somehow deflated. I did feel guilty, knew the killer must have seen her with me at some time. Had somehow figured where she lived, maybe followed her.

She looked at me through glassy eyes, "How ya feeling, Janice?" At first she didn't seem to recognize me, but then she put it together.

Through her mashed up lips, "You weren't kidding about being dangerous."

All I could say was, "Sorry." She shrugged, seemed about to slip off.

Merlano jumped in, introduced himself, asked if she could answer a few questions, that it might help us catch this guy. A garbled, "sure" was all she got out. He asked what the mugger looked like and what he said to her.

Janice seemed to drift off, but mumbled softly, "It was dark, I couldn't see much. He was real big, wore dark clothes, uuh, a stocking cap. Had his hair tucked under it, I couldn't tell the color, but I think dark brown." Merlano let her catch her breath, and then asked how it happened and what he said. "He came from behind a bush near my front door. I thought it was Teddy; he's been following me a lot lately.

But then he hits me with something long, like a bat, knocks me down and starts kicking and saying, 'Here's one for your pretty boy, the snooper. I didn't know what that meant but he kept saying it as he kicked me. Then Teddy shows up, that's all I remember."

Merlano called Teddy in and asked the same questions. He stood near Janice as he answered Merlano. Something came to me, "Did the guy have long hair?" I was surprised to see Janice grab his hand and hold it.

Both nodded at the same time but Teddy answered, "He had a cap on, I didn't see much hair." Janice nodded. Seeing them act as a pair, I thought: Looks like my problem with Janice is over. Teddy is the new knight in shining armor. Guess the fact that he stalked her was forgiven.

Unfortunately, Teddy didn't give us anything we didn't already know about the killer. "When I heard Janice scream I just went at him, wasn't looking at his face, just wanted to get him away from her." They looked at each other and beamed. Teddy was golden. Merlano gave them his card, told them to call if they remembered more details.

Outside, Merlano summarized what we learned. "He must be the same guy, big, dressed in dark clothes. That Teddy's at least 250, so if he says the guy's big, the killer must be huge." I mentioned the long hair but Merlano dismissed that, "It was probably under the cap, plus it was dark. Just didn't see it is my bet."

I let the hair thing go then I filled Merlano in on something he didn't know.

326

"Janice has been hounding me some. She works for
Gator, if you didn't know that. A couple days ago,
she showed up outside my place late, wanted to move
our relationship along, so to speak."

Merlano grinned, "How was she?"

I gave him my altar boy smile, "I remained pure of
spirit, if that's what you're asking. Anyway, I sent her
off, walked to her car to make sure she was okay. The
psycho might have been watching, followed her."

Merlano didn't say anything for awhile. "How'd he
follow her if she drove off in a car? You'd a seen him
driving after her. Your place ain't that far from the
corner, you'd of noticed something. How'd he find
out where she lived?" Before I could answer, he
added, "How often does she drop by? I mean if she's
hunting you every day, he could of spotted her before.
She the bitch in heat type?"

I wagged my head, "That was the first time I'd seen
Janice since this case got crazy, it had to be the other
night."

When I told Merlano that he threw up his hands. "I
got to think on that some."

As he was about to leave I had an idea. "Let's go to
my place, see if we can spot where he hid. Maybe that
will help." He agreed to follow me. On the ride there,
I saw there was a full moon, so visibility would be
good. Any time I looked at a full moon, it reminded
me of Nam, a Hunter's Moon was what they called it
there, made it much easier for Charlie to spot us. I've
disliked full moons ever since. The headlights broke
my thoughts; Merlano arrived, pulled directly behind
my car.

I had an idea on the drive over and got to Merlano fast. "Do you think the killer might have been outside the hospital? Maybe hoping I'd show up?"

All Merlano answered was, "Shit."

He pulled his jacket open and made sure his 38 was handy. As Merlano and I checked for the killer's hide-out, I said, "After we're done, why don't you pretend to leave, then walk back and see if this guy shows up?" He reminded me that the other day I told him to rotate my bodyguards; to have a crew in place at my house at night- but out of sight. So when I arrived after work the other crew would pretend to leave, maybe lure the killer into getting careless.

Knowing that, Merlano said, "I gotta warn the other crew, make sure they don't think I'm the creep. Wait till I get to my car."

Thinking the killer spotted Janice the other night, I retraced from where her car had been parked, trying to find where someone hiding could see her plates. We found a likely place, not far from the street.

Merlano said aloud, "Even with a full moon, the guy would have to be an owl to see anything much farther than this." He had a point. There was no obvious evidence that he was here, but it had to be the right spot. Merlano said, as if to himself, "Tomorrow, we'll get the night crew to stay where they can see this spot." Merlano looked around, "He could of parked around the corner and walked through the yard, been at this spot in a minute or so. Maybe we'll be lucky now that we know he's sneaking around here at night."

We walked to Merlano's car, he got in, made a call on his radio to "Team Foxtrot." He used a jargon of police 10 series codes that basically said, "I will be leaving by car and returning on foot. I'll be coming through the yard directly across the street from Frazier's apartment. Don't get too antsy." His team called in and acknowledged his warning. Merlano looked grim. "Frazier, if this guy comes, it'll probably be soon. If nothing happens in an hour, I'm going to figure it ain't going to happen. I'll call you when I leave. Got it?" I spent the next hour inside, expecting to get a call that they bagged the killer. What I got was a call from Merlano telling me he was on his way home. I spent a fitful night, but had no flashbacks.

SYLVAN

Sitting in his locked office, Sylvan cleaned the rare Meissen figurine with loving, gentle strokes. He thought about the pieces left in Biata's house. It was too bad she got nosey. He didn't like to dwell on the things already done so be began reviewing his next steps, anxious to finish the cat lady but realizing that he made some mistakes. He should have let snooper's whore alone. He never figured she had that big moron following her. He slammed his hand on the desk, jarring the priceless Meissen. He grabbed the figurine, making sure it was safe.

As he caressed the Meissen, a disturbing thought appeared from his subconscious. He realized this notion had been lingering for the past few days, looking for a way to surface. What if I get caught? What if perfect planning wasn't enough? Could they catch him through sheer luck? Was it possible that chaos sometimes played a part in the world order? Sylvan sat back and let his mind drift. After a few minutes, he regained control and a rare smile crossed his normally blank face.

Finally, he sat up straight at his orderly desk and muttered, "There, there, it's going to be all right." And then he thought about the snooper trying to fake him by sending the cop to circle back after they left the hospital and went to his apartment. He whispered, "You're way out of your league, boys, way out of your league." That thought calmed him; he continued to massage the Meissen.

DYLAN

Monsignor Pugh called and asked me to drop by, that he had some news. I hurried over. When he opened the rectory door, I saw the joy on his face. "The annulment went through; Marisol and Jimmer are free to marry in the Church."

Not knowing why, I yelled, "Yee haa!!"

Monsignor looked at me funny but slapped me on the back and added his own yell. "Praise be to God!"

I walked inside and got the rest of the update. "Marisol wants to marry right away and asked me to perform the ceremony at St. Tim. The wedding is next Saturday at 4 pm." And then he winked at me, "Miracles do happen, don't they Dylan. Miracles do happen."

Monsignor Pugh had already called the Keilmann's and told Mary the news.

"How did she react?"

I could see him thinking how to phrase it. "Quietly." But then he added, "When I told her I was marrying them in the Church this Saturday, she finally seemed to relax, at least that's how it seemed over the phone.

I think this is a big relief for her. Now we have to find a way for Jimmer to call and invite her. We might need your help there. You seem to have an unusual connection with Jimmer, almost like a little brother." I agreed to call Marisol first to strategize.

As I prepared to leave, "Say a prayer for me, Padre. Might need one of those 'Hell freezing over moments'." Monsignor Pugh raised his hands, giving me the Sign of the Cross.

I called Marisol and she surprised me. "Can you come over now? Let's not over think this with James." I got there in 20 minutes.

When he opened the door, Jimmer had a hard look on his face. "I see Marisol's trying to double team me, huh? What do you two have cooked up?"

Marisol took the lead. "You need to call your parents and personally invite them to the wedding. I know you'd rather jump off the Walt Whitman Bridge but that's what you have to do. I want Jose to have grandparents."

I jumped in, "Why go through all that work if you can't get your family back together. I know your mom was in the wrong but she's from a different generation. You need to turn the other cheek."

Jimmer got up from his chair, looked at us passively, "Screw you both." He left the room.

Marisol walked me to the door. She smiled, "This is just the first round, Dylan. James is still in shock, this happened so fast. Let him absorb it awhile." Then she got a contented look on her face and added, "Like I did at the negotiating table at work, I'll wear him out. My James has a loud bark but he's just a puppy inside.

Just you wait." She gave me a hug, "You have no idea how much I appreciate what you did for us. I never thought I'd get an annulment, but now that I have it, I want the whole enchilada." I agreed to call in a day or so to see where we stood. I walked to my car wondering if that puppy Marisol talked about might surprise her this time. I wasn't optimistic.

SYLVAN

Sylvan watched the bodyguards leave after the
snooper got home. Listening to his scanner he knew
the other team was approaching on foot and would be
in place in the next few minutes. One idea that
intrigued him was killing the snooper while the
guards sat outside twiddling their thumbs. But his
driving hunger was to get the cat lady. Then he could
take his time with Snooper. No need to rush. Just wait
a month, maybe two or three and wait for the worry to
slip away. He'll get careless, think it's all over. And
then I'll be waiting with Dick Allen's bat. Bang! A
tater to left field. Sylvan let that sink in and nodded: I
like that. But now it's time for the cat lady. He drove
off.

DYLAN

Gator called that night to check in. I told him about the latest on the Voyager cases, there were at least 10 more murders.

"Fuckin' A, this is a real cluster fuck." To a more cheerful topic, I told him about Jimmer's annulment, about my role as mediator for the wedding on Saturday. He weighed in, "I agree with you, no way Jimmer calls his mother. He didn't get that hard-headed by accident. Mary Keilmann is one tough broad. She makes my step-mother look like Cinderella." But then he told me the real reason he called. "Remember that guy William we met at Lost in Time? He got mugged the other night, beat to death."

I let that marinate awhile before asking. "How'd you know it was him, we never got his last name."

Gator had a simple answer. "They mentioned Lost in Time as his employer in the Obit. It's got to be him, right?" And then he added, "Fuckers are dropping like flies."

That prompted me to ask how Janice was doing. "She came back to work already. She said Teddy was driving her nuts, fussing over her so much.

But I could tell she kind of liked it. I think you don't have to worry anymore, Teddy's the man now."

Trying to lighten the moment after all the murder talk, I asked if Gator was going to sneak back to get that Robin Roberts uniform. "Might get a better deal now that William died, maybe the temporary help won't give a shit."

He chuckled in his snorting, distinctive style, "I forgot to tell you, I already tried that a few weeks ago. I learned that William was just the helper. I met the owner; now that was one tough son of a bitch. No way I'll be going back, even for my hero Robin." Before I could respond, I heard Gator's wife yell from the kitchen that dinner was ready. "Got to go, Dylan, talk to you tomorrow."

SYLVAN

Sylvan waited till the cat lady and her snooty friend got back from dinner and had gone safely inside. He made it a point to wave at Sullivan as he passed by earlier. He didn't want him surprised when he showed up later on. He'll think the new priest was visiting one of his wayward parishioners, just doing the Lord's business. Sylvan wasn't worried about Sullivan. But the older guy kept a close watch on the old ladies. He walked with an air of authority. He's the problem. He had given that guy lots of thought. For the past few weeks, he saw lights on in the front room till about 10 pm. Based on the flashing light, it must be the television room. His plan: Let the old ladies get nice and comfortable.

Sylvan knew the cat lady had bodyguards parked about a 100 feet down the street. They weren't far from the Grateful Palate. The old ladies ate there tonight and the cops just stayed put. He counted on them keeping their routine and they did. They were too lazy to move the car, had a bag of doughnuts to keep them busy. There was an alleyway entrance not far from the bistro and Sylvan made his way there.

The previous night he brought a gas can and hid it behind the dumpster. Sylvan fished it out and methodically poured the gas on the back of the restaurant. He wanted just enough fire to cause confusion. He dripped a trail of gas to the alley entrance, lit his cigarette and flicked it. Sylvan nodded as he watched the gas ignite. His eyes glowed as he saw the fire dart toward the rear of the restaurant. He was pleased with himself. It was time to go.

The bodyguards were downing another jelly doughnut when they heard the people yelling inside the restaurant. And then they were amazed to see customers pouring outside and running down the street. They looked at each other: What's going on? The driver got out and asked an excited customer what was up; "Fire in the kitchen, I think. Ain't hanging around to ask, smelled the smoke and took off." The other cop joined him; they wandered over to see if they could help. Sylvan had counted on that too. Cops like to help in emergencies. They'll never notice him going to the cat lady's building.

SULLIVAN

Sullivan saw the priest headed towards him, and then noticed the commotion down the street.

He came outside to greet Father Melzen. "Late night Father?"

The saintly priest smiled, shrugged, "The Lord's servants get no rest. " And then Sullivan asked what was going on down the street.

"A kitchen fire at that bistro, nothing to worry about I think." Pausing as if embarrassed, the priest asked Sullivan, "Would it be too much trouble to ask for a sip of water? I'm parched. I just visited a dying lady around the corner and have a long walk home."

Sullivan nodded, "Not a problem, Father. I got my own supply of goodies. I spend a lotta time here and don't like getting caught short. Come on in."

The priest came inside and watched as Sullivan slipped into a side room and came back with a cup of water filled with ice cubes. "I like it ice cold myself, kills the Philly taste pretty good." He noticed two elevators and fire stairway nearby and commented, "These old places sure need fire escapes. Look what happened down the street. Lucky the bistro is on the ground floor or it could be real trouble."

Sullivan agreed, "This place has all the bells and whistles. Only three people live in this building, each got their own stairway. All got lots of bucks, don't go chintzy on nothing."

Sullivan watched the kindly priest finish his water. "Thank you my son." And then he hesitated. "Could I trouble you for a refill? I'll be happy to get it myself if you point the way." There was a small kitchenette that served as Sullivan's office, also a small bathroom on the side. Sullivan said he'd take care of it, turned to get the refill. The priest followed him inside, pointed at the elevators and asked. "How are our wealthy friends today?"

Sullivan shrugged, "Mrs. Rawley's got a visitor, so it's busier than usual. But I like her, she's a gem. The other tenants, now them two aint much to write home about, if you know what I mean."

The priest nodded, "Most of the wealthy parishioners I've met at Saint Patrick seem delightful. Some people who aspire to wealth can be 'a long day', as the Irish like to say." As Sullivan turned to give the priest his water, he saw Father Melzen holding a huge wrench. Before he could react, the priest closed on him and crushed his skull with the steel bludgeon.

SYLVAN

Sylvan watched the lifeless mass, smashed his head again and said, "Sleep well my son." Sylvan went to the front door and locked it. He whispered, "Now comes the tricky part." He walked into the stairway to see if access was easier from the steps. Slowly, Sylvan scaled the stairway and found what he expected. He looked at the sturdy fire door, realizing it only opened from inside and banging on it would probably lead to a police call. "Plan B it is," he mumbled as he descended. When he got to the lobby, he went to the front door to make certain no visitors had come by. His only worry about setting the fire was that all the neighbors would alert each other to vacate their apartments. But then he decided these wealthy people didn't think about anyone but themselves. When he saw the silent front steps, he knew he was right. He went towards the elevator.

BELDEN

As was his evening ritual, Belden sat reading the Bulletin. The ladies had recently left the TV room and were playing Hearts at the far end of the Library. Mrs. Rawley was a formidable player but Mirella proved a worthy match.

"You're in trouble tonight, Gertrude, the cards are falling my way."

Mrs. Rawley laughed, "Pride cometh before the fall Mirella." They settled into their familiar chatter, making Belden think: What will happen when they catch this killer? Will Mirella stay? Gertrude has come alive since she arrived. It's almost like when Mr. Rawley was alive. And then he heard the elevator moving. He wondered: Strange, why hadn't Sullivan called?

Belden put down the newspaper and moved from his nook outside the library. It wasn't totally unusual for Sullivan to pop up, but he normally called. And that made him think about his sidearm, tucked snuggly at his side. Just then the door popped open and a priest lumbered out.

The priest raised his hand and blurted, "I think Sullivan had a heart attack. I was talking to him on the stoop, he collapsed; you better call an ambulance." The large priest moved closer. Belden hesitated, struggling with years of instinct versus his friend needing help.

He decided quickly, raised his hand, "Hold up, who are you?" Belden watched nervously as the immense priest moved toward him but then he suddenly slowed down. The priest smiled at him as he looked at his out-stretched palm.

He was now only a few feet from the butler. "I'm Father Melzen, the new priest at St. Patrick. I got to know Sullivan over the past few weeks while visiting parishioners in the neighborhood." His tone was gentle, got a concerned look on his face. "Do you want to go see him first or call the ambulance? We better move fast."

Belden started to back up, "I belong to St. Patrick's; I don't know anything about a new priest."

The priest smiled, "When was the last time you went to service, my friend? Monsignor King announced me four weeks ago at Sunday service. Did you attend that day?"

Belden hadn't attended mass for months but did know Monsignor King was the pastor at St. Patrick. But something sounded off. Catholics always used the term "mass" for the Sunday ceremony. The term "service" was more a Protestant phrase. And then he looked more carefully at his visitor. Dylan had said the killer was big, this priest was immense.

Thinking back decades to his military police training, he said, "Move back to the elevator.

I'll call the police as soon as you leave."

The bulky priest was about to protest, but smiled and began to retreat. "As you wish."

When he started to exit, Belden wondered if he'd been foolish. He turned and noticed the old women were watching, motionless at the card table, wondering what Belden was discussing with this strange visitor. But then the priest spun and bull-rushed him, closed the gap between them in seconds. Belden went for his holstered pistol but was too late; the priest plowed into him and knocked him over the small ottoman by his reading chair.

Gasping, Belden yelled, "Code Red" just as the intruder kicked the ottoman aside and pulled out an enormous wrench. Belden grabbed for his pistol, fumbled to aim as the crazed priest crashed the wrench into his shooting hand.

MIRELLA

Mrs. Rawley had moved rapidly to the gigantic doors of the library. Just as they'd practiced, the doors slammed tightly shut, she flipped the powerful deadbolt that locked them firmly inside. And then she fixed the second deadbolt deep into the floor. Mirella had run to the phone and called the police. Even though bodyguards were posted outside, Belden insisted that a call be made, "If the killer had gotten this far, somehow he had eluded the cops outside."

Nervous, Mirella fumbled her words with the police dispatcher. She heard herself say, "We've, we've been attacked, attacked by a priest."

The dispatcher obviously thought this was either a prank or an addled old woman. "Now, ma'am, let's go over this again slowly. You're saying a priest is attacking you?"

Mirella realized she sounded foolish but quickly regained her composure. "Now listen, sonny, I know this sounds weird but check with Detective Merlano. He's had bodyguards on us for weeks now, protecting us from a killer that wears disguises. So, are you going to get off your fat fanny and get us some help or do I have to call Merlano?"

The dispatcher regrouped quickly. "Give me your address. I'll have units there in minutes. Is the priest still a threat or has he left?"

Mirella gave him a summary of what they saw from the library, adding that the butler Belden had been clubbed and might be dead. When the dispatcher asked if they were in a safe place, he got a chuckle from her answer. "He's got as much chance getting in here as the Phils winning the World Series." Just then Mirella heard a loud crash into the thick, cherry wood doors. She turned back to the phone, "He's crashing into the door but it's built like a vault. Hurry up, though, we don't want to test this too long." The dispatcher told her to stay on the line and to keep him apprized on what was happening.

SYLVAN

Sylvan stood over Belden, ready to deliver another blow, when he heard the doors slam. Realizing what happened, he got a crazed look in his eyes as the deadbolts went into place. Frustrated, he charged the massive doors, slamming his 350 pounds into the relentless wall of old growth cherry wood. Sylvan bounced back and then charged again. Realizing no amount of rage would get him inside, he fought to compose himself.

Finally, he conjured up his kindly priest voice to cajole them. "Now ladies, this isn't what you think. Poor Sullivan is dying in the lobby. Your butler just misunderstood and attacked me, I was just defending myself. Open up and we'll sort this out. Let's hurry, now." Sylvan was pleased with himself, he was so reassuring.

But the response he got stunned him. "You filthy coward; if I was younger, I'd come out there and whip you myself. What kind of maniac kills poor defenseless cats? A coward is what you are. The cops are coming; we'll be looking at you in jail before the nights over. Then we'll see who the tough guy is." Sylvan realized the opportunity was lost. He stepped back from the door, tempted to rush one more time.

Instead, he surveyed the apartment, thought: I have to get them out. Now. As he entered the kitchen, an idea came to him. He expertly gathered supplies and moved toward the door. Sylvan became very happy. Just like old times, he thought.

DYLAN

At about midnight, the loud ringing started me awake. My first thought: Flashback. I looked around, saw the familiar surroundings. Still in civilization, I was glad to see. And then I realized what it was, cleared my throat and fumbled my way to the phone. And then the surly voice of Merlano came on, he filled me in on what happened.

All I could say was, "You have to be kidding me. Where the hell were the bodyguards?" He explained about the decoy fire, that the killer had slipped by them. Realizing the depth of this, I suddenly became enraged, "I'm coming over there, Frank, you better get those worthless pieces of shit out of there or I'm going to…" Merlano hung up.

The ride over to Mrs. Rawley's was a blur. I was still half believing this was a nightmare, that what Merlano had told me wasn't real. I saw the fire engines as I pulled down the street. The police had the block barricaded, keeping onlookers at bay. When I saw the crowd, I realized how drawn people were to disaster. Irresistible. It took a call to Merlano to get the cops to let me through. As I strode up, he asked, "You cool down yet? There won't be any shit with the bodyguards.

They fucked up; they know it and you ain't going to
help by rubbing their noses in it. Got me?" I gave the
peace sign.

We walked to what had been Mrs. Rawley's
apartment building. What stood was a charred
skeleton of a once beautiful brownstone.

I looked at Merlano, "What happened, Frankie?"

He shook his head, "Near as I can tell, the killer
faked the fire down the street. The team watching
Rawley's was parked near there. When they went to
check out the fire, the guy must a gotten into the
lobby somehow and clocked Sullivan." He looked
solemn, "His skull's crushed, probably dead instantly.
Must of been a pipe, something heavy." I stared at
Merlano, not saying anything, eyes big. He went on,
"Anyways, then he got up to the penthouse, knocked
out Belden somehow, then set the place on fire when
he couldn't get to the ladies." I still said nothing,
waiting for more.

Merlano looked at me, a sense of dejection in his
eyes. "The ladies didn't make it, Frazier. Place went
up like a tinder box. By the time the Firehouse
figured there were two fires on this street, the place
was an inferno." I could see his anger as he added,
"They never had a chance." I had hoped that there
was a happy ending to this horror story but this
wasn't the night for miracles. I slumped against a
nearby cop car and tried to absorb how bad this had
gone. I wanted to cry for those sweet ladies but anger
held back the tears. My rage was burning, but then
my own guilt overwhelmed me as I thought about
what I'd done.

My breathing labored. I stayed silent as Merlano filled in details.

Some of this theory had come from Belden. He had a broken arm and smoke inhalation but somehow crawled to the elevator, made it to the lobby. Fireman dragged him to safety when they broke in. Merlano got this story from him as the medics worked on him, getting him into the ambulance.

Merlano looked at me, "Belden was pretty wacked-out, so I'm not sure how accurate this info is, shock makes your memory suspect."

I finally shook off my funk, "What hospital?"

Merlano nodded north. "At Hahnemann, I'm heading over there in a few minutes. Belden was lucky, apparently the killer got distracted when the ladies locked themselves in the library. He got too busy setting the fire, never finished him off. Probably never figured he'd get out. He's a tough old guy."

As we were walking towards his cruiser, Merlano added, "He said the killer was dressed as a priest."

I had gathered myself some, looked at him, "This just keeps getting worse. Who would figure a priest?"

And then Merlano added, "He said he wore a hat, a nice Fedora." After a few more seconds, he continued, "My old man used to wear a Fedora to work. This guy's smart, most people trust someone in a hat. Kind a like an authority symbol, a father figure, know what I mean?" I thought of my own dad walking off every morning to work, trusty hat on his head. Even in the summer. Merlano was right; this guy didn't miss a trick.

We road silently as we headed toward Hahnemann. I was thinking about Belden, how careful he was.

But this guy somehow tricked him enough to catch him off guard.

But then I said out loud what haunted me. "I fucked this up royally. If I didn't stick my God damned smart ass into this, none of these nice people would be dead."

Merlano spun his head at me, pulled sharply to the curb, put the car in neutral, and looked at me hard. "Just stop that, Frazier. This guy's a monster, a smart monster. He would of gotten to Mirella if she stayed at her apartment. She would of died in that fire. You did the decent thing, the smart thing, trying to protect her. The rest is just a shit storm."

I wasn't consoled. "But I had no right to involve Mrs. Rawley and her people. Sullivan's dead. Belden, who knows what he'll be like after this. He'll hold himself responsible, that's the kind of man he is. Jesus, Mirella and Mrs. Rawley's are dead! What the hell am I doing?"

Merlano softened a little. "Frazier, you did the right thing. Rawley was happy to help. Based on what my crew said, she seemed happy as a clam. Almost acting like a teenager with a new best friend. She knew the risks, was glad to help. Let's focus that self-pity on fucking this guy up, making sure he never gets a chance to kill again, right?"

I looked at Merlano, a stone cold gaze, "If I get a shot, I'm going to kill this guy." I could see Merlano processing this, but he said nothing.

We went to the valet parking lot. Merlano shrugged, "One of our few perks, no one tickets a police cruiser, even if it's parked illegal." We ambled to the Emergency entrance as an ambulance pulled up.

Both doors flew open as the emergency crew sprung into action. We stepped aside to let the medics do their work. The driver rushed around, threw open the back door, and then the other medic jumped back to help, pulling out two stretchers with old ladies laying on them. I stared dumbfounded. Gertrude and Mirella lay there, looking at me, Mirella finally said, "What took you so long?"

꙳

All I could do was rush over and hug them both. They asked about Sullivan and Belden.

Merlano hesitated, weighing what to say, then answered, "Belden should be okay but Sullivan's dead. I think Belden'll be fine, might be in shock, you never know. He's lucky to be alive." You could see the horror on both ladies' faces. They felt elated they had escaped but now Sullivan's death was a shock.

The medic intervened when he saw his patient's forlorn looks. "We need to get the ladies in the ER. You can walk with us but let's not tire them out. They had a rough night, okay?" We followed as they were wheeled inside. I asked the ladies what the killer looked like.

Mirella spoke first. "A priest, at least that was how he was dressed. He wore a nice hat; but it looked funny on him because he was so big."

And then Mrs. Rawley piped in, "I think he just got his hair cut, he looked groomed."

Both ladies seemed to be enjoying all the attention; it probably prevented them from thinking about Sullivan.

The medics kept shooing us away but Merlano was a bulldog. "Couple more questions fellas, these ladies saw this killer, we need some info, just a few minutes more."

While he bought time, I asked how they got out. Mrs. Rawley smiled, "You can thank my careful husband. We bought the penthouse because it had a vault hidden off the library." She saw my puzzled expression. "The vault had an escape passage with a stairway that led to a tunnel under the garage. He was a cautious man. With our money, he always felt we were a kidnapping target." She smiled beautifully, "He would have been pleased we finally got to use it."

Merlano caught the gist of the escape story and gave Mrs. Rawley a rare smile. "Now that is friggin' outstanding. Oops, sorry about my language."

Mrs. Rawley shook him off. "Since Mirella joined me, I've gotten a true education on colorful language. My dear friend swears like a sailor."

Mirella beamed proudly, "It served me well at work. Cussed like one of the boys."

Merlano asked if they would work with a sketch artist; try to get a description out that police could work with. "Maybe someone will recognize this guy. We need a break." They nodded enthusiastically. The medic shrugged in defeat.

We told the ladies we would check on them tomorrow morning. Merlano added, "We'll have bodyguards outside your room.

No one gets in but the Doc and the nurses." And then we left to check on Belden. We went to the front desk and were told he was undergoing surgery.

When Merlano persisted, the nurse scowled at him. "He'll be knocked out from the anesthesia. Believe me Detective; he won't be making much sense for a day or so."

It looked like Merlano was going to argue but he finally nodded. "See you tomorrow morning, nurse. That tough old bird will surprise you."

I followed Merlano and silently fumed as he met with the bodyguards. He had new teams to guard the three survivors. He gave specific orders. "Nobody gets in but people you know. Any new face, tell them to take a hike. No exceptions. Anyone tries to Bogart you, threaten arrest. No more fuck ups got it? This killer might come back. He's a big guy, like a side a beef. See anyone like that nearby, call me but stay at your post. Wait for back up. I'll have a squad car nearby, out of sight. Remember, this guy will try to lure you away. He's smart. He's been a step ahead of us every time. Won't happen again, got it?"

Suddenly furious, I pushed in front of Merlano, stuck my hands in their faces, "If you fuck this up, you'll have 200 lbs of pissed-off to deal with."

Merlano pulls me away but turns around, looked at the bug-eyed cops, "He aint kidding."

Merlano was quiet as we walked to his car. I was expecting a lecture but he said, "Thing is, this guy's got balls. It's almost like he likes the challenge of killing these people while we watch them. Know what I mean?"

I said nothing, letting him finish his thought. "He's careful, but takes chances. I don't think he can help himself now. He'll go ape- shit when he finds out they got out. He's probably patting himself on the back right now. Thinks everyone's dead. I got to figure how to use that. I got to think on that."   There wasn't anything else to say. He was right, we had to think. We had to make sure this murderer was stopped.

&

It was still early morning when I got home, was thinking about taking a nap. It was useless, my mind was racing. I flipped open my notes and added new details:

The Killer

1. *New disguise- priest.*

2. *Where does he get disguises?*

3. *Wore a fedora*

4. *Cut his hair?*

5. *Used fire again.*

*6. Ask Merlano about arsonists who fit the
description.*

7. Takes calculated risks.

8. Likes the challenge?

9. Thinks Mirella and Gertrude are dead.

10. How does he spot the bodyguards?

11. How to use the botched killing to trap him?

Still antsy, I needed to think about something else so I called Marisol to check on progress with Jimmer. Forgetting that it was early, I could tell by her sleepy tone that I woke her.

I quickly apologized but she cut me short. "The rock has cracked, Dylan. I gave him the silent treatment for two days, he couldn't stand it. Finally he said, 'So this will make you really happy? You know my mother's no walk in the park. Forget that Aunt Bee image in your head. My mother is one tough daughter of a bitch.'" I could picture Jimmer delivering the message. Mariol went on, "So that broke the ice. He's already talked to his father, told him about the wedding. James said his father was speechless, said he thinks he was crying. Apparently he never saw his father cry, so that choked him up. James had tears in his eyes when he told me.

Anyway, he's going to visit his mom tonight and invite her to the wedding."

Starved for good news, I whooped joyfully into the telephone. Marisol started to laugh and that made me crack up. When I settled down, I asked her to keep me clued in. "The wedding will be small, but you are a guest of honor. If we have another child, I will name him, or if it's her, Dylan. You made this happen. Where I come from, people never get divorced, they just move on. From the bottom of my heart, thank you." I hung up thinking at least one of my crazy ideas worked out. Now to catch this psycho.

As I did throughout my life, when I couldn't relax, I went to the basketball court and shot hoops. The sun had been up for awhile but it was still quiet outside. I enjoyed the peace as I dribbled full court, doing lay-ups, just letting my body move. All the facts about the killer rattled around as I began my shooting routine. I started from 5 feet away on each side of the hoop and only moved when I made 5 in a row. Finally breaking a sweat, I moved to ten feet and shot mindlessly. Pretty soon, I forgot about the case and focused on my target. The shots were falling and I remembered the coach who taught me to shoot telling me that shooters are made in the summer. "Good mechanics, constant practice and you'll be a good shooter." It was a life lesson for me, hard work usually beats talent.

Finally exhausted, I drove home and picked up the newspaper as I headed upstairs. I flipped to the obituaries to see if any names popped up that I knew. Halfway through, I suddenly remembered something Gator said the other night.

Excited, I called him to follow my hunch.

My groggy friend answered, "What the hell do you want at 7 AM in the morning?"

I told him about last nights disaster and he listened quietly. "God damn," was his accurate summary.

I got to the point, "What did the guy look like who owned Lost in Time? You said William worked for him, something about being tough. What did you mean?"

Like a good lawyer, Gator gave me a full description of the pawn shop owner. "He's a big guy, more blocky than tall.
Built like a tackle, pulling guard, kind of like that. He had funny eyes, kind of like a snake. He didn't blink much, looked like he was wound tight. Creepy is the right word, he was definitely intense." I told him what I was thinking. Again he added, "God damn." My mind was whirling. But then he jumped in, "Call Merlano, don't do anything stupid; let the cops check him out. Okay?"

I was about to hang up, when I asked, "Did he have long hair?" Gator exhaled, "It was pulled back in a ponytail." I didn't hear what he said next as I went for the door.

I thought as I drove. Should I call Merlano or check it out myself? It was still early, so I parked down the street and walked by the door to see if anybody was inside. The sign said, "Closed" but I noticed the store hours said 9 am till 8 pm, except Sundays. There was no movement inside, still a few minutes before opening time. What to do? I kept walking down the street and headed toward the back alleyway. Wanted to make sure there were no surprises.

I walked by a phone booth as I hit the corner. Was I being stupid? I circled back and stood outside the Bell booth.

When I made my way into the alleyway, I saw a black Chevy van parked behind the pawn shop. I walked closer and peered inside. Is that a police radio? It wasn't the same as Merlano's, older probably. Is he a retired cop? I thought about how this killer seemed to stay a step ahead of us. I circled the car but found nothing else of interest. The backyard was surprisingly neat. No undergrowth like the neighboring shops. I thought about that: The owner is neat, organized, doesn't like mess.

I walked to the end of the alley, circled back to the entrance. It was a few minutes after 9 am, time to pay a visit. The sign now said "Open" but the door was shut. Would I be the first customer? Or was someone already inside? I didn't want any company. I pulled the door open and heard a chime ring. Was that an alert to the owner? Or was it one of the many clocks? So far, I saw no movement. And then my eyes hit the row of costumes. I tightened up as I spotted a priest's cassock hanging on the end. Was it there last time I was here? Another clock chimed, I almost jumped out of my skin. I breathed in deeply, getting set.

SYLVAN

Sylvan was sitting in his office as he heard the door chime. He was reading the newspaper description of his handiwork. "Deadly Fire Claims Elderly Ladies." But he could find no verification that Sullivan and the butler were also dead. The story concentrated on the wealthy woman, Gertrude Rawley. The cat lady was almost an afterthought. She was described as "a companion." Sylvan was troubled. What happened to the men? They could identify me. I have to find out. I can't have any witnesses. And then he thought about the snooper: He's next but there's no need to rush. Sylvan liked that thought. But now to see who's come to the shop so early. Perhaps it was his lucky day. A new project?

As Sylvan moved toward the door, he spotted the tall customer inspecting the rack of costumes. There was something familiar about the profile. And then the stranger turned and Sylvan froze. He couldn't believe his eyes. This didn't add up. He couldn't know. But why was he here? Sylvan was wearing a Cub Scout Leader's uniform. He stood motionless, thinking about what to do. He remembered William had mentioned a couple guys had inquired about Hummels a few weeks ago. Was it him?

Does he know about me? Sylvan ran that through his keen mind. Slowly, he moved into the showroom.

DYLAN

I heard movement and spun quickly. There stood the biggest Cub Scout I'd ever seen. If I wasn't so pissed off and tired, I might have laughed. But I was in no mood for humor. I still had only gut instinct working for me so I had to proceed slowly. But what I wanted to do was charge this monster and beat the hell out of him.

Instead, I said, "Was in here a few weeks ago looking for Hummels. William helped me then."

The oversized Scout nodded, "William met an unfortunate accident. He was killed by a mugger. So senseless, he was a gentle man." This was said in a quiet monotone, almost a whisper. But the quiet tone didn't match the intense eyes. They shone with controlled fury, like a cobra fixated on the flute.

The big man wandered closer. His movement was effortless, like a Summa wrestler ready to battle. I moved toward the costume rack, keeping my distance, putting an obstacle between us.

I looked at the costumes, "Still have the Robin Roberts uniform?" I saw that registered with the giant. But before he could answer, "My buddy was in here the other day asking about it. He's a lawyer but he'd trade that to be a ballplayer.

Loves the Phils. He's the one told me about you.
Mentioned the price went up from the last visit. Too
bad about William. Funny how the old and
defenseless seem to be such easy prey." He looked at
me oddly before I added. "Only cowards would pick
on old people, don't you think?" His reptilian eyes
widened.

He edged closer. This time I did the unexpected, I
moved at him quickly. This startled him, he moved
backward. I looked at him intently, "You didn't
answer me, isn't it cowardly to pick on old people.
Wouldn't someone like that be lower than whale shit
on the evolutionary scale?" I had caught him off
guard.

He walked around the rack and pulled out the Robin
Roberts uniform. "Is this what you were looking for?"
And that made me notice the Scout cap covering his
neatly trimmed hair. Looked like a recent cut, still
sharp, everything in place. A careful, tidy man.

I went at him again. "Still checking on Hummels. A
little bird told me you carry them occasionally. I think
some dead beat stole them from a friend. Thought
maybe he sold them, wanted to see if they turned up
recently." Before he could answer, I moved farther
away, toward the room from where he'd suddenly
emerged. I pointed, "What do you keep back there,
bet it's the good stuff, like the stuff you don't want
the cops to see."

The large man's eyes fluttered a few times, but his
face remained still. He didn't answer for awhile but
then added, "That would be illegal. I run an honest
business.

This is an honorable profession that a few scalawags have given a bad name. Lost in Time operates by the book, meticulous."

Trying to keep him upset, off balance, "What did you do with the Meissen that Biata sold to you? I'd like to see that one if it's still here." This time he wasn't ready, he actually recoiled, was shocked.

But he soon recovered, "I don't know who that is, I don't have any Meissen pieces, never have." I was now close enough to the doorway to see a private office with the door slightly ajar. My nervousness had disappeared, anger was driving me. I turned and bolted toward the office, realizing that if I was wrong, I'd probably get locked up. I pushed open the door and scanned the room. Clocks were everywhere but what jumped out were porcelain figurines stacked above the desk like trophies. I turned to see the human freight train racing toward me.

SYLVAN

Sylvan's mind was a blur. The snooper was asking
questions about William, like he knew I killed him.
How could he know that? Why is he asking about
Hummels? Why is he calling me a coward? Sylvan
thought back to Aunt Anca taunting him throughout
his childhood: I fixed her, didn't I? But still the
snooper baited him. Now he's asking about Biata's
Meissen. Had she said something to him before he
killed her? And now he was moving towards my
office. He remembered back to his football days when
he took care of anyone calling him Ding Dong or Fat
Piece of Shit. He thought of superstar Ricky Silvato
mocking him. Sylvan looked at the snooper's knees
and charged.

DYLAN

The huge man was unbelievably fast. When he was 8 feet away he dove at my knees. My months of training instinctively caused me to pivot and focus. As I spun to my side, I lashed my right knee into the shoulder of the charging beast. Oddly, I remembered Jimmer repeating, "The clavicle is brittle, will snap like a twig, cause incredible pain and disable the shoulder." I heard the sickening crunch but the impact knocked me off my feet. Disoriented, I breathed deeply and jumped to my feet. Where was he? And then I heard him moan. Spinning again, I spotted him lying on his side. He was groaning like a wounded beast. Wary, I backed away and got in front of him. He was cradling his shoulder, in excruciating pain.

I looked at him, "Get up you gutless bastard. This isn't over."

I stepped nearer, kicked him hard in the shin. He winced in pain and began to mumble to himself.

Through his moans, "I'm calling the cops. You broke my shoulder."

I moved a little closer. "If you don't get up, I'll break the other shoulder. Not so much fun when it isn't a defenseless old women, is it?"

The big scout master started to rise, stumbled into the seat by his desk. He kept his head down, mumbling incoherently. I began to have some doubt. Was this pathetic creature really a mass murderer? He turned and sprawled on his desk. He seemed to be in shock. I turned, looked for a phone, ready to call the police. That was a mistake…

❧

As I grabbed the phone, the groaning mass came alive. Lightning fast, he grabbed the closest figurine and swung at my face. I saw the motion and leaned back enough to avoid full contact. Still the glancing blow brought stars and I staggered. As I struggled to regain focus, the monster crashed into me, forcing me to the ground, his enormous weight burying me underneath. Gasping for air, I saw him raising the porcelain club, ready to deliver another blow. Funny how strange thoughts pop into your head at odd times. I recalled my recent lesson with Jimmer when the fat opponent suckered me. As the figurine rose, I thought: Not this time.

The jugular notch is that super sensitive point near the center of the lower neck. Jimmer had trained me to jab this spot if my life depended on it. I thrust my middle and index fingers in the monster's exposed neck. As I drove my fingers deep, I saw the monster's eyes roll back in his head as his breath stopped.

Lightning bolts shot within my assailant's brain; stunned senseless, he fell backwards, freeing me. I rolled to my right, jumped to my feet. Taking no chances, I punched his left ear with all my might. He howled miserably and seemed to deflate. Was he dead? Or just faking again?

I stood over the motionless carcass and noticed the wetness clouding my eye. I reached up; saw the blood staining my fingers. I took my shirtsleeve and rubbed the blood away. My vision cleared but my head ached. I ordered the lunatic to stay down, face to the floor. He didn't budge. I moved in front of him, but far enough away to dodge if he attacked again.

Getting antsy, "If you don't say anything, I'm going to start hitting you again. Counting to three. One. Two."

All of a sudden, a flat whisper, "It wasn't my fault. I was abused as a child. I can't help myself." And that's when I stomped on his exposed hand, mashing it into the floor. As I was about to kick again, I heard the noise behind me, turned.

Merlano had his hands out, "It's over, Frazier. Easy now."

❧

The Bulletin was all over the story. Speculation ran rampant about how many people Sylvan Skolnick had killed. I got some credit for solving the case, was a big shot for a few days at Schultz's, got more free drinks than usual.

Merlano backed me up when Sylvan's lawyer claimed I'd been overly aggressive with his client.

Merlano got quoted in all the news clips, "The guys a psycho, what's wrong with aggressive?" Fortunately, I'd called him just before entering the shop or who knows what I'd have done.

The worst part was Merlano thought the guy had a shot at criminal insanity. "The aunt apparently abused the kid from birth. Locked him in a shed and shit. I mean, totally fucked."

When I was about to go ape-shit, Merlano grinned, "Not to worry, worst scenario, he's locked in the nut house for life. Me, I'd rather get juiced than live with all those sickos. Guys jamming pencils up their dicks, shit like that all day."

I put up my hands, "Enough, Frankie, that image is going to haunt me all day. Please shut up, will you?"

Merlano grinned, "Giving you the real scoop is all. Your worried about this shithead getting' off. Thing is, he's be better off dead that locked up with the loonies." I didn't respond to Merlano's analysis. But, I don't know why, that did give me some comfort.

But something else had been gnawing at me for a couple days. I decided to share it with Merlano, seeing if it made any sense or if my imagination was running wild. "Frankie, what if Sylvan was playing us? What I mean is, what if he isn't insane? What if he knew he might get caught and the whole abused child story was an act? I mean, how can you really prove it, his whole family is dead? What if he just likes killing people?" During my vent, Merlano 's expressive face went from pissed-off to concerned. He finally said, "Jesus, Frazier!"

&

For the next few days I let things get back to normal, did chores I put off during the investigation. I was one of those people who made "to do" lists. Perhaps my German blood made that quirk inevitable. Each day I reviewed the list, crossed off successes and added new tasks. People who are afflicted with this habit are both energized and tormented by the ritual. We felt driven to complete the list. One of my tormentors was, "Call Mac." Since I'd been having flashbacks, I had thought about their source, had narrowed down my deepest regret. I had involved Mac in the hunt for traitors and had almost gotten him killed. His friendship and loyalty to me had put him in peril. We had briefly discussed it after my return from Nam and Mac had graciously dismissed my guilt, seemed almost embarrassed I brought it up. But had I forgiven myself?

I went to my telephone notebook, looked up his number in Portland, Oregon. We hadn't talked in months. Can't put this off anymore, I thought as I dialed. It was 11pm in Philly, so I thought Mac would be done dinner and have little Mike in bed by now. My buddy was completing Medical School, on his way to becoming a Pediatrician. We had talked for hours each day in Nam. We often had duty together and spent the time learning each other's dreams. Mac was a great person, red haired and freckled, brutally honest, funny, a good athlete, the best ping pong player I ever saw and crazy in love with Mary and little Mike.

Despite all these great qualities, he liked me. I missed him.

I heard the familiar voice answer the phone. Mac had a clear, strong, happy voice. There was always a hint he was about to laugh. With my knack for foolishness, we had been a good team.

I greeted him as I had in Nam. "Hey, carrot-top, were you out circumcising goats today, practicing up for the higher primates?"

The familiar chuckle greeted me. "Hey, Dylan, what a surprise! Mary and I were talking about you the other day. I have a conference in Philadelphia next year and was hoping to get together. How have you been, buddy?" We spent the next half hour catching up. I told him about Laura being away but that I knew she was "the one."

Mac laughed, "I could have told you that. She's all you talked about for all those months."

I told him about starting my own company, that I was back sticking my nose where it didn't belong. Mac jumped in, "That's no surprise. You were never so happy as when you stirred the pot. You actually 'lit up' when things got dicey. I'm glad you figured that out and can make a living at it." I didn't say anything, thinking how perceptive he was. And then he added, "Plus you happened to be a born investigator, a natural. Things you noticed or tied together just flew over my head. Damndest thing I ever saw."

That was the perfect intro into why I called, so I took the opportunity. "Mac, what I'm really calling for is to apologize to you. My foolish obsession got you hurt and it could have been much worse.

Don't know about you, but I've been having flashbacks once in awhile. Most of them center on the mess we got into. But what's driving me nuts is how I got you involved when you wanted nothing to do with it. I know I told you that before and you brushed it off. But somehow, my friend, I can't seem to forgive myself." And then my voice quivered and I sobbed, unable to gain control.

Minutes went by. Mac sat silently on the phone, letting me get it out. Finally, he broke the silence and said the last thing I could have expected. "I don't forgive you, Dylan." I started to blather another apology when he stopped me. "I don't forgive you because there's nothing to forgive. What you don't realize is the guilt I feel for not getting more involved. You did everything you could to protect me. But what I realized afterwards was that I was a coward to run away from that. We were Military Police. Our job was to protect the soldiers and I failed at that. You did all you could to isolate me. I'm the one with the guilt. Can you forgive me?" And then we both cried.

Eventually, Mary came to the phone, I heard her push Mac away. "Dylan, I was listening in, sorry. But Mike's also been having flashbacks. He thinks he let you down. I'm happy you called and got it out. I think it's time for both of you to put it behind you. Neither one of you has anything to be guilty about. It was a bad place and a bad war. It's time to forget, time to heal."

I sucked the air back into my lungs, worried I would lose it again. "Mary, tell Mac I'll call again in a few days when I have my hormones under control."

And then I added, "Tell Mac when he comes to Philly for that conference that I'm going to kick his ass in ping-pong. No babying him anymore." I hung up listening to her nice chuckle.

᠅

With that off my chest, good stuff started happening. I attended Jimmer and Marisol's wedding last Saturday. Mr. and Mrs. Keilmann were there, sat in the middle aisle, not up front like normal proud parents. Stubborn bastards! But they were there. Marisol was beautiful, beamed with joy. Jimmer and Jose had identical suits, looked sharp. The snazzy outfit was very un-Jimmer but Marisol must have twisted just right. I winked at him when he walked by, "Super groovy duds, Jimmer." I could see him lifting his middle finger but he caught himself mid-flip out of courtesy for Monsignor Pugh.

He mouthed, "Douche bag." I chuckled out loud. From the altar, Monsignor Pugh gave me a correctional glance. It was a great day.

That is, until I got home late that night and had a midnight call from my buddy Nut. He cut to the chase. "I've got bad news for you, Dylan."

I gave him my characteristic response, "Not interested in bad news, Nut. I'm trying a new diet of nothing but positive vibes. Okay? Call somebody else." Nut didn't laugh and I could tell he was letting me get my lines out.

And then he finished, "This you'll want to know, Dylan. Percy busted out of jail.

I know the warden from our Green Beret training days. He told me Percy talked about you a lot. He didn't say anything threatening exactly. He just kept talking about you. I thought you should know."

He went on to explain that MP's in every nearby state were on the alert. That local police got his picture; spread it around everywhere. That he figured Percy would be caught pretty soon. But he made me nervous when he told me he was headed home, had leave for a few weeks, and that we "should catch up." We made plans to meet in a couple days. I hung up and went to the couch and turned the TV on. Waiting for Johnny Carson to come on, I realized that Nut wasn't coming home just to visit. He was coming to protect me. And then I thought: Did I lock the front door? To clear my mind, I thought about Laura. She would be home in a couple weeks. She called last night and sounded sensational. I had slept like a baby and then had a blast at Jimmer's party tonight. Life was good. Except Percy was coming.

EPILOGUE

Although this story is a product of my fertile imagination, some of the plots are based on real life occurrences. There was a predatory serial killer in Philadelphia in the late 60's who stalked unsuspecting teenagers. This real fiend owned a tobacco shop near the University of Pennsylvania campus. The killer frequently dressed in odd costumes and preyed on lonesome males who found some solace in his warm, smoke-filled shop. Multiple young men were found buried in the tobacco shop basement. Hence the inspiration for Sylvan Skolnick.

Identities are altered to protect the guilty; many of the insurance investigations in this story are based on true events. There are many odd people out there and I happened to cross paths with them as I pursued my early career investigating insurance claims that appeared fraudulent or extremely odd. I kept a folder throughout my career labeled "Nuts." From that fun folder, many of the characters made their way into this tale- and without much exaggeration. It was the most amusing job I ever had.

Parts of this book are humorous--the Vietnam references are more somber and come from "flashbacks" to another book "Dylan's Nam" which will be published in the future. I am a former MP and Vietnam veteran. It was not a happy time to be a soldier. Many stories have been written to highlight the sad way many returning soldiers were treated. I came through the experience unscathed but the "flashbacks" mentioned throughout this book are meant to honor the struggling heroes of that unpopular war who returned home to an unsympathetic country.

Made in the USA
San Bernardino, CA
09 February 2014